LAURA
MONSTER
CRUSHER

Wesley King

LAURA

MONSTER CRUSHER

Wesley King

PUFFIN

an imprint of Penguin Canada Books Inc., a Penguin Random House Company

Published by the Penguin Group

Penguin Canada Books Inc., 320 Front Street West, Suite 1400, Toronto, Ontario
M5V 3B6, Canada

Penguin Group (USA) LLC, 375 Hudson Street, New York, New York 10014, U.S.A
Penguin Books Ltd, 80 Strand, London WC2R 0RL, England
Penguin Ireland, 25 St Stephen's Green, Dublin 2, Ireland (a division of Penguin
Books Ltd)
Penguin Group (Australia), 707 Collins Street, Melbourne, Victoria 3008, Australia
(a division of Pearson Australia Group Pty Ltd)
Penguin Books India Pvt Ltd, 11 Community Centre, Panchsheel Park, New Delhi –
110 017, India
Penguin Group (NZ), 67 Apollo Drive, Rosedale, Auckland 0632, New Zealand (a
division of Pearson New Zealand Ltd)
Penguin Books (South Africa) (Pty) Ltd, 24 Sturdee Avenue, Rosebank,
Johannesburg 2196, South Africa

Penguin Books Ltd, Registered Offices: 80 Strand, London WC2R 0RL, England

First published 2017

1 2 3 4 5 6 7 8 9 10   (RRD)

Copyright © 2017 by Wesley King

Jacket design: Lisa Jager
Jacket image: (trees) Yuriy2012 / shutterstock.com ; (letters) Vera Holera /
shutterstock.com
Manufactured in the U.S.A

Library and Archives Canada Cataloguing in Publication

King, Wesley, author
Laura monster crusher / Wesley King.

Issued in print and electronic formats.

ISBN 978-0-670-07002-2 (hardcover).—ISBN 978-0-14-319782-9 (epub)

I. Title.

PS8621.I5653L39 2016   jC813'.6   C2016-900947-5
                                            C2016-900948-3

Visit the Penguin Canada website at **www.penguinrandomhouse.ca**

For my Opa,
whose memory remains in all that he built

Chapter One

Duck, Duck, Goose ruined my life.

It happened way back in first grade, but I still remember it perfectly. I was wearing my favourite knitted red sweater and these really awful matching scarlet track pants—not sure why that outfit was allowed by my parents—the combination made me look like a particularly large and plump strawberry.

Our usually strict teacher, Mr. Bugbutter, surprised us with the news that we were going to play a quick game of Duck, Duck, Goose before home time, and the class happily marched down to the gym with me at the lead. I loved Duck, Duck, Goose more than anyone. Well . . . I did. That was about to change.

We sat in a circle, and I tucked myself in between Teresa Little and a really shy kid with a super freckly nose named Daniel Pittwell. Portia Carson was selected to go first. She stood up slowly, scanning the group for the perfect target. I saw her eyes dart from one face to the next like a predatory lioness. I watched her circle the group, tapping one nervous person after another with an almost whispered "*duck*," and then, as she passed out of view behind me, I tensed, ready to move. I already knew what was coming. She slapped me on the head with those dainty, little, manicured fingers and shouted, "Goose!" The game was on.

I scrambled to my feet and took off around the left flank. You're always at a disadvantage as the goose, of course; the picker is up and running. But I had a strategy. Take the inside track—force the picker wide. It gained you valuable seconds.

The plan worked perfectly. Portia Carson had to go around me, and I grinned wolfishly as I rounded the circle at a full sprint. I had a slight lead. The game was mine.

I think Mr. Bugbutter saw it coming first. I saw him look at me and then at Daniel Pittwell, who was sitting beside the now vacant spot in the circle. Mr. Bugbutter's big brown eyes widened, his mouth opening with a desperate warning, but he was too late.

With a last burst of energy, I flung myself toward the opening—butt first.

I don't know what happened. Maybe I was too competitive. Maybe I slightly miscalculated my jump. But whatever the reason, I over-sailed the opening and landed directly on poor, innocent Daniel Pittwell.

I should probably mention that I was the biggest girl in class. Actually I was the biggest kid in my grade. I was at least four inches taller than Daniel and probably thirty pounds heavier. He never had a chance. I heard a loud crack in his arm, Daniel started to scream—he was flattened beneath me on the floor at this point—and there I was, sitting on his stomach and looking around at a circle of horrified faces.

For years, they called it the Strawberry Squish. And the Dead Duck Disaster. There were a lot of names. But most importantly, that was the day they all realized something they would never again forget: Laura Ledwick was very large.

And worse yet, they never let me forget it either.

Six years later I left Newcastle Elementary for the last time, basically skipping down the hallways to the tune of the final bell. My family was moving to the next town over, Riverfield, in late August, and I would spend eighth grade at a new school. My dad had found his dream fixer-upper there, and we were making the short move to undertake the new project. My uncle Laine already lived in Riverfield with my aunt Sandra and their two kids, and he had recommended the place to my dad as a promising opportunity. I still hadn't even seen it.

Most kids probably would be at least a little upset to be moving so suddenly, but I was thrilled. Portia Carson had naturally evolved into some sort of evil Barbie Doll, and she'd led her minions in a six-year campaign to remind me that I was fat. I'd had many names myself over those six years: Laura Largebottom, Laura Lardo, Laura Lumpy . . . you get the idea. Alliteration is always popular with bullies. Easier to remember, I guess.

Like I said, I was happy to leave Newcastle behind, although I knew that I was going to miss our house. I had this pale-yellow room with bright-pink unicorn border that hadn't been changed since I was a baby. I know that sounds completely awful, but it felt like home. The bedroom was really small though: I couldn't even fit a desk in there, and considering I loved to write and draw, that was a big issue. I had to use the floor, or sometimes the window, which probably confused my neighbours and didn't help my reputation of being the reclusive, chubby girl who almost killed an innocent first grader.

To make matters worse, one of my aunts—my mom's mean older sister Tara—also liked to refer to me as the Closet Monster when she came over and saw my tiny little bedroom. Not overly nice, considering I clearly had weight and self-image issues, but it was kind of true.

Overall, my years at Newcastle Elementary were long and painful and mostly unpleasant. I had hobbies to keep my mind off of things: writing, drawing, working on the house with my dad, and softball. Ugh, never mind the last one. But when I saw other kids laughing with friends and playing in the schoolyard, I would get jealous. And upset. No one wanted to make friends with Laura Largebottom and no one wanted to become a new target of Portia Carson. So I was alone.

Even the town was bad, to be honest. Newcastle looked like an evil fantasy kingdom: ominous black smoke clouds would drift out of the old car plant down by the lake, blocking out the sun, sticking to windows and clothes, and generally making everything smell like burning rubber. I felt like I was living in Mordor. Combined with my super-bully Portia Carson, I was definitely ready to start somewhere new.

And then we pulled into the driveway of our new house.

"You have to be kidding me," I said.

Chapter Two

The house was perched at the end of a sleepy little dead-end street that was appropriately named Raven's End. There were only six old-fashioned brick houses on the street, all backing onto a dense forest that wrapped around the entire town. My parents had bought the house at the beginning of summer and insisted that it be a surprise for my brother and me on our first day—September 1st, only two days before the start of school. Now I could see why: they wanted to make sure someone was already living in our old house so we couldn't run back to it and refuse to ever leave. Clearly Uncle Laine hadn't actually looked at the house before he recommended it.

"Seriously, this isn't the house, right?" I said.

The house was awful. The exterior was painted white, but the paint was peeling off everywhere and flying into the wind like artificial snowflakes. The steep roof was a patchwork of missing black shingles and exposed wood, while a large, rotting porch wrapped around the front of the house. The windows were worse. They were dark and grimy and one of them was even covered with a piece of plywood. Then you had the sprawling front lawn, which was at least a foot high and spotted with menacing thistles.

I was literally looking at a horror movie.

"Surprise," my dad said happily.

My dad is a big man with a bit of a gut and a thick brown moustache. I like to call him Stache. His wispy chestnut hair is thinning and he's almost fifty, but he's got crazy amounts of energy. He's the one who likes renovations. This was his big dream. A fixer-upper.

I guess my mom was equally to blame. She didn't really like Newcastle either and quickly jumped on board when my dad suggested the move. She got in a fight with this woman on the parent council and decided she hated Newcastle. When she gets in a fight with someone, it lasts for like twenty-five years, so we didn't have much choice.

She is an aesthetician, so she does people's nails and waxing and things like that. My dad is an accountant, and he would still be commuting to the same job in the city, but he had the week off so he could try to get as much done around the house as possible. He likes to consider himself a handyman and always does everything himself.

"Is it bad?" my little brother asked.

I should probably tell you about my brother. His name is Tom, and he's nine years old with sandy-blond hair and these really cool icy-blue eyes. He's also blind. Not completely. He sees sort of different shades of black. Shapes sometimes. I'm way overprotective of him, but we have kind of a weird relationship where we just say things that should be faux pas. Like I call him Bat Boy and he calls me Giant Girl.

"It's bad," I said. "It looks like our old house, except condemned and haunted."

"Oh," he replied.

"It's not that bad," my mom said, giving me a disapproving look. "You should see the floor space. Its twice the size of our old house."

I made a face. "And eight times as decrepit."

My father rubbed his big, calloused hands together eagerly. "Not for long," he said. "I'll have this place looking like a dream in no time flat. You just wait."

I looked up at the ugly two-storey house looming over our car.

"Good luck, Stache."

My bedroom was worse. First of all, I had to walk up the narrow old staircase with floorboards that groaned and complained like an African bull elephant was trying to climb the steps. I could see this house was going to be great for my confidence.

"Just needs to be nailed down," my dad said, coming up the stairs behind me and noticing my sour expression.

"Or burned down," I muttered.

Then I opened the door to my room. I've never seen so many spiderwebs. They looked like drapes. I would have needed a machete to get in there.

"No," I said firmly, turning to my dad.

I hate spiders. Hate them. I'm not a girly girl by any stretch—I think I wore a dress once when I was six, and that was for a wedding. But spiders are my weakness.

Stache peered into the room for a moment. "I'll clean yours first."

When my dad has a mission, get out of the way. He plunged into spider city with a broom and some garbage bags, and ten minutes later I could actually tell it was a room.

He walked out with a big grin, wiping his hands together. "All yours, sweetie."

"There's a spider on your shirt," I said.

He looked down and squashed it with his hand.

"Ew," I said, stepping around him and cautiously walking into my room.

It did look spider-free. It was actually a lot bigger than my old bedroom, with a large double window looking out onto the woods behind the house and lots of space for my bed and dresser, along with the new desk my parents had bought me. There was even a walk-in closet. I wasn't much of a clothes person, but who doesn't like closet space?

My mom followed me in. She was definitely a clothes person. She liked to do her makeup and hair and always wore lots of jewellery. We didn't have much in common.

"What did I tell you?" she said, putting her arm around my shoulders. "I made sure you got this room. Haven't you always wanted a walk-in closet?"

"I guess," I replied. "I only have, like, ten shirts."

She smiled. "We'll buy you more. This is a new start for all of us. You can go to school on Monday and make new friends and leave the miserable bullies in Newcastle behind. This is going to be great, Laura. Trust me."

I watched as a surviving spider lowered itself from my ceiling.

I looked at my mom, and she forced a smile. "Eventually."

When she left, I reluctantly started unpacking my stuff from the small trailer we'd lugged over here. My parents had basically bought all new furniture for the move, and there were already huge boxes scattered around the main floor when we arrived—dropped off by the store. Everything was a bit rushed: we'd only officially gotten possession of the house last week as it had taken the summer to close and finalize everything with the bank, so there wasn't a lot of prep time. The rest of our stuff had already been moved here through the week by Stache, so all we'd brought with us today were clothes and other random personal possessions. For me that wasn't much. Besides my clothes, I had some books, a laptop, two big boxes of trophies, and another small box of collectibles—random things that I'd kept, like a pen that was my grandpa's and an old coin I d found the night my nana died. I was always close to my grandparents. Just my dad's mom, Grandma Elly, was left now.

After hauling everything upstairs, I started hanging my clothes up, marvelling at how much space I had now. Walk-in closets were kind of cool. It was definitely old-fashioned though: large white wooden panels covered the bottom half of the closet, while the top half and ceiling were finished with regular plaster. I didn't even want to know how many spiders had been in here. I shoved the trophy boxes in the bottom corner and was just turning to leave when I noticed something written on one of the panels. I leaned down for a closer look. There were small, crooked words carved into the wood:

It's not too late.

"Oh . . . perfect," I murmured, looking around uneasily. It looked like the words had been carved into the panel with a pocket knife or something. But what did it mean?

Frowning, I shook my head and went to unpack my last box. Just one more creepy thing in a creepy house. Maybe it meant it wasn't too late to move out of here again. But could my parents be convinced? Judging by the way my dad was basically skipping around the house, I sincerely doubted it. I would just have to try and settle in. Somehow. I left most of my little collectibles in the box, at least until I could get my dresser up here. I did pause and gingerly pick up the old black pen, thinking about my grandpa Roger. I wished he was here. He would have snuck me some German chocolates and laughed about how I could become a biologist here, specializing in spiders. I missed his laugh.

I put the pen back in the box and climbed to my feet, deciding to check out the yard. Maybe there was a pool or something. I walked over to the window and looked outside, scanning the forest that encircled our overgrown backyard. It was mostly tall, narrow oak trees, packed tightly enough that it grew dark just a metre into the woods, even during the daytime. Thick brush filled the space between the trees, as well as squat pines that blocked out much of the sunlight breaking through the overcast sky. It wasn't a happy-looking forest. I probably wouldn't be hiking very much.

I was just turning away when I saw a strange flicker of colour. I squinted, trying to peer into the shadows. Leaning close to the glass, my eyes fell on a particularly dark one. As the shadow took shape, the sunlight caught another flash of pale blue. Eyes.

Suddenly the shadow became a recognizable form, and I realized with trembling hands that a man was standing in the forest, staring right at me.

Chapter Three

I froze, unable to scream or move or even look away. The man was tall, but it was difficult to see much else of his face beyond those piercing blue eyes as he was wearing a loose-fitting hood or cowl. The hood flowed back into a long cloak, making his shape indistinguishable as well. But there was no mistaking a second glint of light at his waist, where the tip of a gleaming sword protruded from the cloak. The shadowy figure just stared at me for a long moment, his cold eyes locked on mine, and then he stepped back into the darkness and disappeared completely. When he was gone, I slowly moved away from the window, feeling my skin crawl.

"You're imagining things," I whispered.

"Laura!" my mom called. "Come help your father with your dresser!"

I took a last look outside, trying to stay calm. Nothing. I must have imagined it. But as I hurried out of my bedroom, I had the distinct feeling that something was watching me.

We ate dinner that night sitting on boxes of furniture in the living room. Stache was covered in so much dust that he looked like a statue in progress. My mom tried to brush off my account of a shadowy figure watching me in the woods, telling me I was clearly imagining things because I was shaken up about the spiders and that it would take a few days to get used to the new house. Thanks Mom.

In fairness, I did have a bit of a history with some . . . creative concerns. I mean, I have a pretty developed imagination, and I am kind of a worrier. Okay, I worry a lot. I asked for a carbon monoxide detector for Christmas when I was four—which was totally valid, by the way— and then I also had a theory that we had a possible sinkhole beneath our house and tried to prove it by digging a hole in our yard to inspect the soil content when I was nine. I also have a lot of nightmares and check on Tom ten times a day.

And the more I thought about it, the more I realized she was probably right. It could have been a shadow from a tree or something, and I was just a little freaked out from the message in my closet. It was probably nothing. I decided to forget about it.

I popped a french fry in my mouth and looked at Tom. "How's your room?"

He shrugged. "Seems all right. I think I heard a mouse in the walls."

"You did not," my mom said sharply, though she did glance at my dad.

He nodded. Tom had amazing hearing. If Tom thought he heard a mouse, there was probably a mouse. One time when Tom was five years old we lost our cat, Muffin. We searched the entire town for three days, and then my mom finally told me that Muffin wasn't coming back. I cried for another two days after that.

A week later Tom and I were in the backyard playing house—I always made him be my butler—when he suddenly looked up and said, "I hear Muffin."

Our old house backed onto a forest too, and I ran to the back fence and listened for a few minutes, not hearing a thing. I patted his shoulder.

"Muffin's gone, Tom," I told him sadly.

He shook his head. "She's crying."

I still thought he was imagining things, but Tom was persistent, so I got Stache and the three of us set off into the woods. We walked for at least five minutes before I finally heard a faint, weak-sounding meow filtering through the trees. It was another five minutes before we found Muffin lying on her side next to a tree, covered in dirt and almost completely unable to move. We rushed her to the vet, and Muffin—who was already sixteen—lived for two more years after that.

And I never forgot how Tom had found her.

"I think this house has a lot of potential," my mom said, obviously changing the subject.

I scanned the living room. Like most of the house, it was in rough shape. The mossy-green paint was peeling, the stucco ceiling was covered in yellow water stains, and the windows were so filthy you could barely see out of them. Dark hardwood ran through the entire main floor—except for the kitchen—but it was dusty and dirty and cracked.

A huge red-bricked chimney stretched like a pillar right

up to the second floor, though I noticed it didn't actually have a fireplace. It must have gone right beside my bedroom to the roof. I wondered why they would have a chimney with no fireplace.

My dad followed my gaze. "Yeah, not sure what the point of that is," he said thoughtfully. "But I think it may actually be a support structure, so have to leave it."

"When was the last time someone lived here?" I asked.

"Six years ago," my mom said. "Got it for a steal. The last owner . . . gave it to the bank, and they sold it as an estate sale. We only got to see it once, but we fell in love."

Tom took a bite of his burger. "He disappeared."

"What?" my mom asked, looking at him. "How do you know that?"

He shrugged. "I heard you talking on the phone with Grandma last week."

She glared at him. "I was outside."

"The window was open."

I turned to my parents, frowning. "The last guy who lived here disappeared?"

"Sort of," Stache mumbled.

"They don't suspect foul play," my mom added brightly.

I popped another fry in my mouth. "Super."

My mom waved a hand. "It's no big deal. Every house has a story. Trust me, once we get this place fixed up—"

She was suddenly interrupted by a loud, booming knock at the door. My mom jumped and almost toppled right off the box. There was another pounding knock.

"Maybe he's back," Tom whispered.

"Enough," my mom said. "Honey?"

"On it," Stache said, wiping off his hands and heading for the door.

I glanced at the curtainless windows, thinking of the shadow I'd seen in the woods. I watched nervously as my dad approached the door. He pulled it open.

"Ha!" he said. "I was wondering if you'd come by, you big lug."

Stache was suddenly embraced in a hug by an even larger man. Stache was huge: six foot four and about 250 pounds, with big hands, and a strong jaw. But his brother was even bigger. He was about the same height, but while my dad had a gut, Uncle Laine had muscles bulging out of his usual button-down plaid shirt. He had a thick black beard to match his hair and big, friendly brown eyes. Despite his intimidating appearance, he was almost always in a good mood and was my favourite uncle by far. I was happy we were now living in the same town with him and Aunt Sandra and my two younger cousins.

Uncle Laine clapped my dad on the shoulders and started into the living room.

"There's my girl," he said, wrapping me in a strong hug as I stood up to greet him. It was like being hugged by a bear. He looked down at me. "You like it?"

"It's something," I said.

He laughed. "Just needs a little loving. I'll help your dad out when I can."

He quickly gave my brother and my mom hugs as well and then plopped himself down on one of the boxes.

"Sandy and the kids would have come, but it was already getting late. We'll have to have you over sometime next week for dinner. I got off a bit late tonight, or I would have come earlier. Got to get as many shifts in as I can."

Stache frowned. "Why do you say that?"

Laine forced a smile and shook his head. "Closing the factory down. Got a few months and that's it."

"That's awful," my mom said. "When did they decide that?"

"Been a long time coming," Laine replied. "I knew at least six months ago. Been trying to find something new, but no one's hiring around here. Not a big lug who's been working the same job for twenty-five years, anyway." He waved a hand. "Never mind that. Something will come up. It's going to be a lot better now that you guys are around."

He shot me a lopsided grin.

"Maybe we can go hunting."

"No," I said immediately.

"Tom came with me once last year, remember?" he said, patting Tom on the shoulder.

"That's when I saw the hole," Tom agreed.

My mom sighed. Tom had told everyone he'd seen faint light in the shape of a hole in the woods that day, which was highly unlikely for any number of reasons. Laine just ruffled his hair.

"Exactly. So you'll come along next time, Laura?"

"I'll just look at the deer, thank you," I said.

He laughed. "Fair enough. Don't worry, we'll find something to do."

There was something strange in his voice, but I couldn't pick it out. We talked for another half an hour or so after that, and then Laine said he had to get back home to help put the kids to bed. We gathered at the door to see him off, and he gave everyone a last hug before climbing in his old beat-up black truck and pulling out of the driveway. He smiled when he waved and drove away, but I could tell he was a bit off. Obviously he was thinking about the factory.

"I hope they'll be all right," my mom said as she closed the door. "Sandra doesn't work either. If they don't find something, they're going to be in trouble."

"It'll work out," my dad replied, heading for his tools.

Stache is the perennial optimist. He strapped on his tool belt and rubbed his hands together eagerly, looking around. "What should I do next?"

That night I lay down on my mattress—we still had to put my bed frame together—and tried to be positive. I was mostly thinking about spiders crawling on me, but I was trying. Maybe the weird message in my closet didn't mean anything. And maybe I imagined the shape. And maybe the last guy who lived here just decided to move or something. It was possible.

And maybe, just maybe, the kids in my school would all turn out to be good friends. There might not be a Portia Carson at my new school. Maybe they viewed plumpness as a sign of wealth and power. It was unlikely, but I didn't know. And until I did, it couldn't hurt to dream.

I could even try dieting again. I'd tried plenty of times before, but after two weeks of being completely miserable and not seeing the slightest change in my reflection, I usually just gave up. My mom said I just had big bones, which was fine, except apparently they made my butt big too. Go figure.

I'm a pretty big girl in general, taller and heavier than all the girls in my grade and probably most of the boys as well. My grandma Elly always tells me I'm pretty, and she might be right. I have long, wavy chestnut hair that falls down past my shoulders, bright-green eyes, and fairly good skin—most days anyway. My grandma says I could be a model, and she doesn't ever add the *if*. I love my grandma.

She lives in the city, which is about a forty-minute drive from here. She is seventy-one, but she still lives all by herself in a big old house and has for almost ten years since my grandpa passed away. She is proud and fiery and fiercely independent. Some of my favourite weekends were spent at her house, going to movies and taking walks in the park. We went to visit her before we moved.

"Are you excited?" she'd asked me from the kitchen, where she was making food as usual. You weren't allowed to sit in my grandma's house without eating something. She was always baking or making soup or something like that.

"I guess," I said reluctantly, reading a book at the table.

She glanced at me. "I want you to promise me some-thing."

"What?"

"I want you to promise me that you'll give yourself a chance."

I frowned. "That's not the problem. The problem is no one else does."

She shrugged and turned back to the stove. "Not in my experience."

She always said that. I guess it was an easy way to end an argument, since she was fifty-eight years older than me. But maybe she was right. I was pretty hard on myself.

I decided to make the most of the move. I was going to start eating right again. And exercising more. I used to play softball—I was the best youth player in the state—but I kind of quit that. Long story.

And hey, with some new clothes and a new look, I could even be popular. Laura Legs. Laura Lovely, maybe. I pictured myself wearing a white tank top and fitted jeans like Portia used to. Laura Lovely. Wouldn't that be nice?

And then I heard it. Rattling. It sounded like a screen door smacking against the frame in the wind. Maybe a loose windowpane. There was just one problem.

It was coming from my closet.

Chapter Four

I did not sleep that night. Not a wink. The rattling would continue for a few minutes, then stop just long enough for me to start dozing off, and then start again. Admittedly I was not brave enough to go investigate—the spiders could have returned. So I just rolled around and closed my eyes and pretended that there wasn't something rattling in my closet.

As soon as the morning sun filtered through my still curtainless window, I climbed out of bed and slowly crept toward the closet. The floorboards creaked the entire way. Stupid, insulting house. I eased the closet door open, ready to take off screaming down the hallway if a raccoon jumped out at me. When it was about a foot open, I peeked inside. Nothing. I pulled the door open the rest of the way, frowning.

It looked exactly the same as yesterday, when I'd put my ten shirts in there. Great. Now I was sure I had a haunted closet. I remembered what Tom had said—the last guy who lived in this house had disappeared. Maybe the closet ate him.

I stepped inside and looked around, trying to figure out what could have been rattling. The house had to be at least a hundred years old—maybe there was a draft in the walls or something. My eyes fell on the two boxes that I'd shoved in the bottom corner of the closet yesterday, both labelled Softball Trophies. I stared at them for a moment. I always wanted to throw them out, but it felt weird to just toss something that I'd put so much work into. The problem was that every time I saw the boxes I had this feeling of regret gnawing its way around my stomach. It wasn't overly pleasant.

I plucked a black graphic T-shirt with a moon and two stars on it from a hanger—still looking around suspiciously—and quickly threw on some jeans. All my clothes fit the same way: loose and unflattering. I always preferred that to tight and very unflattering.

But I did have my favourites. Most of my graphic T-shirts were space-themed—I have a thing for sci-fi—and generally black, navy-blue, or grey. Colours always led to easy references for bullies—yellow was the sun, red was the Kool-Aid man, and so forth. Once I wore blue jeans and a green shirt, which did not go over well—Portia called me Planet Earth all day, and started pointing out where countries would be. The U.S. was on my stomach . . . she wasn't very good at geography. My jeans were usually either ripped or worn or faded, because I hate clothes shopping. That's not just because I'm big either—it's just that my mom *really* likes to shop and we end up spending the whole day at the mall. It's exhausting. Taking one last peek into the closet, I went downstairs, scowling as the steps groaned beneath my feet.

My parents were already eating breakfast in the kitchen. They're both early risers—actually, I doubt my dad had even slept. He had heavy bags under his eyes, and he was drinking out of the actual pot of coffee. He had probably been up all night painting.

"How did you sleep, Laura?" my mom asked glancing up from the paper.

She was already fully dressed and her shoulder-length blond hair was done up in elaborate curls. She always wears dark eye shadow and mascara to make her blue eyes pop, and she'd even added a little scarlet lipstick today. I often looked at my mom and wondered what had happened to me. She was slim and petite, and she looked like a model in her old high school photos with her long golden hair and fair skin. Tom looked a lot like her, while I definitely took after Stache. Big bones, strong jaw, stronger hands.

I wish I got a *bit* more of my mom. Maybe the petite part.

"Great," I said, putting some bread in the toaster. "Minus the rattling in my closet. There must be a crack or something. I could hear wind."

Stache looked up immediately. "I'll check it out after breakfast."

"I'm sure there's nothing rattling in your closet," my mom said patiently. "You were probably dreaming."

I scowled. "I was not dreaming. I have a haunted closet." I went to grab the peanut butter. "What are we doing today?"

"Your father is going to continue working. We can help him with the painting later. But first we're going clothes shopping, just like I said. We need to find you and your brother something new for your first day of school tomorrow. It's going to be fun!"

I exchanged a resigned look with Stache. "Hurray."

Five hours later I was standing in front of the bathroom mirror wearing a tight new purple top and a pair of very snug blue jeans. The saleswoman said it was trendy. I said it was cruel. I tried putting my hair in a ponytail and then straight and then I just gave up.

I started to cry. I'm embarrassed to say it. But once in awhile I looked at myself and bawled. I don't know why. Today, it felt like I was going to go to school the next day and get picked on, and my parents would be ashamed, and my teachers would pity me, and all because I eat too much breakfast or something. It's not a good feeling.

I watched as the tears rolled over my cheeks, round and fat, and then dripped off my chin, not even making it to the floor because they hit my fat body on the way. I roughly wiped them away, but seeing my bulky arm poking out of my T-shirt only made the hot tears flow faster. I stifled a sob, trying to get ahold of myself.

"You okay?" a quiet voice asked from outside the bathroom door.

Tom was very perceptive about my crying. He could tell if I was crying from anywhere in the house, and he always came to find me. Like I said, he has crazy good hearing. One of the reasons I call him Bat Boy.

I wiped my eyes and nose and opened the door.

"Yeah," I said sheepishly.

"Wow," he said, stepping back. "You look good."

He always liked to tell me I looked good. It was his little joke, I guess.

"Thanks," I muttered. "You too."

He was wearing new jeans and a cool graphic T-shirt I'd picked out for him.

He ran his hands down his shirt. "You think so?"

"Definitely," I said. "The girls are going to go crazy over you."

He wrinkled his nose. "I'm nine."

"And a real catch," I said, my voice cracking just a little.

It does that after I cry sometimes.

Tom suddenly reached out and squeezed my fingers. He also always knows exactly how far away I am. Sometimes I think he can see more than most people.

"It's going to be fine."

"I know," I said. "Just a little nervous, maybe."

He smiled, revealing his sparkling white teeth. "Me too. But I'll be the most popular kid at school by next week. The captain of the football team always is."

"That's true. And I'll be the head cheerleader, so I don't know what we're worrying about."

"Exactly." Tom suddenly frowned, looking past me. "Do you see that?"

I turned around. There was nothing there but the bathroom wall with its flaking green paint and brown water spots. "Where?"

He pointed at the wall, near my waist level. "Light," he said.

"There's nothing there, Bat Boy."

He shrugged. "Strange. Now if you'll excuse me, I'm going birdwatching."

Tom also liked to come up with ironic tasks that he had to hurry off to. I shook my head as he strolled back down the hallway, using his hands for guidance. He really was a strange boy.

But he was also a brave one.

I flicked off the light and went to my room. I was done crying.

That night I lay in bed—my dad had somehow found the time to build it—splattered in white paint and thinking nervously that I was going to school the next morning. The house was coming along. We painted the living room that evening after we got back from the mall, and I'm pretty sure my dad was now hard at work installing new kitchen cupboards. The man didn't sleep.

I was busy wondering what my new school would look like when the rattling started again. There was no doubt: it was coming from my closet.

Again, I didn't investigate. I really am a wimp. I just lay there and once again pretended that nothing was rattling. Where was Bat Boy when I needed him?

The morning dawned, and only then did I creep over to the closet and peeked inside. Still nothing. This was getting weird. But I didn't have time to worry about haunted closets—it was the first day of school. I changed into my new purple top and blue jeans, grimacing as I tugged them on. It felt like the stitching was about to blow.

I made my bed, grabbed my backpack, and started for the door. On the way I glanced out the window, just to make sure there wasn't a shadowy figure standing in the trees. I stopped immediately. There wasn't a man out there. There was something worse.

Two yellow eyes were watching me from the deep shadows of the woods.

They were large and pale, with thin, vertical black pupils like a snake. I hurried over to the window to get a closer look, but by the time I got there, the eyes had blinked closed and disappeared. I stood there for a moment, scanning the woods. Great. Now there were yellow snake eyes in my backyard. This new house was awesome

Shaking my head, I went to the bathroom to get ready, convincing myself that it was just a particularly large cat. After fixing my matted chestnut hair and putting just a bit of blush on my cheeks—something my mom insisted I do—I went downstairs to eat some breakfast. I know most people eat breakfast before getting ready, but if I went down there on the first day of school without looking semi-presentable my mom would insist on doing my hair and makeup for me. I tried to avoid that as much as possible.

"You look nice," my mom said brightly as I walked into the kitchen. "Maybe I could just curl your hair a little—"

"No," I said firmly.

She returned to her paper, looking disappointed.

"I just saw yellow eyes watching me from the forest," I said.

She didn't even look up. "Was it a cat?"

I paused. "Possibly."

"Maybe it was whatever ate the last owner," Tom suggested.

"Tom," my mom said, scowling at him. "Don't encourage your sister."

I plunked some bread in the toaster. "I saw eyes," I muttered.

She looked up and smiled. "You're just nervous for school."

"Of course I am," I said, glancing down at my tight purple shirt. "I look like fat Barney."

Tom laughed and spit out a chunk of English muffin. He covered his mouth.

"Oops," he said.

My mom just sighed.

After breakfast, I brushed my teeth and put on a brave face as I stared at my reflection in the mirror. I flattened my hair again, wishing it would just stay down and cover my cheeks and make me look skinny. You can do this, I told myself. It has to be better than Newcastle.

My mom always drives us to school because of Tom, so we climbed into her van and set off. We drove in near silence through Riverfield, which was a little smaller than Newcastle. It was nice enough, I guess.

The main street was about a five-minute drive from our house, and it was old-fashioned and cozy, with red-brick shops and cafés and little boutiques. The surrounding houses were all Victorian-style wood and brick homes like mine, many with white picket fences and neatly manicured gardens. The whole town had the feeling of being a century or two behind.

I saw a few kids along the way and snuck little peeks at them out the window. I really hoped they were in high school, because they all seemed cool and old. One girl in particular caught my eye. She had long, glistering raven hair and this perfect tanned skin, and she was wearing black yoga pants and a tight, blue T-shirt. She had to be at least in tenth grade.

I was not looking forward to meeting that girl in high school.

We pulled into our new school a few minutes later: Riverfield Public School. It was an old, one-storey structure of sun-blasted red bricks and black metal doors. Colourful cut-outs and pictures dotted the windows in the kindergarten section.

It looked like a happy place.

"Better than the old school?" Tom asked.

I paused. "Possibly."

My mom piled out of the van and pulled open Tom's door. She never helped him get out though. He liked to do it himself. He usually used his walking stick whenever we went somewhere new, but he didn't want to bring it today. He told me he liked people to try and guess if he was blind first. He has a strange sense of humour.

"School doesn't start for five or ten minutes," my mom said. "I'm going to take Tom to meet his Educational Assistant. You can just go around back to the yard. Have fun, honey."

"Yeah," I said skeptically. I hugged my brother. "See you later, Bat Boy."

"Go get 'em, Giant Girl," Tom said, squeezing my arm.

With that they were gone, and I was on my own in a strange new school in a strange new town with a purple shirt that was desperately trying to escape my body.

This should be good.

I wandered around to the yard and saw that a fair number of kids had already gathered outside, waiting for the bell. The older ones were standing in scattered groups. Some of them looked at me with raised eyebrows, but no one laughed or said anything derogatory. That was a good start. I tried to look as natural as possible as I shuffled along the brick wall, heading for the door. When I was eight years old, I made five rules for bullied people and stuck them on my bedroom wall to remind me. They were:

1. NEVER bring attention to yourself.
2. Boys are mean . . . girls are evil. Avoid them.
3. Smaller lunches are better. Fewer fat jokes.
4. Don't react to insults. It only makes it worse.
5. Remember that no one bullies you at home.

Not the most inspirational, I guess. But they made sense at the time, and I'd sort of followed them ever since. I figured it was probably best to use the same rules here.

I was just settling into what I figured was an inconspicuous location when I noticed two other girls standing by themselves near a portable. They looked a little nervous. There was something about the way they were standing right against the steps and cautiously glancing around that told me they weren't overly popular. One had long auburn hair that was tied back in a nicely braided ponytail, light freckles, and she was wearing a jacket over a white shirt and snug jeans. The other was a skinny, short girl with caramel skin and shoulder-length black hair. She was dressed a bit more plainly with a black sweater and loose-fitting khakis.

I briefly made eye contact with the auburn-haired girl and then stood awkwardly against the wall for a moment, wondering if it was time to abandon my rules. I wasn't very popular at my old school. And by that I mean I didn't have any friends. Like none. I was sort of reclusive, since I always assumed everyone was making fun of me, and because my rules forbid me from going near boys or girls, my options were pretty limited. But it was a new school and a new town. Why not try something new?

It took another few minutes to muster up the courage. My stomach was doing backflips as I snuck glances at the two girls and debated if I could actually do it.

But I knew if I didn't talk to them on the first day, I wouldn't do it, period.

And so I walked right over to them. They looked confused as I approached.

"Hey," I said. "I'm new here. Just thought I'd say hello. Laura, by the way."

The two girls looked at each other.

"Uh, Shal," the girl with the auburn hair said. She had big hazel eyes and a nice smile. "Well, Michelle, but people call me Shal. And this is Mia." The short girl waved shyly.

"Hi," I said, nodding at her. "Do you mind if I hang out until the bell?"

I fully expected them to tell me to go away. I was already preparing myself for it and trying to justify that I was at least proud I had tried something new.

Shal shrugged. "Sure."

"Really?" I asked. "I mean, thanks. I like your hair, by the way."

She immediately touched her hair. I recognized the instinct. It was from someone who was worried about how they looked. "Really? I've never worn it like this before."

"You should," I said. "It looks really good."

"Thanks," Shal replied, blushing. "I like you already."

This was easy. I already liked Riverfield way more than Newcastle.

"No problem. So whereabouts do you guys live—" I stopped.

They were both staring behind me, their eyes wide. I slowly turned around.

There, walking around the school in her yoga pants and blue shirt, was the girl from the street, flanked by three well-manicured minions. Her dark eyes immediately flicked toward me, and a smile split her lips. I knew that smile. It was the same one that Portia had worn every day she saw me. It was the smile of evil.

I slumped. "Perfect."

Chapter Five

I should have known it was too good to be true. There's always one. Portia Carson was more your typical blond cheerleader type: flawless skin, perfectly flowing hair, clothes that my mother would never allow into her house. This girl was all raven hair and dark eyes and annoyingly beautiful features. This was going to be bad.

"Tell me her name isn't Portia," I whispered

"No," Shal said. "It's Allison Black."

Of course it was—the perfect name for a villain. She walked right by us, sparing just a quick glance and still wearing that evil smile. She made a comment I couldn't hear, and the three girls beside her giggled. They sounded like cackling seagulls. I glanced at Shal and Mia. Except Mia was gone. Vanished. I frowned at Shal, who just shrugged.

"She doesn't like confrontation," Shal said quietly. "If Allison Black or any of the popular kids even look in our direction, she takes off. I call her Mia Mouse—she always disappears when predators approach."

"Is she gone?" a quiet voice asked.

"Yes, you big coward," Shal said, and Mia reappeared from the other side of the portable, looking at the ground in embarrassment.

"It's true," she murmured, her slender little hands fidgeting nervously in front of her. "But Shal's afraid of her too."

"Well, obviously," Shal said. "She's terrifying. But I don't run away."

"You're just too slow," Mia replied.

Shal paused. "Shut up."

"Well if you're too slow, I'm in trouble," I said, watching as Allison joined a larger group of kids by the basketball court. "How come you guys aren't popular? You're just as pretty as those girls."

Mia and Shal looked at each other.

"Is she patronizing us?" Shal asked.

"Probably," Mia said. "But I like it."

"Me too," Shal agreed. She turned to me and smiled. "Would you like to officially join our group? There aren't many perks. We get made fun of a lot, we sit alone at lunch, and we spend our weekends at my house listening to my mom talk about how many parties she went to when she was our age. Boys don't really look at us, unless it's to throw their pudding cups at our heads. That aside, we do share lunches, and Mia's mom makes some awesome sandwiches. Anything else?"

Mia thought about that for a moment. "Not really."

"Thanks," Shal muttered. "So what do you say?"

They both looked at me expectantly. I grinned.

"I'd love to," I said. "And I make some pretty good sandwiches myself."

"Perfect," Shal said happily. "Now, I have a whole lot of gossip to catch you up on. First things first. Allison is the queen bee, but she does have some competition. Ashley Tumwick is the main one. She's almost as pretty, and her family is rich."

I listened happily as Shal discussed just about everyone in the school. I didn't really care about the gossip. I was just thrilled people were talking to me. I'd been at my new school for five minutes and accomplished more than I had in eight years at my old one. Sure, my closet was haunted and there were yellow eyes watching me from the woods. But overall I was starting to think Riverfield was pretty awesome.

And that was before I ran into Liam R. Kelp.

There were only twenty-seven eighth graders in the entire school, so Mia and Shal were obviously in my class. Of course, so was Allison Black. She also sat right behind me, which was slightly unfortunate, but she seemed too preoccupied talking to a boy named Carl Hemwing to pay much attention to me. Well, she did snicker when I said my name in the little introduction game—probably because she was thinking of alliterative nicknames—but it was still a lot better than Portia Carson.

The desks were assigned by our teacher, Ms. Haddock, so Mia and Shal were spaced out around the room. It would have been nice to sit next to them, but I didn't want to get caught talking anyway. That would definitely violate rule number one.

After the introductory games and outlines of the curriculum, we had recess, and then we finally came to our first subject: geography. I was excited: geography was one of my favourite subjects. I stopped by my locker to grab my note-book and hurried to get to class before it started without me. I was just reaching the classroom door, peering back to make sure I had closed my locker, when I walked into someone.

My notebook toppled to the ground, and I looked up in horror to see an equally stunned boy with thick black glasses. I recognized him from the front row. I braced myself for a mean comment. I hadn't been watching where I was going, and I'd almost run him over. He was going to say something insulting about my size. I knew it.

"Sorry about that," he said, flashing me a shy grin. He quickly snatched up my notebook, which I had already taken the liberty of labelling GEOGRAPHY! YAY! He read the label and then handed it to me. "I guess we're the nerds of the class."

"Yeah," I murmured, taking the book. "Sorry."

"Sweet shirt, by the way," he said. "Laura, right?"

He stuck his hand out, and I tentatively shook it.

"Liam R. Kelp," he said, and then paused. "Not sure why I told you my last name. Or my middle initial. Can I do that again?"

I smiled. "Laura T. Ledwick. Nice to meet you."

"So you're new to town, right?"

"Yeah. It's nice."

He shrugged. "I guess. It's pretty quiet." He glanced into the class and saw Ms. Haddock preparing to start. He gestured to the door. "After you," he said, smirking.

"Thanks," I replied, flushing and hurrying inside.

I snuck a peek at him as he sat down in the front row. He was as skinny as my left wrist, had a mop of messy almond-coloured hair, a freckled, pointy nose and those thick black glasses. Not to mention his last name was a slimy ocean plant. But there was something about him. And the more he spoke, the more I liked him.

He answered just about every question. Clearly a brainer. I knew the answers too, but I was afraid of being pelted by an eraser. Not Liam. He put his hand up again and again, even when people snickered and gave him dirty looks. I was already in love.

Okay, maybe not love, but you get the idea. Let's just say I smiled a lot when he walked by. And I kind of watched him play some sort of fantasy card game with his two friends, Paul and Steve, at afternoon recess. And I wanted to marry him.

Anyway, I thought I was being secretive, but before the end of the day Mia and Shal had already nic-named me Laura Lovesick, giving me yet another name to add to my collection. I didn't mind this one.

You might be thinking I'm a terrible sister by now, but I did keep a distant eye on my brother in the yard too. He mostly had to walk around with an Educational Assistant, but I did see him talking to a few classmates. I certainly wasn't going to go over there. The last thing he needed was an overprotective, pudgy sister following him around the schoolyard.

When we were driving home that afternoon, I asked him how his day went.

"Not bad," he said. "They already asked me about football. I told them I'd have to see how my schedule plays out."

My mom looked in the rear-view mirror, clearly

confused. "They want you to play football?" she asked, hesitating just a little. "Like . . . on the team?"

I smiled. Not a bad day overall.

That night we went to dinner at my uncle's house. He lived in a smaller place on the north end of town, tucked onto a little suburban road. I noticed his house was a little run-down, and the normally tidy front yard was overgrown and wild. That was surprising, since my uncle always seemed so full of energy. Clearly he wasn't doing yard work.

When we climbed out of the car their dog, a beautiful golden retriever named Stella, ran out to meet us. I had always wanted a dog, but my mom was allergic to them. The only pet we'd ever had was Muffin, and after she died, I didn't really want another one. It was too sad saying goodbye. I'd had enough of that with my grandparents.

Aunt Sandra met us at the door, and after a flurry of joyous hugs, she led us right to the dinner table. She was a very pretty woman who seemed a bit tired herself. Her long russet hair was frayed and her normally cheerful blue eyes looked worn and cloudy. I could tell that the factory closing down was having a big impact on both of them.

"How are you?" she asked, heading to the kitchen to get dinner.

Uncle Laine walked in, trailed by my cousins, Emma and Peter. They were only five and nine years old, and they were really cute with their jet-black hair and big blue eyes. I had seen Emma running around at school earlier but hadn't gotten the chance to say hi. I smiled at them and turned to the kitchen.

"Pretty good," I said. "Getting used to everything, I guess."

Aunt Sandra smiled as she walked back in with a ham. "It always takes some time. Can you help me with the vegetables, dear?" she asked my uncle.

There was noticeable tension in her voice.

He gave me a lopsided grin and went to help her, and I turned to my cousins.

"Hey, guys," I said. "How's school going?"

"Good," Emma said immediately. "I like my new teacher. Peter doesn't. He said his teacher is mean."

Peter nodded. "She is."

"It happens," I said. "Everything else okay?"

Peter shrugged. "I guess. Mom and Dad have been fighting—"

"Okay then," Uncle Laine said, coming in with two big plates of steaming vegetables. "That's not happy dinner talk." He put the plates down. "Everyone dig in! I'm starving. Got to work a night shift tonight."

"Really?" my mom asked. "I didn't know you had to do nights."

"Oh yeah," he said. "Have been for awhile now. Tom, what do you want?"

"A bit of everything," Tom replied.

"That's my boy," Laine said, dumping some food on his plate.

Aunt Sandra gingerly sat down beside Laine at the table, still looking slightly agitated. I wondered what was wrong as I filled my plate up and dug into the ham.

"It's delicious," I said.

"Thanks, sweetie," she replied, pouring some red wine. A little rivulet spilled over the lip of the glass, she poured so much. "How's the house coming along, Pat?"

"It's coming," my dad said, already digging into the roasted potatoes. "Gonna take a lot of work, but it'll be worth it. Laine was right: it has a lot of potential."

"And a lot of spiders," I added distastefully.

Laine snorted. "I knew you'd like it. Anything else of interest in there?"

"Well, I've already heard mysterious rattling, found a warning carved into the wall, seen yellow eyes watching me from the woods—"

"She has a vivid imagination," my mother cut in, glaring at me.

When I'd shown her the warning, she told me that clearly the person living in my room before me had been equally "creative," as she called it. I had just scowled and left it alone—clearly my mother was going to be no help. She wasn't one for conspiracies.

"Rattling?" Laine asked, glancing at me. "What bedroom are you in? I took a walk through there a few months ago—didn't mess with the spiders, of course."

"The one with the walk-in," I replied. "Facing the backyard."

I saw him glance at Tom, as if surprised, and then back at me. "You didn't want the bigger one at the back of the house? I figured Tom would take the one with the closet."

I shrugged. "Mom said I should have the walk-in. Not that I use it."

"Yeah, I guess it makes sense," he said slowly. "What's the rattling coming from?"

"I don't know yet. Probably a ghost trying to escape my closet."

Laine was silent for a moment, and then he just laughed and shook his head. "Nothing would surprise me in this town."

"What do you mean?" Tom asked.

"The old guys tell stories," Laine said casually. "Things they've seen in the woods . . . stuff like that."

"Oh," I said. "Thanks for encouraging us to move here."

Laine waved a hand. "Just old guys seeing things. You want more, honey?"

Emma nodded and he scooped some potatoes on her plate and gently kissed her forehead. He might have looked like a bear, but I've never seen a more affectionate parent than my uncle Laine. I knew he'd do anything for his kids, which explained why potentially losing his job was having such a big impact on him.

The rest of the dinner was normal enough, and when we all stood up at the end, I felt my belt straining. Thanking Aunt Sandra profusely, we all went to get our coats on. I stopped at the bathroom on the way, which was just beside the kitchen. On the way out, I heard a quiet conversation and stopped at the door, listening.

"I just don't know why you have to work again tonight," Aunt Sandra was saying.

"I told you," Laine replied. "We need the money."

"Well, why am I not seeing it?" she asked, her voice rising just a little.

"It's a bonus at the end. I explained all this. It adds to the severance payment."

"I just wish you'd stick around a little more. The kids miss you. And look at this place. I'm embarrassed to have your family over."

"It looks fine! They had fun—"

Feeling rude, I loudly opened the door and hurried to the front. The conversation stopped immediately. Throwing on my jacket, I joined Tom and my parents just as my uncle and aunt came to say goodbye. Peter and Emma were already watching TV.

My uncle gave me a big hug. "Good luck with the haunted house."

"Thanks," I muttered, hugging my aunt. "See you guys soon."

We went out to the car and waved to them as we drove down the road.

"That was awkward," Tom said.

"Yeah," my mom agreed quietly. "I'm a little worried about them."

"They'll be fine," Stache said. "Laine will figure out something."

"I hope so," I murmured, staring out the window.

Later that night I sat in my room at my brand-new desk and looked at a picture of Liam R. Kelp online. That sounds bad. I just glanced at it, really. His profile picture was him standing with his arm around his mom. Literally asking for someone to make fun of him. It was official.

I really did love him.

I'd exchanged cellphone numbers with Mia and Shal, but I didn't actually expect them to call me. As a result I almost fell off my chair when my phone rang at 10:15, and I quickly closed Liam's page, as if whoever was calling could see what I was doing.

"Hello?" I said tentatively.

"Hey, Laura," Shal said. "What's up?"

"Uhh . . ." I replied.

Anything but staring at Liam. Anything but staring at Liam.

"Cleaning my room?"

"Are you asking me?" Shal said. "Never mind. Mia's on the line."

"Hi, Laura," Mia said brightly. She actually kind of sounded like a mouse too.

"Hi," I said. "What are you guys doing?"

"Just talking," Shal replied. "Were you thinking about Liam when we called?"

"No," I said way too quickly.

They both giggled.

"She's in love," Shal said. "You can tell."

"I am not in love," I replied sternly.

Shal snorted. "Don't be so embarrassed. Mia can't even look at a boy without blushing."

"It's true," Mia said sadly. "And Shal likes Carl."

"Mia!" Shal said. "That was classified."

"Isn't Carl the guy who always talks to Allison Black?" I asked.

"Maybe," Shal murmured. "Your crush doesn't have to be realistic."

I clicked on Liam's page again and smiled. "I guess not."

"Are you looking at Liam's profile?" Shal asked.

"No," I said quickly, closing it again. I knew that was going to happen. "Besides, you could get Carl. You're just as cute as Allison and three hundred times nicer."

"Don't lie to me," Shal said. She paused. "You really think—"

Then I heard it. Rattling. I slowly turned to my closet, tuning out Shal as she talked about a possible love affair with Carl. The rattling grew louder.

"Sorry, guys, my mom needs me," I said distractedly. "I'll see you guys in the morning."

I didn't even wait for them to respond. This time the lights were on, and I wasn't curled up in bed. There was no excuse. I wanted to see what was making the noise.

I crept toward the closet door and gently pulled it open. The rattling grew even louder. I nervously scanned the closet and froze. One of the white wooden panels was shaking back and forth. It was the one with the message carved on it.

I crouched down and slowly ran my fingers along the edge, and I was halfway down the side when I felt a sudden catch. A little square on the side of the panel popped inward if you pressed on it. Well, I'd gone this far. I pressed the square all the way in, hearing a click, and then pulled the panel open. My eyes widened.

"I'm really starting to dislike this house," I whispered.

Chapter Six

I was looking into a tiny wooden room, tall and narrow and unmarked except for what looked like a crude lever on the opposite wall. The walls were made of a light wood, and I realized that the room must have been built inside of that overlarge, fake chimney that dominated the living room downstairs. I just crouched there for a moment, trying to wrap my head around what I was seeing. There was a room in my closet.

I knew I should probably go wake my parents, but I was a bit hesitant. For one, I'd seen enough movies to suspect that this door would somehow disappear by the time I got back here, and my mom would just pat my shoulder and tell me how the stress of moving was causing me to hallucinate again. I was really getting sick of those comforting pats. Besides, a secret room in my closet might come in handy if I ever managed to get popular or have a social life. I figured I might as well investigate.

I crawled through the panel and stood up in the small room, looking around curiously. Maybe it was a hideout built during the war or something. Maybe there used to be a witch living in this house who had to hide whenever the peasants came around. The possibilities were endless. I ran my hands along the three wooden walls, which were worn and smoothed from wear. Inevitably my eyes fell on the lever. It was nothing more than a small plank of wood attached to a rusty old cog, but what it did, I had no idea. Perhaps there was another secret room behind this one?

I reached out for it, the much smarter side of my brain telling me that it probably wasn't a great idea to pull a lever without knowing what it did.

But I don't listen to the smarter side of my brain nearly as much as I should . . . probably because it's usually telling me to eat some celery and go for a jog. My hands found the old lever, and with a final guilty look back into my closet, I pushed down on it.

Yep, I'm an idiot.

The room suddenly plummeted downward, and I realized with a feeling of complete and utter stupidity that it wasn't a room: it was an elevator. And it moved fast. My socked feet started floating off the floor as the elevator dropped like a stone. I frantically tried to grab onto something. My grasping hands found the lever, and I clutched it desperately and screamed as the elevator just kept falling. I tried to pull the lever up but it wouldn't budge. I was trapped.

My panicked brain started to wonder if the elevator was even attached to anything, or if I was literally just plummeting down a hole. What if it went on forever? What if I smashed into a lake of lava? My body just kept rising higher and higher off the floor, and I gripped the lever, my knuckles turning white, and screamed until my voice was hoarse. I pictured Stache and my mom when they found the elevator shaft in my closet, when they realized what had happened, when they told Tom. My eyes started to water and then tears streamed freely from my face, heading up instead of down and soaking into my hair. It was all over. I was going to die. I remembered the warning carved into the panel: it's not too late. I really wish they'd been a little more specific.

And then, suddenly, I saw light. White light.

I assumed I must have died, since any light under the earth would obviously be the fiery red of lava. There was no other explanation: I must have died. Except why was I still falling?

The light grew brighter and suddenly the shaft slipped away at the front of the elevator. The elevator only had three walls—the front was completely open. I wasn't staring at endless rock anymore. I was staring at . . . a landscape. For a second, I forgot I was even falling. I just looked out in bewilderment as a massive green expanse opened up in front of me, stretching for miles in all directions and seemingly meeting distant, towering rocky walls on all sides. It didn't make any sense: I saw what looked like homes and roads and even a brilliant blue lake shimmering in the light. But how was there light? I peered up, leaning out just a little to get a better view, and saw something shining far above, nestled against the ceiling of stone that stretched farther than should have been possible. None of it made any sense.

And then I looked down and saw that the beautiful green landscape was rushing toward me at breakneck speed. I was going to smash into the ground.

I screamed again, even more desperately than before, clawing at the wooden ceiling of the elevator to see if there was any way out. My body was still weightless, powerless, and the ground rushed ever closer. I was going to smash into it.

It happened slowly, so that I didn't even really notice it at first. I started feeling heavier, and my kicking socked feet touched the ground, my grip on the lever loosening. The ground started to approach a bit more slowly, and I realized with a tinge of hope that the elevator might not be broken after all. In fact, I was soon gliding along at a comfortable clip, and when it finally touched down, it was just a gentle bump in the tall grass. I leaned against the elevator wall, unable to move. My entire body was shaking violently.

I found myself looking at a winding dirt pathway running out from the elevator, cutting across an emerald meadow of tall grass and tiny flitting butterflies. Squat farmhouses lined the pathway like patches of flowers, and in the distance a huge stone castle, white as ivory, perched on a rocky outcropping, bordering a quaint town and that crystal clear lake that glinted in the blazing light of whatever was up on the ceiling. I even think I saw a bird wheeling around overhead, though it looked abnormally large and blue.

But most notable of all was the little old man sitting in a rocking chair beside the elevator, smiling at me through a beard like a snow-covered thicket, tiny yellow stumps of teeth just visible through the brambles.

"So it was you," he said thoughtfully. "Eldon won't be happy."

I stared at him for a moment before finally finding my voice. "What?"

His eyes were grey and stormy, not matching his frail appearance or smile. "You're the one," he said, looking me up and down. "Eldon said it had to be wrong. That the house had made a mistake and would fix it. But you're here, and that means it's you." He chuckled. "The other ones are going to have a field day. And at such a time, too."

I gingerly walked out of the elevator, testing the spongy ground with my toe. Yep, it was real. I turned around and looked up, feeling my stomach drop to my toes when I saw just how far I had plummeted down in that elevator. The dark opening in the cavern ceiling was just a pinprick.

"Was it fun?" the old man asked, following my gaze. "I've never been."

I turned and looked at him again. "Who are you?"

"Porton," he said, extending a frail, wrinkled hand. I shook it out of habit, and I felt him test my grip. He was much stronger than he looked. "I'm a Watcher . . . one of fifty. We keep an eye on the doorways. Of course, you're one of fifty too." He laughed again. "But they weren't expecting you, my dear. I can tell you that. On that note, you should get along. Head for Arnwell Castle. Well, it's a training ground these days, really, I suppose. If you want to call it that."

"A training ground for what?" I asked nervously, my eyes on the great stone castle in the distance. How was any of this possible? How was I under the ground?

He smiled. "You'll see."

I looked back at the elevator, thinking maybe it was time to get out of here. Porton obviously guessed my thoughts, because he smiled and folded his frail hands in his lap.

"You can go back, of course. But I don't recommend it. Have you seen the yellow eyes yet?"

I frowned. "Yes."

The smile disappeared from his face. "Then go to Arnwell. Your time has come."

I held his gaze for a moment, locked on those stormy eyes. There was something in his soft voice that told me he was the kind of man you wanted to listen to. That he meant what he said. I shifted, still looking out over the strange landscape in front of me. Rocks and boulders and stalagmites rose from the grass like quiet sentinels, watching me.

"Will you at least tell me where I am?"

"Of course. You're in Derwin, one of the last five realms in the Under Earth. The smallest of the five, but perhaps the most important."

He smiled again when he saw the look of incredulity on my face.

"I suppose you never thought there was life beneath your feet?"

"But . . . how can that . . . I don't get it."

Porton nodded. "Understandable. Be content for the moment to know that there have always been two worlds, and only one has ever really known about the other." He gestured to the gleaming white castle. "Now go. Eldon is waiting."

I had a million more questions for the frail old man, but I sensed he wasn't going to answer any more. I was still tempted to get back on the elevator, but could I really just ignore this now? There was an entire world in my closet, and I figured I might as well get some answers before I risked my life on that rickety, old wooden elevator. I certainly wasn't coming back down ever again, not on that death trap.

"Okay," I murmured, and then I started down the pathway.

I looked around numbly as I went, trying to figure out if I was dreaming. The cavern, if you could call it that, was almost endless, rolling with lush green hills and tranquil woods and babbling streams cutting through the landscape like ribbons. The air was warm but comfortable, and almost unnaturally still, as there was no wind underground. It was the strangest and most beautiful place I'd ever seen, made all the more so by the glittering white castle that looked like a stalagmite of pure ice in the distance. I saw a few lizards perched atop rocks, as if sunning themselves—all with big, glassy eyes and dark skin. Multicoloured birds flitted around overhead, perhaps nesting way up on the cavern ceiling, which loomed over everything like a great canopy of storm clouds. The whole scene was earth-like but distorted: the lush meadows pockmarked with stone outcroppings, the forests with purple leaves mixed in the greenery, and the sky that ended in hard stone.

Soon the squat houses I had seen before appeared around me, perched in the grass like cute little toadstools. Most were built of grey stone slung into place with mortar, though their roofs alternated between planks of wood or straw or even looser brush tied into bundles and laid over the stones. I wasn't even sure what you would need a roof for, considering the ceiling that covered the entire realm surely didn't allow rain, but what did I know? I also wasn't sure why people were living in a hole in the earth, so it was all relative.

It wasn't long before people started noticing me too. Villagers poked curiously out of open windows or peered at me from tilled wheat fields, while small children stopped playing to stare and whispered amongst themselves. I awkwardly waved at a couple of little girls in dresses and they ran away. I felt like the Closet Monster again—I could picture my aunt laughing at the irony that I had literally emerged from the closet.

The houses grew closer and closer together, and the pathway soon turned to dirty white cobblestone as the scattered farmhouses became a bustling village. Now there were people everywhere: they looked normal enough, though a bit behind the times. The women wore coarse brown dresses and hide boots, and they all stared at me and whispered. There were only a few men, who wore the same kind of woollen peasant clothing, and many had thick beards and thicker arms. Some of them just laughed when they saw me, which would have been insulting except that I'm sure I did look pretty ridiculous with my pink-and-white striped socks, red pyjama pants, and blue hoodie.

I did notice one peculiar thing about the people of Derwin: many of them had weapons. In fact, almost all of them did. Swords and knives were sheathed at their waists, and some even had broadaxes slung on their backs, the metal blades banged up and worn. Others wore necklaces with fangs on the end, and I'm pretty sure one of them had a yellow eyeball on a chain, which almost made me vomit right there in the street.

Arnwell Castle was growing larger ahead of me, and I saw now that it was bordered by tall walls and parapets, though the arched gate was open. It sat on a small hill overlooking the lake, which bordered the edge of the town and stretched out a long way in the distance. I was again struck by how incredibly clear the water looked . . . it was as still as glass and marked only by some old boats lazily fishing off the rocky coast. The entire village looked like one of those cheesy postcards your grandma sends you, minus the strange abundance of weaponry and the fact that this particular village was deep underground. Which were fairly important points, I guess.

Finally reaching Arnwell's gate, which was almost seven feet high, I stopped and looked through the opening into a huge courtyard. It was completely packed with . . . boys. The white stone walls bordered three sides of the courtyard, while the castle itself took up the fourth, looking over everything like a watchful teacher, proud and silent.

The courtyard was built of the same white cobblestone as the castle, but it was scuffed and worn and stained in places with a dark liquid that might have been blood. It was also filled with the strangest array of things I have ever seen. There were crude wooden rings for sparring, logs to jump over, ropes to swing on, massive carts to push, and weapons everywhere. But that wasn't even close to the weirdest part.

Scattered in between all those items were fake creatures stuffed with straw. They were stitched together with what looked like thick leather, and all of them were scarred with rips and tears and gashes. Straw was poking out of the wounds like gushing blood. I saw one that looked like a troll, another a goblin, and some larger ones that looked like dragons and ogres. Little stuffed creatures with wood-framed wings were scattered everywhere, and there was even a huge fake spider that did not make me happy at all. I eyed the creatures, standing there uneasily as the young men slammed axes into the creatures' heads and fired black-feathered arrows into wings.

I noticed now that while many of the assembled warriors were wearing brown peasant clothes and long hooded cloaks, many others were wearing jeans or track pants and tight-fitting T-shirts, revealing muscular arms. All of the latter were boys, though I did start to notice a few girls amongst the hooded warriors. Now I was really confused.

Who were these people, and why were they attacking monster scarecrows? I tried to step against the wall to avoid being seen, but I was too late.

A tall boy with curly black hair and a strong jaw spotted me first, standing up straight and letting his massive battle-axe rest on his shoulder. He was wearing a Star Trek T-shirt, which would have been awesome if he wasn't holding that axe.

He nudged the boy next to him, and one by one, the word seemed to filter through the crowd, and the fighting stopped. I would have assumed that would have been replaced by talking or gossip or something, but no. They all just kind of looked at me, eyebrows raised in confusion or doubt or who knows what. I wanted to run away, but that probably wouldn't help my first impression. So I kind of just stood there, smiling like I had walked into someone else's party and was now going to slowly let myself out again.

I never got the chance.

The crowd suddenly parted, and a tall man with a long cloak swept through it like a stalking predator, his hood draped over his strong shoulders. I immediately knew it was the man from the woods behind my house, because there was no mistaking those eyes. They were as bright and clear as the lake, and they made the hair on my arms stand up when they fell on me. He was really cute for an older guy but grim; a white scar ran from his forehead to his chin, passing right through one of those icy blue eyes. He was grizzled with stubble, and his dark hair fell right to his shoulders, framing proud cheekbones. Without even asking, I knew this must be Eldon. I stood there rooted to the spot as he stopped in front of me, his eyes passing once over me and then resting on mine.

"It's as I feared," he said quietly. "The spell is broken."

Chapter Seven

I waited for him to say something else, but he just stood there for a very long moment, looking at me like I was a bug. The gathered warriors around him still weren't speaking, though some exchanged meaningful looks, their expressions dark. I shifted uneasily, and then decided to break the silence.

"Do you mind explaining who you people are?" I asked, trying to sound braver than I felt. I tucked my hands in my pockets to hide the trembling, but my knees were shaking even worse than my hands. I really hoped they didn't give out.

Eldon just stared at me, obviously trying to decide what to do. I suspected he had half a mind to shut the heavy iron gate and tell me to go home, but clearly something was stopping him. Finally, he spoke.

"These," he said, gesturing around him, "are the Monster Crushers. Well, some of them are. The rest are their guardians, or as we call them, their Swords."

I looked at him with what I'm sure was a blank expression. "The Monster what?"

"Monster Crushers," he repeated quietly, "the warriors

that protect this planet from the horrors beneath their feet. They are chosen from across the surface world by a spell as old as the homes they live in—a spell that until this day has chosen warriors capable of bearing the Iron Hammers and defending the earth from monsters." His blue eyes narrowed. "And those Monster Crushers have just been dealt a very dangerous blow."

"Because of me?" I whispered.

"Yes," he replied coolly. "Because of you. The Monster Crushers do not choose their members. We are bound by law to let the houses choose, as the spell is supposed to only allow those worthy to find the secret doors and enter Derwin. And because of this same law, we now have no choice but to train you as a Monster Crusher."

I laughed. I didn't mean to, but it just kind of came out. Surely he was joking. There was no way I was going to live down here and hit fake monsters with swords, just as I was sure there was no way they'd want me to. I looked around, shaking my head. Almost all of the boys looked like they were captains of the football team: square jaws, defined muscles, stern looks. I looked like an absent-minded grandma who had just wandered out of the house in her pyjamas. Except I was also thirteen, which I'm pretty sure was younger than anyone else in that courtyard.

Eldon didn't laugh. No one did. In fact, they just looked angry.

"You can't be serious," I said, turning back to Eldon.

"I am. Like it or not, the spell has chosen. Even if I believe it has finally been broken, I cannot make that decision myself. That's up to the Brotherhood. And so I will train you, girl, to the best of my abilities. And then I suspect you will die, and we will all have to live with the consequences of what happens after that. What is your name?"

"Laura Ledwick," I whispered.

Eldon nodded. "Very well, Laura Ledwick. Come with me."

He turned and strode back toward the gleaming white castle, and I just stood there, looking around incredulously. Was he serious? There was no way he was serious.

Eldon stopped and turned around, his eyes narrowed. "Now."

I hesitated, and then very reluctantly followed him, trying to ignore the disbelieving stares as I shuffled through the courtyard.

"Are those like . . . accurate?" I murmured.

I was staring up at the elaborate murals that covered the great hall of Arnwell Castle, which was a massive, domed room dominated by a beautiful marble floor and a ring of golden statues of what I could only guess were past Monster Crushers. Every one of them was a man: tall, strong, and proud. Their cold eyes watched me from all sides.

But the statues were the least of my concern. The murals on the wall depicted actual battles between the Monster Crushers and their foes: grotesque trolls with mossy-green skin, yellow orbs for eyes, and shocks of black hair swung stone clubs at brave young men with iron hammers and gleaming steel armour. Dragons flew above the scenes, while hordes of goblins swept like a green tide toward the Monster Crushers and the hooded Swords that stood beside them.

"More or less," Eldon said, finally turning to face me.

He had led me straight to the great hall from the court-yard, his steps echoing around the massive room as he stalked into the middle.

"You must have questions," he continued. watching me closely.

I snorted. "That's an understatement."

"Let me give you the brief version. And then we can discuss your training."

I opened my mouth to say something, but he ignored me and went on.

"When humans first appeared on this planet, some-where in the northeastern heart of Africa, they went many ways. North to Europe, east to Asia, south to the tip of the continent. Those you know. But humans went one other way. Down."

He suddenly turned and started walking again, and I hurried to keep up.

"Early humans always gravitated to caves, as you know, but some decided to go deeper. They went deep enough that they discovered places like this . . . places where the world reset again and where water pooled into lakes and even tiny patches of vegetation grew in the dim sunlight that filtered through the cracks."

He gestured to a painting at the far side of the hall, where some early humans were walking with a torch through the darkness.

"It was a difficult road to take, but they had an advan-tage. No predators, no competition, and from very early on . . . magic."

He stopped in front of another line of statues: hooded men with serious eyes and scraggly beards. They looked like wizards.

"The ground beneath them hummed with magic . . . it was hidden down here in the darkness. They began to find new ways to create light with alchemy and spells, real light that could grow crops and scare away the shadows of the Under Earth."

He clasped his hands behind his back, looking thoughtfully at the statues.

"Ten of these great openings in the Under Earth were found—the foundation for the ten realms, of which Derwin is the smallest. For centuries, the ten realms grew in peace. The people of the Under Earth wanted no part of the endless wars on the surface; instead they worked together to build the most complicated series of tunnels ever devised by man. Any tunnels created by surface humans are but a pinprick of what they created. Most thought we would long outlast the surface humans here. We could journey up to take seeds and livestock and building techniques, and continue living down below. In fact, the surface humans forgot we were here. We were ignored. And that's how we liked it. Thousands of years ago, we decided to keep it that way."

I frowned, scanning the murals. "So what happened?"

"We realized we were not alone," Eldon said quietly, following my gaze.

A little ways down, there was a disturbing picture. Yellow eyes flashed from the darkness, just like the ones I had seen in the forest behind my house. Slit-like pupils, like a snake, watched from the shadows. I felt my skin crawl as I realized the implications.

There were monsters behind my house.

"One day our tunnels merged with one the humans had not made. A crude tunnel reeking of rotting meat and death. The diggers followed it, and they soon realized there were other realms even farther beneath the earth. And there were not humans there."

I followed the murals and saw the monsters emerging from the darkness, their eyes flashing like candles.

"There are many types of monsters," Eldon explained. "Some as wild as animals, most as evil and insidious as the worst of humans. I do not know which side was more to blame: we hunted them, and they hunted us. But we had no idea of the horrors we were unleashing. There were so many of them. They spread through the Under Earth, and many of our people were wiped out. Five of the ten realms were overrun by monster armies. Hundreds of thousands of our people were lost. The Brotherhood—an ancient order of wizards that oversees all people of the Under Earth—knew it was only a matter of time before they spread to the surface and claimed the entire earth as their own. The monsters' realms were so deep they didn't even know of the surface back then, but of course, our tunnels would lead them right to it. We had doomed the surface humans as well."

He turned to me, and his blue eyes flashed with pride as he spoke.

"That was when the Brotherhood, led by Warlin the Wise, created a desperate defence against the monsters. He knew the people of the Under Earth could not do it alone;

they needed reinforcements from the surface. They needed Monster Crushers."

We slowly walked along the mural, and I saw hooded men forging weapons while others built elevators and winding stone staircases to the surface. I saw one grim bearded man creating a secret door in a walk-in closet, and I wondered vaguely if it was mine.

"There are fifty locations on the surface that we have tunnels to," Eldon explained, "created throughout the centuries. In those places, fifty houses were built to shelter future warriors, each endowed with a powerful spell to select only worthy Monster Crushers. These warriors would find the entryways when the time was right and come to Arnwell Castle for training. The Brotherhood wanted surface humans for two reasons: they would defend the entryways to their homes with everything they had, and they also didn't know enough about the monsters to truly fear them. Our children had lived entire lives in terror of the creatures, hearing stories from their wet nurses. But the surface humans could not possibly know what they would face until it was too late."

He stopped in front of a golden statue of a particularly tall boy with tousled hair and a massive hammer slung over his back, his biceps bulging where they emerged from a tunic. He looked like a male model or something.

"And so those fifty young men became the first Monster Crushers. Each Monster Crusher received a group of Swords: five warriors chosen from both worlds to help them guard their tunnels and fight the wars of the Under Earth. They all trained here, and they fought and died bravely for hundreds of years after, and still do. Each is responsible for his own location, and no other. Monster Crushers cannot help another, nor can their Swords, for fear that they would leave their own tunnels unguarded. The Monster Crusher and his Swords must defend their tunnels, or doom the surface world."

Eldon turned to me.

"Throughout all that history, only one location on the surface has ever had monsters leave the tunnels and kill civilians. That same town has been the centre of countless wars underground and has been the site of more battles than any in our long history. It is the focal point of the war, and today, it is the only place on earth where we know monsters are on the surface. Do you know what town that is?"

"I have a guess," I murmured.

"Riverfield: home of the very first Monster Crusher, Daniel the Dragon Killer, and the home of some of the most famous Monster Crushers in history. Three of the statues in this room hail from your town. And that is where Laura Ledwick has found the elevator and thrust herself into the middle of the longest war in the history of mankind."

I just stood there for a moment. I didn't know whether to laugh at the ridiculousness of the story, cry that I was here, or just run away like I should have done twenty-five times by now. But instead I just looked at the statue, and then back at Eldon.

"Can't we just pretend I didn't find it?"

For the first time, Eldon laughed. It wasn't really an amused laugh, but it was something. It echoed around the massive room, and then he shook his head sadly.

"No, Laura. We can't pretend. When someone comes through, they must be trained, and then they must be tested by the Brotherhood. It's the law. The Brotherhood are almost all gone, their magic faded, but the Monster Crushers were built on that law, and I won't change it now. You will train to fight, and if you pass the tests, you will wield an Iron Hammer, and the identities of your five Swords will be revealed to you. What happens then, I do not know. But I have an educated guess."

His smile was gone again.

"I am sorry, Laura. But you are the newest Monster Crusher, and you must do your job. If you don't, the monsters will kill you regardless. When you opened that panel, you sealed your fate. And ours."

I stared at him. That didn't seem very fair. I had so many questions I couldn't even pick one. There was no way I was ever coming back down here. I was going to go home, push everything I had in front of that secret panel, and pretend I had never seen any of this. Which, of course, led me to the one question I really needed to ask.

"Is my family in danger?"

"Yes," he said. "But so is everyone else's if you don't protect Riverfield. I have Swords from the Protectorate, as well as your Swords, watching your house already—"

"Who are they?" I interrupted.

He frowned. "There are ten Swords here that serve as our Protectorate, which means they patrol the tunnels around Derwin and if necessary can help out on the surface, though I usually only do that in special circumstances, like now. As for your Swords, their identities are protected until you pass your training. Suffice to say you are guarded. But the monsters are coming forth from the darkness in ever greater numbers, and we can't protect you forever." He suddenly reached out and took my arm. "I can promise you one thing, Laura Ledwick. If you don't go to the monsters, they will come to you."

He released my arm and abruptly started for the courtyard.

"It's time to go home. Return tomorrow night when the panel rattles."

"Why does the panel rattle?" I asked. "How do you do that?"

"I don't know," Eldon said. "I've always wondered that myself. It's part of the spell I suppose, but I would be lying if I told you I really understood magic. It rattles at certain times only, and only for certain people—the ones who are supposed to find the door. After that, it rattles for the Monster Crushers when they are called to do their training. It is the same for all fifty houses across the world. It always seems to know when the best time is . . . which should be around when you go upstairs to bed."

"What if someone else hears the rattling? My brother—"

"Then you will tell him it is just the wind and move on. Understand?"

I thought about that. Tom had super hearing, but at least he was a heavy sleeper. As long as it only rattled at night, it should be fine. But that didn't mean I wanted to come back.

"Get going," Eldon said impatiently. "Return as soon as the door rattles."

"But—"

"You will be training, so you might as well wear comfortable clothes. You will train for four hours, so take a nap beforehand. You will not be getting a lot of sleep. And tell no one of any of this, or there will be consequences for you and whomever you tell."

"I didn't even agree—"

He stopped at the doorway. "And before I forget." He pulled a dusty old book out of his cloak; it was thick and bulky, and the cover was marked with a small rectangle with three diamonds in the middle. "Take this. *The Complete Guide to Monster Crushing*. It was created by the Monster Crushers of Riverfield that came before you. Read it."

I gingerly took the book, staring at the symbol. "Can I just—"

He led me into the courtyard, and I blinked in the light.

"See you tomorrow, Laura. I hope you are a lot more capable than you look."

I scowled. "Thanks."

With that, Eldon swept back inside, his cloak billowing out behind him, and I was left in the courtyard surrounded by those same confused stares. Tucking the book under my arm, I hurried out into the village, my cheeks burning as the whispers finally started.

"She has a guide!"

"It can't be."

"You don't think he's actually training her, do you?"

I hurried all the way through the village, ignoring everyone, and started jogging down the dirt pathway, clutching the book to my chest. By the time I reached Porton and the elevator, I was drenched in sweat. He raised his bushy white eyebrows in surprise.

"Back so soon?"

"Yeah," I muttered, walking past him. "Am I going to die on this thing?"

He shrugged. "I certainly hope not."

"That's reassuring."

I walked into the elevator and reluctantly put my hand on the lever.

Porton smiled. "Have fun."

Frowning, I pulled the lever, and the elevator suddenly shot upward. I dropped the book and grabbed the lever with both hands as the elevator flew toward the cavern ceiling, barely slower than it had plummeted down in the first place. I watched as the realm of Derwin started shrinking away below me, the white spot of Arnwell Castle becoming as small as a droplet of rain. I caught a glimpse of some massive mechanical contraption on the cavern ceiling, blazing white, and then the elevator disappeared into the shaft again. The climb was seemingly endless, too dark to see, and my stomach roiled as I flew upward, clutching the lever in terror. Finally the elevator slowed again and settled into place right where I had started, the small panel still open to my closet.

I immediately crawled through, grabbing the book on the way, and then swung the panel shut behind me. I sat there on the floor for a long time, holding the book and trying to comprehend what I had just seen. None of it made any sense: sorcerers and goblins and Monster

Crushers. Realms beneath the earth. And yet here I was, leaning against an elevator shaft in my closet. It was almost too much to deal with.

I tossed the book in the corner and started out of my closet, shutting the door behind me.

"Laura?"

I almost jumped through the ceiling. My mom was poking her head through the door, a pink sleep mask pulled up onto her forehead. I glanced at my alarm clock . . . it was after eleven.

"Oh," I said, trying to recover. "Hey."

My mom frowned and walked into the room. "What are you doing?"

"Just organizing the closet," I said absently, dusting the door frame with my hand.

I don't know why I didn't tell her about the elevator. But something told me that it would not be a good idea, and I would at least read some of the book before I decided what to do. Eldon had been pretty clear in his instructions.

"I see," my mom said, raising a manicured blond eyebrow. She was wearing her striped white-and-pink pyjamas, which matched my socks. "Let's sit down."

I followed her out into the bedroom, taking a last peek at the dusty old book poking out from behind the trophy boxes in the corner. My mom sat on the bed and patted the mattress beside her. I reluctantly sat down, my eyes still on the closet. This was not the best time for a mother–daughter chat.

"Were you having nightmares?" my mom asked quietly.

I used to have nightmares a lot growing up. I think it had something to do with the bullying at school. I'd lie awake for a while thinking about the things they'd said and what I should have done differently and how I wished I looked like Portia Carson, and when I finally slipped off, I would dream of shadowy things attacking me or falling off cliffs or just waking up alone. I also had lots of dreams of losing Tom, which isn't good for an overprotective sister. Needless to say I'd woken up screaming or crying a whole bunch of times in my life, and my mom or Stache would come in and wait with me until I went back to sleep.

"I was in the closet," I pointed out.

She shrugged. "I thought maybe you went to hide in there."

"I stopped doing that when I was ten," I muttered. "I'm fine."

She gently took my hand. "You know, Laura, I'm really proud of you."

"What for?" I asked, frowning.

"You didn't complain once about this move. And you went to school today and you were brave and you made new friends. You know your father wanted to renovate and I had a little . . . thing with Brenda, but that's not the only reason we moved. We also moved because we wanted to give you a fresh start. A chance to make friends and get away from that awful Portia Carson. And here you are doing just what I had hoped for."

I glanced at her. "You moved here for me?"

She nodded. "It was part of the reason, to be sure."

"I didn't know that," I said quietly.

She leaned over and hugged me. "Well, now you do. Get some sleep, honey."

"Will do." I thought of something as she started for the door. "Mom?"

She looked back.

"Thanks," I said.

She smiled and closed the door behind her. I thought about what she said for a moment, and then decided I had better try to get some sleep. I took a quick look out my window, saw nothing, and then plopped onto my bed, staring at the stucco ceiling. Monsters took shape in the pits and I turned on my side, pulling the blanket up to my eyes and huddling there like I used to when I was a kid. I knew one thing for sure.

Eighth grade was going to be even more interesting than I thought.

Chapter Eight

When I woke up the next morning, I rolled out of bed, blinking sleepily. It had been at least 5:30 a.m. when I finally drifted off, which meant I'd only slept for about an hour and a half. I was so tired that for just a second I forgot all about the secret door in my closet.

But it all came rushing back as soon as I looked over at my window and saw the thick canopy rustling in the wind, just visible through the opening in my new curtains.

It could have been a dream, I decided. As long as the secret door in my closet was gone, I would never have to think about monster crushing again. So I tiptoed across my room, fairly certain that the door would have vanished with the arrival of morning. I snuck a peek inside the closet and then knelt down beside the panel and felt for the little catch. The catch popped inward and the panel swung right open just like it had last night.

Once again I was staring into the elevator, the lever beckoning for me to pull it.

"Okay then," I said, quickly closing the panel.

It's not too late stared back at me as I shut it.

"Thanks for the heads-up," I muttered.

I grabbed a pair of faded old jeans and a blue T-shirt that would have inevitably led to some sort of blue whale reference at my old school and then hurried back out of the closet, shutting the door firmly behind me. After changing, I opened my newly installed brown curtains all the way to let some sunlight in. It was too fast to be sure, but I thought I saw big, yellow eyes instantly vanish in the woods. The same eyes that had emerged from the darkness in the mural in Arnwell Castle. Monster eyes.

I wanted to tell my parents about the secret door. Or at least Tom. But I remembered Eldon's ominous warning, and the threat in his cold blue eyes, so I just went downstairs like everything was perfectly normal. I did not want to make enemies of Eldon and his scary hooded warriors. I just wanted them to leave me alone. I did tuck the dusty old book into my backpack on the way—just in case I had some time to read it at school. Something told me that it might be a good idea to read as much of that guide as possible.

And if the door did rattle, I was going through. I had to tell them they had the wrong girl.

Tom was already sitting at the kitchen table eating breakfast. He always ate the exact same thing: an English muffin with strawberry jam. Not sure where he got that, but I decided to join him today.

"Jam's in the refrigerator door," Tom said absently.

He freaked me out when he read my mind like that.

"Ready for day two?" I asked, grabbing the jam.

"Yeah," he said casually. "Day one was pretty good. You?"

"Same," I replied, loading an English muffin into the

toaster. "I managed to make a couple of friends, so I can't complain. Where's Mom?"

"Getting ready," Tom said. "She seems nervous."

My mom was starting at a new salon today, and she didn't always get along with other women, so it was sort of a recipe for disaster.

"I am not nervous," my mom said, storming into the kitchen.

Her blond hair was meticulously combed and curled and complemented by two shimmering gold earrings. She tended to fake tan once in awhile, so she didn't have the same pasty skin as her children. But she must have sat in there too long yesterday, because she looked a little burnt. She stopped and turned to me.

"How do I look?" she asked, fixing her blouse.

"Lovely," Tom said.

She sighed. "Thank you, Tom. Laura?"

"Lovely," I said. "Like you just came from the beach. And forgot sunscreen."

She scowled. "I think the beds are stronger here. Are we all ready?"

The toaster popped. "Not exactly," I said, glancing at it.

"Well, eat your breakfast in the car," she replied hurriedly. "I don't want to be late." She opened the door to the basement where the sound of banging could be heard clearly. "We're going!"

The hammering stopped. "To bed?" my dad asked.

My mom rolled her eyes. "It's morning, dear."

"Oh," he said. "Well, have a good day!" The hammering started again.

"Your father has officially lost it," my mom said.

"Join the club," I muttered, slathering my muffin with jam.

Shal and Mia and I met up before the first bell and stuck together for most of the day. I managed to get in a bit of reading between subjects, and I even tucked the bulky guide into my desk so I could read it during math. As Ms. Haddock wrote out some equations on the board, I slouched down a little and opened the guide. Most people around me seemed to be either quietly chatting or dozing off, so no one noticed. Well, Liam was watching Ms. Haddock eagerly and taking notes, but that was no surprise. Making sure Shal or Mia wasn't looking over, I started reading. The handwritten table of contents was first.

Contents

Frowning, I carefully turned the page, which felt almost brittle. Everything was written in flowing black script, but it didn't look like a normal book. Lines were crossed out, sentences were added in, and notes were scribbled in the margins. It looked like five different people had written the first page with five different pens. I read the title.

The Complete Guide to Monster Crushing
By
Daniel the Dragon Killer AND Gregory the Giant's Bane
AND Thomas the Goblin Terror AND Ivan the Ogre Crusher
AND Paul the Imp Chaser

I flipped through the book. All the sections were the same. Different people had added their own notes and histories throughout the book, creating a confusing mess of scribbles.

This should be fun, I thought vaguely.

I flipped back to the first page.

If you are reading this book, you have been selected as the next Monster Crusher in Riverfield. You may be wondering what that means. The complete history and guide to becoming a successful Monster Crusher are contained within this book. You have three jobs:

1. *Keep the monsters OFF the surface.*
2. *Guard the tunnels and keep their existence a SECRET.*
3. *PROTECT the people of the Under Earth.*

How do you do all that? By crushing monsters. Before you continue, please flip to the Guide to Monsters section. It's time you see your enemies.

This is not cool, I thought, flipping to page 151. A picture of a grotesque-looking creature filled the page, sketched with pencil or charcoal. The creature was hunched and bent, with a bald head, pointed ears, and rows of sharp teeth. It wore a metal cap and was holding a crooked black sword. I read the explanation.

Goblin
These fell creatures come in many shapes and sizes. They are the most common monster in Derwin. When attacking, try to keep the hammer from swinging too far from your body, or they will sneak in and stick you with a knife. Short swings are best.

There were a few scribbled notes in the margins, but one in particular caught my eye:

I find a strong overhead blow is best.
Don't listen to Daniel—he was killed
by a goblin.

I frowned and turned to the next page. There were more monsters like the ones I had seen in the murals and in the courtyard: trolls, imps, ogres, dragons, giants, sea creatures. I saw more huge spiders that made my stomach turn. I flipped through the monsters, getting more and more concerned as I saw fangs and claws and swords.

Liam answered a question and someone behind me groaned. Glancing back, I saw Allison leaning on her elbow, looking completely disdainful. Her dark eyes flicked toward me and then fell on the book. I quickly moved it out of her view.

"What are you reading?" she asked quietly.

"Textbook," I murmured, turning back to the front.

What was I thinking? Never make eye contact with a bully.

"I see," she said.

For a few minutes I just stared at the board, too nervous to open the book again. But after awhile I heard Allison whispering to Carl, and I continued reading, turning to the Great Monster Crushers section.

One thing in particular caught my eye.

To ensure that only a worthy Monster Crusher would ever discover the elevators, the Brotherhood put a spell on all the houses. Only the next Monster Crusher can live in that bedroom and discover the panel. Once they open it they are without question the Monster Crusher, and training can begin immediately.

* Take care of my bedroom, by the way.

* It's my bedroom now.

*Not anymore. P.S. I carved a message in the panel.

* Saw that. Maybe you could have been a little clearer? Like: if you go in here, you have to kill monsters.

I sat back in my chair, my hands shaking. Eldon was right: the spell must have been broken somehow. I flipped through the rest of *The Complete Guide to Monster Crushing*. It seemed each Monster Crusher had written his own story, and I found at least twenty blank pages at the back. There were blank pages scattered throughout the book, actually. I guess the future Monster Crushers were supposed to add to the tome. I tucked the book back into my backpack after math, looking around nervously to make sure no one noticed.

I really needed to talk to Eldon. I still wasn't sure if I believed any of this, but even if it was true, I knew one thing for sure: I was definitely not the Monster Crusher.

Chapter Nine

I was so shaken by what I had read that I forgot about the possibility that my clothing choice would make me a target. But Allison and the other girls made the blue whale connection pretty fast—I saw them look at me and giggle from across the classroom as we ate lunch—but since I saw it coming it kind of bounced right off. Must have been the blubber. Better yet, Liam was wearing a red-and-blue plaid shirt that made his eyes really pop. He even looked at me. Possibly behind me. But still.

Mia, Shal, and I spent the rest of lunch hiding out in the far corner of the yard gossiping about people I didn't even know. Not bad gossip. More like, "I think Carl was talking to Ashley today" and "Did you see Carl's hair?" and "Carl is such a flirt." By the way, Shal did most of the gossiping. Mia and I were just the moral support.

I still wasn't exactly sure why Shal was unpopular. Mia was very shy and ran away from popular girls, so that made sense. But Shal was pretty and wore nice clothes and gossiped, which as far as I could tell were the basic ingredients of popular girls.

I made a mental note to ask Mia.

"I don't know what he sees in her," Shal said, picking grass and watching Allison talking to Carl. "I mean, yes, she's beautiful and popular. But she's so . . . evil."

Mia was sitting cross-legged beside me. Some of the blades of grass Shal was picking were flying into her hair, but I think she was too polite to mention anything. Shal certainly didn't notice. "I think the beautiful and popular thing helps," Mia said.

I snorted. "Just slightly. But Carl just hasn't had a chance to talk to you yet."

Shal glanced at me, running a hand through her long auburn hair. "You think?"

"Of course. If he talked to you, he'd forget all about Allison."

Shal smiled. "So not true, but thank you. What about you and Kelp?"

"What do you mean?" I asked, feeling my cheeks burning.

"Have you figured out a way to tell him you love him yet?" she asked coyly.

I sighed. "I was just going to yearn from afar for awhile. Like five to ten years. Or when I wake up and look like Allison Black instead of a beluga whale."

Mia giggled. "Sorry," she murmured.

"You're gorgeous," Shal said, waving a hand in dismissal. "Liam would be lucky to have you."

"As his bodyguard," I muttered. "I think I outweigh him by fifty pounds."

"It's not your fault he's a twig," Shal said.

I glanced at Liam, where he was playing his fantasy card game with Paul and Steve near a portable. Apparently, the three of them played the same game every single recess and lunch.

I thought about going up to talk to him and imagined Paul and Steve snickering that the huge new girl had a crush on their friend. Liam would get embarrassed and ignore me, and I would be reminded once again that I just wasn't one of the pretty girls. I felt my stomach twist, and I turned away again, picking at the grass.

"Let's talk about something else," I muttered.

"Fine," Shal said. "What would you name your kids—"

I laughed and threw a clump of grass at her.

And then came last recess. In my experience, it was often the worst one. I think kids get bored or something and decide to cause trouble. Who knows. But there I was sitting in the back corner of the yard with Shal and Mia when Allison Black and her flock of seagulls set off toward us. There were even a few boys trailing the pack. Never a good thing.

Mia Mouse was gone in a flash. She was like a ninja.

"We really need to work on that," Shal muttered.

"What's up, girls?" Allison said as she approached. She was wearing dark jeans and a white top that contrasted sharply with her long raven hair. Her eyelashes were plumped up with mascara, making her dark eyes seem big and mysterious. She really was unfairly beautiful. Her legs and arms were toned and muscular, and she didn't seem to do any running or anything—not at school anyway. She seemed to just gossip and watch the boys play sports.

Carl was standing behind her, along with Tim and Mike. Oh, great. Shal was already red as a fire hydrant.

"Nothing," Shal said quietly.

"Just hanging out with your new friend?" Allison asked, sitting down beside me. "Can I join? Unless you were making out or something."

"Gross," Tim said. Carl snickered.

Shal definitely noticed.

"So what are we talking about?" Allison asked, smiling cruelly at us. "Boys?"

"No," Shal said immediately.

Too fast.

Allison turned to her. "You were, weren't you? I thought I saw you looking over at us. You have a crush. Who is it?" She looked at the three boys with them. "One of these guys? Tim, maybe?"

"No thanks," Tim muttered.

Allison looked taken aback. "You don't think she's cute?"

This was particularly cruel. Allison was like an evil genius bully.

"Yeah, don't you?" one of the seagulls asked.

Her name was Ashley, and from what Shal told me she was second-in-command. She looked kind of like Portia Carson: blond hair, blue eyes, lots of jean skirts. She was almost pretty enough to challenge Allison, and Shal told me there was sometimes a little friction between the two.

"No," Tim said curtly. "She's an ugly ginger."

Shal couldn't hide it. Her big hazel eyes welled up with

tears the second the words left his mouth. He might as well have punched her in the stomach.

"Now you made her cry," Allison said with just the slightest knowing grin. She climbed to her feet. "Let's leave them alone. Maybe the new girl can cheer her up. Better to be an ugly ginger than an ugly whale."

Yep, I knew it. The group set off across the yard, laughing as they went. Other kids fled from their path.

"What a sweetheart," I said, turning back to Shal.

Shal was already standing up. "Thanks for the help. Some friend you are," she said sarcastically.

She hurried off toward the school, and I was left in the corner alone.

"What's wrong?" my mom asked me during dinner that night.

She'd bought new plates today and had insisted on making a nice roast to celebrate. It looked delicious, but I wasn't very hungry. I was just picking at a small slice on my plate.

"Nothing," I muttered.

Tom was chewing on a boiled carrot. "She's sad."

"Yes, I realize that," my mom said. "But why?"

"The room all right?" Stache asked worriedly, looking up from his dinner. "Did you find more spiders?"

"I'm fine," I said.

Stache nodded and returned to his roast. His wispy brown hair was matted against his forehead with sweat, and even his moustache looked sweaty. He was working fast though. The cupboards were installed, and he'd even slapped a coat of paint on the kitchen walls. There were still boxes piled along the counters, but it was starting to look like a normal kitchen.

"I'm sad too," Tom said, poking around for another carrot.

My mom turned to him. "Why?"

"There's a pile of garbage below my window. It's a real eyesore."

My mom sighed, and I cracked just the slightest bit of a smile. Tom was obviously trying to save me from anymore questions from my mother. When she thought something was wrong, she would keep asking until she got an answer.

Stache must have been only half-listening.

"Garbage?" he said. "I'll check it out after dinner."

"You do that, dear," my mom said. "Now, Laura, are you sure you won't—"

"Can I be excused?"

Stache looked at me in surprise. My plate wasn't finished, which was a rarity.

"Yeah," my mom said, sounding worried. "Sure."

I wrapped up my plate, put it in the fridge, and headed upstairs. As I went up the stairs, I could hear Tom say to my dad, "Love the paint in here. It smells like it was perfectly applied."

"Thanks, Tom," my dad replied proudly.

I shook my head and closed the bedroom door behind me.

I spent the rest of the evening in my room, thinking about Shal. She didn't talk to me the rest of the day. She didn't even look at me. After school she just hurried off with Mia—who at least snuck me a little wave—and didn't look back once.

I thought not having friends sucked. Losing them after a day was worse.

I'd spent most of my life giving bullies the silent treatment. You just took their insults and tried not to get angry and then cried about it in the safety of your room. Sounds kind of strange, I know. But the few times I let my temper get the best of me with Portia, it hadn't really worked out. If I yelled at her, the rest of the school looked at me like I was a maniac. The one time I really lost it and hit her, she acted like I was a murderer, and I got detention for two weeks and a very awkward meeting with the principal and my parents.

But Shal was right. I didn't stick up for her. And deep down I knew it was because a small part of me was happy I wasn't the one being targeted. It was selfish, and it wasn't what a friend was supposed to do. And when you spend your whole day fighting off fat comments, it really hurts when you get home and have to call yourself a coward.

And so I lay in my bed thinking about Shal and Mia and Allison until Tom and my parents went to bed. It was after ten when the rattling started. I slowly climbed off the bed, the issues at school instantly forgotten. I had bigger things to worry about.

Tucking the guide under my arm, I walked into the closet, my eyes on the rattling wooden panel. I crouched down, found the catch, and gently swung the panel open.

Stepping into the elevator, I carefully put the book at my feet, grabbed the lever firmly with two hands, and, against my better judgment, pulled it.

At once the floor swept away beneath me, and I plummeted through the earth like the night before, trying not to scream. Closing my eyes, I tried to count how long the descent was, and I was around forty-five seconds when white light suddenly flared across my closed eyes, and I opened them to see the lush greenery of Derwin racing toward me. The elevator slowed, and I stepped out to find Porton sitting in his rocking chair, smiling at me through that scraggly white beard.

"Welcome back."

Chapter Ten

I hurried through the town, aware that the villagers were staring at me even more curiously than last time. They had probably assumed I was never coming back.

The streets were bustling again, and I took a closer look at the village as I walked through it, noticing ash-covered forges, small butcher shops, and even a packed tavern. The entire realm of Derwin might have been dropped a few hundred years ago on the surface and been totally normal, aside from those strange weapons sheathed to belts and thighs and the dangling yellow fangs that seemed to be a fashion statement here. I did also see a boy walking a blue lizard, which was odd.

"Is that your pet?" I asked him.

He glanced at me, grinning. "Yep. Called him Eldon."

"Like the mean guy at the castle?"

The boy nodded. "Best Sword in the Under Earth. Eldon Rein. My father always said he could kill ten goblins without breaking a sweat, and that's with his hands."

I knelt down to pet the lizard, and it nuzzled my fingers. "What does your father do?"

The boy's smile slipped away. "He was a soldier. He died last year from a goblin."

"I'm sorry."

"Yeah. I'm gonna be a warrior though. I'll make 'em pay. Say . . . you're the one they're all talking about. From the surface. You're training to be a Monster Crusher?"

"So they tell me."

He nodded thoughtfully, eyeing me up and down. "First girl ever. Last one from your place didn't last long. Paul the Imp Chaser. He was nice . . . met him once—he knew my dad. Got killed too fast though. Was a good fighter, just had a nasty temper and a bit too much pride, my dad said. You best be real careful."

"Thanks," I said softly, giving the little lizard a last head rub and setting off.

I reached the arched gate to Arnwell Castle and saw that the Monster Crushers and their Swords were training again, the ring of steel echoing through the stone court-yard as they sparred or tossed weapons onto the cobble-stone and scooped up new ones.

Eldon stood in the middle of the organized chaos, overseeing the training and shouting orders, and when he saw me, I'm pretty sure he sighed. He wore the same brown cloak as the night before, and the dark stubble on his cheeks was even thicker.

It looked like he hadn't slept.

"Did you read the guide?" he asked me coolly, walking over. Some of the other warriors stopped training to watch us.

"Some of it," I said, looking down at the book. "It's a little . . . strange."

"It will get stranger," he replied quietly. "And you read about the spell?"

"Yeah. There's obviously been a mistake."

He smirked. I tried not to stare at the puckered scar that ran down his face.

"We thought the same when we saw you move in. We had . . . hoped that perhaps you would quickly move out again, or that fate would change slightly and have your father come through. But when you arrived in Derwin, your fate was sealed."

He turned away and started walking through the crowd.

"As was ours."

"So it was you. I thought so. Have you been watching my house from like the second I moved in, or what?" I asked, hurrying to catch up.

"Yes," he said. "And we're not alone."

He led me to the far side of the courtyard, and I stared up at the towering castle. I noticed now that the white stones were dirtier than I had thought; there were spots of charred black near the base and even large chunks missing. But being underground it was safe from the effects of any weather at least, and the gleaming white stones still caught the light of whatever was up on the ceiling. The castle must have been thirty metres tall and twice as wide. Dark, narrow windows watched from above.

"Listen, Eldon, we really need to talk—"

"I agree."

He raised a calloused hand, and the warriors stepped immediately in front of us, moving in almost disconcerting unison. I took a closer look at the Monster Crushers and their Swords this time. The Monster Crushers, which I had figured out were all the boys in regular clothes, were mostly in their teens or early twenties, while there was a much bigger range for Swords, who were easy to pick out because they all wore those long cloaks like Eldon. Of those, the youngest was probably fifteen or sixteen, while the oldest was a huge, barrel-chested man with deep-green eyes and endless scars running across his pale face. Most of the scars were clumped together in fives. Claws.

Of the assembled warriors—both Swords and Monster Crushers—only seven were women, but they looked like the scariest ones of the group. One in particular caught my eye; she had crimson hair that draped to the small of her back and probing blue eyes that popped from her ivory skin. All the Swords seemed muscular and grim, even beneath their cloaks, with swords and axes and bows strapped to their backs and thighs. Some wore black padded armour, while others wore just simple beige tunics and coarse wool pants beneath their cloaks.

Eldon lowered his hand. "As you all know, the Riverfield door has opened, and this . . . girl has emerged."

"Laura," I murmured.

"Laura," he said, looking a little annoyed. "The Brotherhood's laws are clear: whoever comes through the door is the Monster Crusher."

I saw a ripple of discontent move through the group, and felt my skin prickle uncomfortably as they all stared at me. I'd had enough. It was time to get out of here.

"Listen," I said, turning to Eldon. "I just came here

today to give you this book back and tell you that you have the wrong girl. Clearly I am not the Monster Crusher."

Eldon shook his head. "If only that were true. But you live in the room, you have come through the door, and you stand here now. You are to be trained, whether we want it or not. We cannot afford to ignore a new Monster Crusher, even if it's . . . you."

"What does the Monster Crusher even do?" I paused. "Okay, stupid question. But really. What difference does one person make? Why do you need one so badly?"

Eldon suddenly drew his gleaming sword from the sheath and used it to point at the nearest stuffed monster, which looked like some sort of enormous coiled serpent.

"There are three kinds of monsters," he said. "Wild, subservient, and leaders. Wild monsters are dangerous, but they are exactly that . . . wild. They are animals, and of little use to either side. Wolf hawks, sea creatures, walkers, spiders—"

"Spiders?" I cut in nervously.

He raised an eyebrow. "You don't like spiders? Then you'll hate the ones below the ground. They're about two metres wide and like to prey on humans."

Ignoring my terrified expression, he continued, pointing at another stuffed monster that I recognized as a wiry goblin, though it was covered in stabs and tears.

"Subservient monsters are the most common in the Under Earth: goblins, ogres, and imps. They're not overly bright, but they're smart enough to take orders. They're also vicious, violent, and extremely dangerous. But all sub-servient monsters have one important weakness: kill their leader and they will flee, no matter what. Sometimes that's just the biggest goblin, ogre, or imp. But when there's a large group, there is always a true leader. And that is where you really come in."

"I'm confused," I said.

Eldon started walking toward the other side of the courtyard, pointing his sword again, this time at a much bigger creature with a patch of black straw stuck to its head. A troll. The other warriors watched in silence, barely moving.

"The last type are leaders. Those are the ones you should fear. There are only three kinds: trolls, giants, and dragons. Thankfully there have been no giants or dragons in a hundred years, but trolls are bad enough. They are clever, evil, and seem to be getting larger. There are rumours that a new troll king has taken power not far from Derwin. I suspect he is the one who sent those monsters to watch your house. You see, the Monster Crusher must kill all monsters and keep the tunnels secure. But they have one job in particular: kill the leaders. So you, Laura Ledwick, have one main job to prepare for: to kill the troll king. Do that and you buy us all some time."

Oh, perfect, I thought. I shook my head, incredulous that he was even talking about this. I looked down at my protruding stomach and lifted my hands, frowning.

"But I'm not a warrior—"

"Not yet," Eldon agreed calmly. "But I will do everything I can to make you one. You will return every night to conduct training—"

"I can't do that," I objected. "I have school. I kind of need to sleep at some point."

"Take naps," Eldon said.

"But—"

"The monsters are on the move, Laura. That's why the house has chosen another Monster Crusher."

"I can't—"

"If you don't, Riverfield will be exposed to the monsters. Your family and everyone you know will be in danger."

I hesitated, looking around at the warriors. "What would I have to do?"

"It's very simple: learn how to crush monsters."

Eldon suddenly walked past me, heading for the obstacle course.

"And we start now."

Chapter Eleven

I followed him to the start of the strange obstacle course that was laid out across the courtyard. My mind was still reeling. There was no way this could all be real. And yet there was a castle looming over me, a group of strange warrior people watching my every move, and some sort of fake sun creating daylight underground. It was tough to argue.

"The Monster Crusher must possess a few virtues," Eldon explained. "Strength, courage, and a sharp mind. Monster crushing isn't just bashing things in with a hammer. It's strategy. It's a mental battle against the monsters. And it's facing your fears."

He stopped and looked out over the various obstacles.

"What are you afraid of, Laura?"

I thought about that for a moment. I was going to say spiders, but that wasn't really the only thing. I was afraid of evil pretty girls and losing my brother and seeing myself in the mirror every morning. So I just shrugged and looked at the ground.

"Lots."

I thought Eldon might be mad, but he just nodded.

"Good answer. You will have to face some tests before you earn the Iron Hammer. We don't risk them on just anyone. We have lost a few in the past with Monster Crushers who weren't ready. So we begin here."

I looked out over the obstacle course, feeling my stomach tighten. I didn't usually do well with physical exercise. Not anymore, anyway. "What is it?"

"We call it the Warrior's Way," he explained. "It measures your readiness to fight monsters. It tests your speed, your agility, your strength, and most importantly, your weapons skills. Monster Crushers and Swords have trained on the Warrior's Way for three hundred years."

I nervously checked out the course, sweat already beading on my forehead.

Eldon gestured to the first obstacle—a row of ten logs that had been laid out like train tracks, though each stood half a metre off the ground. It would be tough just getting over them, never mind with any speed.

"You will proceed clockwise through the obstacle course," he said, slowly walking forward. "The row of logs first—a test of agility and speed. From there you will move through each obstacle, always remembering to kill the monsters along the way. If any survive your attack, then you fail. There will be weapons laid out for your usage."

The other warriors had formed a loose ring around the course, watching with folded arms and very skeptical expressions.

"So I just . . . run through it?" I asked, wringing my hands together.

"That's it," Eldon replied, sounding dubious himself. "We will use it a lot for your training." He glanced at me. "I imagine you don't do much . . . fighting."

I snorted. "Or running, walking . . . moving."

He sighed. "A true Monster Crusher can do this course in less than two minutes, slaying the monsters on the way with perfect killing blows. If you do it in five minutes today, I will be happy."

I turned to the first obstacle, feeling my skin tingle with nerves. I didn't want to do it, especially in front of a crowd, but I didn't seem to have much choice. I figured I should at least give it a try. Maybe I was a warrior. I had never actually tried to be one.

"Are you ready?" Eldon asked quietly.

I paused. "I guess."

"Begin!"

It was bad. Like terrible. The only sport I ever played growing up was softball, which, like I said, I was actually really, really good at it. I was the best hitter in the state— better than any boy my age. I hit my first home run when I was eight years old, which isn't even supposed to happen in girls' softball. I remember the field going dead silent as that ball sailed over the fence. I think my coach fell off the bench.

I quit when I was eleven though. It's going to sound stupid, but I got sick of the snickers as I rounded the bases. I got sick of looking at myself in that uniform knowing I was the biggest girl out there. I got sick of the boys making jokes on the bleachers. My dad was devastated when I gave it up. My coach too. But I just wanted to hide. I didn't like people watching me.

Well, so much for that.

The first part was to jump over those ten pesky logs. I tripped on the first one. I tried to run over it and just didn't get my right leg high enough. My sneaker hit the log with a painful thud and I toppled forward, pitching over the next one and hitting the cobblestone ground very hard. My whole body throbbed with pain, especially my toe.

I heard mumbled laughs echo around the courtyard. I already wanted to quit. To get up and storm out of there and go home. But I thought back to the boys on the bleachers, laughing at me while I ran the bases. I thought back to Portia Carson.

No. I was going to finish this stupid course.

My cheeks were burning as I pushed myself up again. I barely managed to step over the rest of the logs, moving very slowly and carefully. The next section was five wooden barriers to roll under, and I almost fell again as I gingerly ducked under them, moving even more slowly. At one point I was supposed to swing on some ropes over a wooden frame filled with water. I just walked around it, ignoring Eldon's annoyed shouts.

The fake monsters were worse. I couldn't even string an arrow. When I finally did, it flopped out a metre in front of me and clattered along the stones. I stabbed a fake ogre with a sword and got the blade stuck in the coarse wool fabric. After failing to pull it out, I just moved on, feeling the humiliation build. I wanted to cry, but the sweat was stinging my eyes, and I was too busy squinting against the salty burn. I just kept moving. I managed to push a large cart over the red line painted on the stones pretty fast, but I knocked over most of the spears during the agility part. They just kept falling one after another. Hitting my hips. My waist. My thighs. My fat arms. My entire fat, bulky body.

When I finally got back to Eldon, the laughter wasn't mumbled anymore. The only one who wasn't laughing was the redhead, who was looking at me scornfully.

Well, her and Eldon. He just stared at me for a long, awkward minute while I clutched my sides and doubled over, sweat pouring out onto the ground.

"Ten minutes . . . the longest I have ever seen in two decades of training. That's enough for today," he said, barely hiding his disgust. "You can go home."

The warriors immediately returned to their training, leaving me standing there alone, grasping my thighs. I knew it.

Someone like me could never be the Monster Crusher.

I was just slinking back through the gate, completely humiliated, when I heard someone fall into step beside me.

"You forgot the guide," Eldon said quietly.

I looked back at him. "Give it to someone else."

"There is no one else."

"I can't do it," I said, feeling my voice cracking. "Weren't you watching?"

He walked toward me, the book in one outstretched hand.

"You have to," he replied calmly. "The house chose you—"

"I don't care," I cut in. "I'm sure it will pick someone else."

Eldon just held the book out, and I reluctantly took it. He looked at me for a moment, his hard blue eyes softening just a little.

"I wasn't happy when I saw you. Nor with what I saw today. But a few months ago there were no monsters anywhere near the surface. Now they are watching your house."

He looked off toward the distant cavern walls.

"Something has changed, Laura. The monsters have purpose. They have direction. You don't look like a Monster Crusher, I agree. But we will just have to hope you can act like one. I know you don't plan on coming back. I can't say I blame you. But I can tell you this with certainty, Laura: if you don't come back, the monsters will come to you."

"So let me tell people in my world to get ready—"

"That I cannot allow," Eldon said, shaking his head. "No one in your world may know about the Under Earth. The Brotherhood were very clear in their instructions."

"Why?"

"My people have survived thousands of years apart from the surface humans, treasuring our way of life. If your people found out about all this, they would harvest the Under Earth for everything it's worth. They are already doing that now. No. We want to keep our world a secret." He met my eyes. "By whatever means necessary."

I sensed the implied threat in his tone. If I told anyone, they would be in danger. And so would I.

"I sincerely doubt the monsters could conquer the surface—"

"They multiply very quickly," Eldon said. "And they grow to adulthood within a year. And remember this: they didn't always have swords and bows and arrows. They stole those from us." He grabbed my arm. "You must be ready to fight."

Eldon held my gaze for a moment, and then he walked back into the courtyard.

I watched him for a moment, and then hurried all the way back to the elevator, giving Porton a quick nod before I stepped inside and pulled the lever, racing back toward the surface.

When I finally lay down in bed that night—after peeking out my window and seeing no yellow eyes—I thought about the look on the warriors' faces. It was the same look Portia Carson had given me every morning for six years. The one the girls on my softball team gave me when I rounded the bases. The one I gave myself in the mirror some nights after a particularly bad day at school.

The one that said, "You're just a pathetic fat girl."

I didn't want to go back. I was tired of that look. But once again, I had a feeling that Eldon was telling the truth. Like it or not, I had to try.

I flicked on my light and rolled over, opening *The Complete Guide to Monster Crushing*. I fell asleep with the lights on, my cheek pressed against the dusty old pages.

Chapter Twelve

I had a lot of alone time at school the next day, and I used it to sit on the portable steps and read more of the guide. Shal still wasn't speaking to me, and she had walked right by me that morning with Mia before the first bell. It stung, but there wasn't much I could do. It was hard to apologize when she wouldn't even come near me.

I figured I'd at least use the alone time to do something productive. I still wasn't sure I wanted to go back to Derwin, but I did want to read more about the other Monster Crushers. Specifically what had happened to them. So I sat there on the cold steps during first recess and read the end of each section in the Great Monster Crushers. Each ending had been written by the following Monster Crusher. It wasn't good news.

Daniel the Dragon Killer was killed when he chased a retreating army of goolins into the Dead Mountains. He was ambushed there and downed with arrows.

Gregory the Giant's Bane was ironically killed by a giant (this was after he killed Ogg the Terrible and got his name).

Thomas the Goblin Terror was killed by a giant spider in the Shadow Tunnels. He walked into the nest while searching for Bandar.

I closed the book, grimacing. This didn't seem like a job I wanted, never mind if I could actually do it. But on the way to school that morning I'd heard something on the radio that was very, very concerning. A hiker was missing from Riverfield. Apparently he'd been off in the woods that bordered the town last night and hadn't come home.

I turned the radio up and listened carefully until the report finished.

"That's comforting," Tom said from the back seat.

I glanced at my mom.

"I'm sure he'll turn up soon," she said, though she looked perturbed.

I didn't say anything, but I was definitely wondering if something with bright-yellow eyes had found the missing hiker. I wanted to at least tell Tom and my parents to stay out of the backyard, but I knew I couldn't explain why.

I just had to hope Eldon and the Swords were keeping watch around my house.

As I sat on the steps thinking about the missing hiker, I glanced at Shal and Mia talking in our usual spot in the far corner of the yard. Shal was picking grass and Mia was sitting beside her cross-legged, probably listening to her talk about Carl's haircut. I wished I was sitting over there with them. At least it would have been a distraction from everything else that was going on.

As it turned out, Shal might have been talking about me this time, because she glanced over, saw me looking, and immediately flushed and turned away. Mia followed her gaze and gave me a shy little wave and smile. I returned it and went back to my book.

I hoped Shal would want to be friends again soon. I could really use some.

I ate lunch alone as well. Shal and Mia were sitting and chatting at Shal's desk, so I was stuck eating my bologna sandwich by myself and listening to Allison and the other girls gossip behind me. They were still leaving me alone, so I guess I couldn't complain.

Apparently I wasn't worth the effort. That was fine by me.

I did sneak a few glances at Liam while I ate. He was sitting with Paul and Steve, of course, but they didn't play their card game inside while eating lunch. They just talked quietly and laughed, making sure not to attract too much attention from the other boys. Steve was thin and wiry like Liam, with messy blond hair and a lot of acne. Paul was stockier, with closely cropped brown hair and an endless supply of striped golf shirts.

I watched as Liam snickered at something and adjusted the thick black glasses that sat perched on his freckled, pointy nose. He glanced over at me, and I quickly went back to my sandwich, feeling my stomach knot and twist. Better to be alone, I decided.

You can't get hurt that way.

So I just kept to myself the rest of the day, reading the guide and wondering what would happen if an ogre wandered into Riverfield. I think I would run the other way.

When the final bell went, I packed up my pencil case and books into my backpack. We didn't have any homework tonight, so I could leave the textbooks at school. That was always a nice feeling.

I actually quite liked Ms. Haddock—she was very enthusiastic and excitable, though she was oblivious to all the gossip and teasing and bullying happening in the class. I think she was too nice to believe her students would do such things. I waved goodbye to her and started for the hall, lugging my bag along with me.

Liam's locker was on the way to mine, and I snuck a quick glance at him packing his books away as I hurried by. Naturally he looked up right at that moment, and I felt my cheeks flush pink. Shooting him a very awkward smile, I quickly walked on, looking away.

"Settling in?" he asked.

I paused and turned back. I'd been caught.

"I guess," I said. "Always takes awhile."

"I've been here my whole life, and I'm still not settled in," he replied, smirking.

"That's comforting."

He laughed. "Sorry. Seems like you made some friends, at least."

"I did," I said, glancing down the hall at Shal and Mia. "I seem to have lost them again."

"That was fast."

"I have a way with people," I muttered.

He shrugged. "You seem nice to me. That said, I was never a good judge of character. You could be an alien in disguise, for all I know." He closed his locker. "Well, best of luck getting those friends back. You can always hang out with us at recess, though we do just play card games. You might want to try your other friends first, if you ever plan on being popular, that is. If not . . . then welcome to the team."

I laughed. "Thanks. See you tomorrow."

"See ya, Laura," he said, swinging his bag over his shoulder and starting down the hall.

I continued to my locker, trying to hold back a grin. My arms were tingling. Liam had talked to me, and this time I didn't even need to run into him. He'd even said we could hang out at recess! It wasn't exactly the "I have a huge crush on you, Laura Ledwick" that I'd been hoping for, but it was something.

I wish I could have told Mia and Shal.

I was just packing my books away when something caught my eye. I turned around and saw Mia scurrying down the hallway, looking terrified. Frowning, I glanced past Mia and saw Shal by her locker with Allison and two other girls standing in front of her. Shal was flushed bright red, and I could tell she was fighting back tears. Obviously Allison was teasing her again, probably about Tim or some other boy. I turned back to my locker. I didn't stand up to bullies. Actually it was rule number one. And I had a pretty good thing going on here: I could go an entire day with just a few snickers and muted comments. But I thought back to what Shal had said: some friend you are.

I'd never had friends before, but I knew I wanted some. I guess it was time to abandon rule number one. Grimacing, I closed my locker and started for Shal.

As I closed in, I heard Allison saying, "So you do like him? I'll tell him, don't worry. I know Tim said you were gross, but he might come around. Or maybe you like Carl?" The other girls snickered. "Should I ask him out for you?"

"Hey," I said, appearing behind them. I think my stomach had given up on backflips—it was too scared to move. But I'd gone this far. "Why don't you pick on someone your own size?" I paused and looked down at myself. "You know . . . figuratively."

Allison turned to me, looking at her friends in disbelief. "Like you?"

"Yeah," I said. "All three of you are about right."

Allison smirked. "Why don't you stay out of this? We were just talking to Michelle about some of her crushes. Maybe you know . . . does she have a thing for Carl?"

I rapidly thought back to every teen movie I'd ever seen. What was the cool thing to say here?

"She doesn't waste her time with eighth graders," I replied. "But if she did, she'd probably be dating Carl right now." Ha. A classic zinger.

Shal looked at me with wide eyes.

Allison didn't like that one. She suddenly scowled and looked me up and down.

"And what about you, tubby? You have a crush too?"

I smiled. "None of your business. Now why don't you

run along? Maybe you girls can buy new skirts and talk about eye shadow."

Shal was slowly shaking her head in the background. Allison narrowed her eyes.

"All right," she said softly. "I guess I'll see you around. Come on, girls . . . let's go buy some skirts. We should enjoy the fact that we can fit in them."

With that she stalked down the hallway, the other two girls throwing me dirty looks and hurrying after her. When they were gone, Shal turned to me in disbelief.

"You just told off Allison Black," she murmured.

"Yeah," I said, not quite believing it myself.

"You're going to regret that."

"Probably."

Shal looked away. "I'm sorry about what I said. I was just upset."

I shrugged. "You were right. I'll be a better friend from now on. You know . . . if you still want to be friends."

She grinned and gave me a hug. "Definitely."

Shal, Mia, and I decided to walk home that day to catch up on everything we'd missed in the last twenty-four hours, and so that Shal could tell Mia all about my confrontation. My mom hadn't minded—actually she was beaming when I took off down the sidewalk.

"And then get this," Shal said, coming to a stop, "Laura goes: why don't you go buy some skirts and talk about eye shadow?" She grabbed her sides, giggling.

Mia looked at me, her eyes wide. "Are you serious?"

I shrugged. "It's tough to think on the spot."

Mia covered her mouth and giggled before suddenly turning serious. "She's not going to ignore you anymore, you know that, right?"

"Oh, don't bring down the moment," Shal said.

"It's all right," I replied. "I'm used to it anyway."

We were walking down the main part of town, which was just a bunch of old brick buildings that had been converted into nail salons and clothing stores and restaurants. The salon where my mom worked now was in one of these buildings—I decided I should probably drop by someday. Shal said she lived close to downtown, while Mia was about halfway between here and my house. That meant I had the longest walk, of course, but I figured I could use the exercise before training tonight. I was going to stay well clear of the woods, however.

It was a warm September afternoon, and there were quite a few people walking along the sidewalk. I decided I really liked Riverfield. You know—minus the monsters. I noticed a blond waitress serving two people in a café glance at me as we walked by. She gave me a strange look and turned away. I frowned, glancing back at her. That was weird.

"I have to ask," I said, turning to Shal. "Why does Allison give you such a hard time? It seems like she goes after you more than anyone. It doesn't make any sense."

Shal immediately stopped laughing and looked away. "Long story."

"Come on. Mia?"

Mia hesitated. "It happened in third grade."

"Fourth," Shal corrected.

"Right," Mia said. "Back then Shal and Allison were best friends."

"Best is a strong word."

Mia glared at her. "Do you want to tell it?"

Shal paused. "Continue."

We were out of the shops area now and into the residential section. Most of the houses here were very old-fashioned with original brick and dark windows. An elderly couple on a rickety front porch watched us walk by.

I felt their eyes following me.

"They were friends," Mia went on, "and they used to dress up and do their hair and all that stuff. Back then, there used to be a boy named Aaron at the school."

"He was the Carl of fourth grade," Shal added.

"Right," Mia said, rolling her eyes. "Anyway, they both liked him."

"In fourth grade?" I asked, frowning.

Shal waved a hand. "You know how it is: kids think it's funny to say that they're dating someone but never even look at each other."

"Not really," I said.

Shal scowled. "Just continue."

"Well, Allison apparently was dating this boy Aaron when he decided he liked Shal more. So Shal and Aaron started dating or whatever and Allison got mad. Oh, and Shal also beat her at a beauty pageant that year—"

"You said you would never mention that," Shal snapped.

"And so Allison got jealous and turned people against Shal by calling her ugly and saying she had a thing for everyone and I guess also that she was a bad dresser—"

"We get it," Shal muttered.

I rubbed my forehead. "So you're saying Allison hates you because you stole her boyfriend in fourth grade and won a beauty pageant?"

Shal nodded. "Pretty much."

I broke out laughing. "That's the dumbest thing I've ever heard."

"I know," Shal said. "But she's very sensitive to that stuff. Low self-esteem, I guess. I don't know. Of course, she turned into the beauty queen and I turned into a freckled Irish terrier."

"You should see her pageant pics—" Mia started.

"No!" Shal cut in. "Never. Anyway, that's the story. I haven't been popular since. Upsets my mom more than anyone, I think. She's the pageant queen who got me into this mess in the first place." She slowed down in front of a big, red-brick Victorian-style house with a white picket fence. "Well, girls," she said, "it's been a slice. I'd invite you in, but I have to go hide all the pictures first. Want to do something this weekend?"

"Sure," I said. "But I do want to see those pictures."

"Bye," she snarled, heading inside.

Mia and I just laughed and continued on. It was another ten minutes to her house, and then we parted ways too. She was strangely quiet about her own family, but I did gather that she had two younger brothers and that her dad was very strict. She'd only moved here from the city two years ago herself and said it had taken her awhile to adjust.

I waved as she went inside and started for home. Leaving the main area of town, I was forced to walk on the shoulder of the road and turn south toward Raven's End, the very last street in town. The forest hugged the road a little more closely here, though it was still interspersed with homes. I watched the trees warily as I walked.

I was just turning onto Raven's End, when I saw something move in the woods. I slowed down, looking around. The street was empty.

I picked up my pace again, peering into the forest. The trees were densely packed and obscured by heavy brush, so it was very dark; all I could see were shadows.

And then one of them started to move.

I slowed down just a little, my skin prickling. The shadow slowed down with me. There was something there. I started walking faster, and the shadow followed.

Panicking, I looked ahead and saw the first house on my street, another ancient Victorian-style home. The woods wrapped tightly around their backyard, and as I walked by the house, momentarily blocking me from the woods, I broke into a jog.

I just wanted to get home.

But when the forest closed in again on the other side, I still saw the shadow. I ran faster and the shadow sped up. I was just about to break into a full sprint when I remembered what Eldon had said: the Swords were keeping watch. Maybe it was just one of their guards. I slowed down a little and glanced at the trees.

"Hello?" I said. "You don't have to follow me everywhere. Just watching the house at nighttime would be nice. Hello?"

I stopped and peered into the woods.

"Are you there?"

Two large, pale-yellow eyes suddenly snapped open, less than three metres from where I was standing. In the shadows, I thought I saw sharp teeth catching the light.

I didn't wait to see anymore. I broke into a full sprint, not even looking behind me. I ran all the way to my house, threw open the door, and slammed it shut behind me.

I stood there shaking for a moment, pressed against the door.

My mom poked her head out from the kitchen. "Did you enjoy your walk, dear?"

"Yeah," I said quietly. "It was great."

Chapter Thirteen

I spent the rest of the afternoon in my room, sneaking constant glances out my window. I was particularly hoping I would see one of the Swords so I would know that my house was being protected. Of course, I was also keeping a watch out for pale-yellow eyes and making sure none of my family members went outside.

This was not cool.

In between glances, I read more of the guide and learned all about the Iron Hammer—the massive weapon that every Monster Crusher used. It looked as big as I did. I read the note below the picture.

The Iron Hammers
Forged by the Brotherhood for the specific use of the Monster
Crushers, the hammers are the most feared weapons in the
Under Earth. Six diamond-shaped rubies are set into the
sides of the hammers, and they glow red when used
against our enemies, as if enjoying the battle. The hammers
were forged with spells and magic, and they are capable of
a great many things. They are light and swift, and when

needed, they possess a strength that no weapon can match. But the spell seems to be fickle: it only reflects the spirit of the Monster Crusher who holds it.

The Hammer of Riverfield has killed Scarab, Ogg, and many other great foes, so handle it with care.

I frowned as I read the paragraph. Handle it with care? I sincerely doubted I could even lift the thing. Surely they would figure that out soon and realize it might be a good idea to find themselves another Monster Crusher. One other area caught my attention:

The Hammer is a weapon—it is not a victory. Daniel forgot this and he paid the price.

I was just getting up to check the yard when my mom called up for dinner. Sneaking a quick peek at the woods and seeing nothing, I headed downstairs, wondering if the yellow eyes were just beyond my sight in the shadows.

I joined Tom and Stache at the table—Stache had actually made it to the dinner table on time today, though that was probably just because my mom had yelled at him. As usual he was covered in dust and paint and dirt and who knows what else. Even his moustache had white paint in it. My mom plunked a big, steaming plate of chicken wings on the table. Despite the whole yellow-eyes incident, I was starving, so I immediately started to load up my plate.

Dinner at my house is like a police interrogation. My mom fires off a rapid stream of questions, and I do my best to give her the shortest answers possible so that I can avoid telling her the truth without actually lying. It's an art form.

Tom was sitting across from me eating Brussels sprouts. He really loves Brussels sprouts. Like savours them. It's weird.

"How was your day, Tom?" my mom asked, turning to him.

"Not bad," Tom said, poking around for his Brussels sprouts. "I made a friend. Shannon."

"Told you," I said knowingly.

He frowned. "Not that kind of a friend. She's just very nice. She told me she liked my shirt. I told her I liked her shoes. She thought it was funny. We laughed."

"I see," my mom said, frowning. "Laura?"

"Got an A on a math quiz," I replied curtly.

My father looked up. "Congratulations."

"Thanks, Stache," I said. "Tom, you want my Brussels sprouts—"

"Hold on," my mom cut in. "That's very good, Laura. What else happened?"

Here we go. She wanted to know about bullying. It was nice of her to ask, I guess, but it's not something I love talking about. Especially in front of my dad. He lives in his own little happy world where his daughter is a beautiful princess loved by all.

"That's really it. Just fighting off the boys like usual."

"What boys?" my dad asked with his mouth full.

My mom sighed. "I think she's joking, dear."

"Oh," he said. "Good."

"Who were the girls you walked home with?" my mom asked.

"Shal and Mia."

She wiped her face with a napkin. "Were you fighting with them yesterday?"

Sigh. She was very perceptive, I had to give her that.

"Yeah, but we're good again," I said. "Just about a girl at school. No big deal."

My mom hesitated. "Is she . . . picking on you?"

"Not yet," I said calmly, taking a big bite of a chicken wing. "Probably tomorrow though. We had a bit of a show-down today." I stopped and looked at the chicken wing. "I probably should eat something healthier in prepara-tion, actually."

"What for?" my dad asked, sounding indignant. I love Stache.

"I'm preparing for a marathon," I said sarcastically. "But if we could just hide the snack food, that would be super. When ten o'clock hits, no bag of chips is safe from my wrath."

My mom nodded. "Of course. I could probably stand to lose a few pounds myself. I'll start buying fresh fruit instead."

"Great," Tom muttered.

I smiled and tossed a Brussels sprout at him. It bounced off his forehead.

"Very nice," my mom said.

Tom frowned. "I would have eaten that."

As I lay in bed that night, the guide beside me, I realized I had to make a decision. The door would start rattling again soon, and Eldon would be waiting. Could I really go back in there after that disastrous training session yesterday?

All the reading I had done had said the exact same thing: the Monster Crusher had to be a mighty warrior, protecting both worlds and keeping the tunnels secure. The only one who didn't look that big in his picture was Paul the Imp Chaser, and apparently he'd been killed three weeks into the job. I clearly wasn't the Monster Crusher. Maybe it was better if I just didn't go back.

Of course, there was also the issue of the yellow eyes in the woods. If that was some sort of creature hunting me, it wouldn't stop just because I decided not to be the Monster Crusher. Was I putting my family at risk? Did I even have a choice? What if they just came and took me back to Derwin to train against my will?

My mind was racing as I glanced over and saw 10:30 on my alarm clock. The door still wasn't rattling. Maybe it wasn't going to rattle tonight, and Eldon was giving me another day to think about it. If that was the case, I definitely appreciated it.

I placed the guide on my nightstand, put on some fluffy red-and-white pyjamas, and flicked off the bedroom light. But as I got into bed, I heard something strange. It wasn't rattling. It was voices. I immediately stopped and listened.

The voices were coming from outside my window.

I slowly crept to the window and peeked through the curtains, but it was too dark to see anything. I stood there for a moment, trying to decide what to do. What if something was out there? What if it was coming into my house? Should I wake my parents? Would they think I was completely nuts?

I frowned and thought about something else. I was hearing voices. I sincerely doubted monsters could speak, and if they could, it definitely wouldn't be English. It had to be the Swords. I decided to ignore it and go to bed.

I was just climbing onto the mattress when I heard the voices again.

There was no doubt: there were people outside, and they were getting closer. Were the Swords trying to come in? Was there a problem? I had to make sure they didn't come inside and wake my family. It was going to be hard to explain a group of hooded warriors to my mother. I thought about taking the elevator to Derwin to see if I could find Eldon, but if that was him outside and he was trying to get my attention, he might wake up Tom while I was gone. Thankfully Tom was a *very* heavy sleeper, but if he woke up, he would hear the voices for sure. The Swords didn't know about his hearing, and I definitely didn't want Tom wandering down there. I had to go check it out before someone else did.

Thinking that I was never going to get a good night's sleep in this new house, I crept down the stairs. I wished I had some sort of weapon to bring with me. Why did I get rid of all my baseball bats? Pale moonlight was filtering in through the windows, and it was eerily silent as I crossed the living room—well, aside from the creaking floorboards. I headed for the family room, where the door to the backyard was located. On the way I scooped a big rolling pin off of the kitchen counter; it would have to do.

Stache had been painting the family room all day, so there were no curtains on the large rectangular windows. As a result the moon was illuminating the entire room, and I could make out the dark, brooding wall of the forest at the edge of the yard. My right hand tightened on the rolling pin as I approached the door. The voices had stopped.

I reached the glass door and pressed myself against it, listening for movement. All I could hear was the wind rustling through the leaves, as if whispering for me to go back. I really didn't want to go out there, but I had to have a look now or I'd never be able to sleep. I slowly turned the old bronze handle, lifting the rolling pin with the other hand.

I eased the door open and peeked outside. Nothing. It was a cool night, and the wind cut through my flannel pyjamas and chilled me right to the core. I was just closing the door when I heard them again: quiet, rasping voices. It was hard to make out what they were saying, but it sounded like, "We need your help."

"Eldon?" I whispered. "Is that you?"

Brandishing the rolling pin, I stepped out onto the sprawling back patio. The cement slabs were crooked and cracked and covered with weeds, and they felt very cold on my bare feet. I took a few steps from the door, peering into the heavy darkness.

"Eldon?"

That's when I heard the rusty hinges on the back door slowly closing. I instantly straightened, feeling tingles running through my entire body.

There was something behind me.

I turned just in time to see the door click shut. Standing in front of it was a creature I recognized instantly from the guide. Its skin was a mossy, sickly green, like it had just emerged from a swamp, which only added to its witch-like hooked nose and protruding mouth, flashing with yellow teeth. It was wearing a rusted black chest plate marked with dents and scratches and holding a crooked sword in one of its slender hands. I recognized the eyes from the woods: large and yellow, with pupils like a snake.

I just stood there, unable to scream or run or fight. The goblin lifted the crooked sword over its head with two hands, ready to bring it down in a killing blow.

"Bad move, Monster Crusher," it whispered in a raspy, awful voice.

That woke me up. I turned and ran just as the goblin swung the sword, and I heard the metal clang off the concrete. I sprinted for the edge of the house, trying to get to the front door. Forget Eldon's warning—I was going to lock the doors and call the police.

I was just turning the corner toward the front when a second goblin charged out of the shadows with a long black spear. I saw him just in time to dive face first into the grass, narrowly avoiding the deadly sharp tip as it sliced through the air where I'd been standing. I slid across the damp grass and then tried to scramble back to my feet as the goblin turned toward me, its big yellow eyes flashing in the darkness.

It stabbed at my stomach with the long spear before I was even up, and I just managed to knock the point aside with the rolling pin, slamming it downward. The spear jammed into the grass, getting caught in the dirt, and I got up and took off running again.

"Help!" I screamed. My parent's room was upstairs in the front of the house, but Tom would hear me and wake them. "Help!"

The first goblin suddenly crashed into me, knocking me right off my feet. I hit the ground hard, the rolling pin flying from my hands. I rolled over a few times and then flopped over hard, lying flat on my back. I looked up in terror as the goblin stepped over me, raising the sword once again. I saw its sharp yellow teeth glinting in the moonlight as it smiled, and I knew it was about to kill me. I didn't even have a chance to scream.

The sword was halfway down when a black arrow tip suddenly emerged from the goblin's stomach. The goblin looked down in shock, grasping at the wound, and then toppled forward. I just barely rolled out of the way as it crashed into the grass beside me.

The second goblin turned in panic as a shadowy figure came sprinting out of the woods, drawing a gleaming silver sword. The goblin never had a chance: the shadowy figure easily dodged a desperate jab of its spear and plunged the sword into its stomach.

As the goblin hit the ground, the shadowy figure tucked the sword into a sheath and walked toward me. As soon as the figure came close, I recognized crimson locks protruding from her hood. She looked down at me in disgust.

"This is why you should be training," she said quietly. "Two goblins should stand no chance against a Monster Crusher. Get up."

"They were coming into my house—"

"They will never enter the house," she cut in coolly. "They're afraid of the Brotherhood's spells. They wanted to draw you outside and ambush you. Which you foolishly fell for."

I climbed to my feet, staring down at the dead goblin beside me. A light flicked on upstairs. "My parents are going to see the bodies—"

"I will take care of the bodies," she snarled. "And I will be sure that we add a few extra Swords here to keep watch. Clearly you need the help. Lie to your parents. You don't know how close you just were to putting your family in danger. When Eldon tells you something . . . *listen.*"

With that, she grabbed the goblin's collar with one hand and dragged him toward the trees. I watched her disappear into the shadows and then hurried to the back door. I had just stepped inside when Stache and my mom rushed into the family room.

"Laura!" my mom gasped. "What were you doing outside?"

Tom stepped in behind them, looking very upset.

"Sorry," I mumbled sheepishly, "I heard something back there. I thought it might have been the hiker. I went to have a look and a stupid bat flew right by and scared me."

Stache hurried to the back door and looked outside, locking it as he did. I glanced outside, alarmed, but the girl had already removed the other goblin. Stache turned to me.

"Why didn't you wake us?"

I shrugged. "I didn't want to wake you for nothing. Sorry."

My mom wrapped me in a quick hug and took my face in her hands, looking over me. "We're just happy you're okay. Please don't go out there by yourself at night."

"I won't anymore," I muttered. "It's all right, Tom."

He was giving me a weird look from the doorway. "You sounded really scared."

"I don't like bats. No offence."

Tom didn't look convinced, but he obviously decided to let it go. "Well, I'm just glad you're all right, Giant Girl."

"Thanks," I said. "I'm going to get back to bed. Sorry again."

We all headed back upstairs, and I gave them a little wave and closed the bedroom door behind me. I leaned there for a moment, trembling. That was too close.

Eldon could have warned me that the monsters were going to try to kill me so soon. But he was right: I was already involved, whether or not I wanted to be. I could try to get my parents to move, but what if the monsters followed? What if they started attacking Riverfield because I hadn't done my job? And how could I possibly convince them to move without telling them about the Under Earth anyway? There's no way Stache would just give up on his dream house.

No, I was definitely going to be here for awhile. Which meant I really only had one choice.

I threw on some light track pants and a T-shirt, grabbed the guide, and crawled through the panel into the elevator. If these monsters were going to come after me, I better figure out how to start crushing them. After plummeting back to Derwin—still shutting my eyes to try to keep from vomiting—I hurried into the meadow.

"Are you all right?" Porton asked, his stormy grey eyes narrowed in worry.

"Yeah," I replied. "But only because that Sword was there."

"That's her job," he said wryly, leaning back in his chair. "So what now?"

"I think I better start training," I murmured.

Porton smiled grimly. "I agree. They'll send more than two next time."

Chapter Fourteen

An hour later I collapsed onto the cobblestones, sweat dripping over my shaking hands. Even though the air was cooler than I thought it would be, I was completely drenched. I'd gone through the Warrior's Way three times now, and I wasn't getting any better.

Eldon had actually looked concerned when I first walked through the gate, and he had reiterated to me to always stay in the house at nighttime, no matter what.

"The monsters are creatures of darkness. Why do you think we never dim the sun sphere?" he asked, pointing upward at the massive mechanical contraption on the cavern roof.

"What is it?" I asked curiously.

"A creation of the Brotherhood, thousands of years ago. Half magic and half alchemy, like I said, but the secrets of its creation were lost centuries ago. There are five sun spheres remaining in the Under Earth. They bring life, and they keep away death."

"Where are the other five realms?"

"Scattered across the globe," he said. "There are two

under your North America, while the largest is the original, under Africa. There is one under your Antarctica, and the last is beneath your China."

I shook my head, frowning. "And how do all these Monster Crushers get to Derwin every night?"

"Most stay for longer and then go home for a few weeks. But we have trains running throughout the Under Earth . . . different than yours, maybe, but similar. They run on coal and reach incredible speeds, so we can stay in relatively good contact with the other realms. You can take one to visit the other realms, if you complete your training."

I thought about that, looking out at the sprawling cavern. It still seemed impossible that all this could exist. The sparkling lake, the forests, the wheat fields.

Eldon obviously guessed at my thoughts. "For surface humans, it's hard to believe. They know the underground as dark and lifeless. But if you were born here, it's frightening to imagine an open sky. A yawning blackness that sweeps over the landscape. For us, it feels like we might just float away into that darkness and never return."

"I guess," I murmured. "How many of you are there?"

"Derwin is the smallest of the five realms: there are only about twenty thousand people here. The greatest is Eran, the one beneath your Africa: half a million live there. In all, maybe three million."

"And how many monsters?"

The smile disappeared from his face. "Countless."

After that, he had ordered me to get right back to training. As I stumbled and tripped and sweated, he shouted out information for me to remember:

"There are sixteen tunnels in Riverfield that we know about—both those created by us and those created by the monsters. It is your duty to protect them all and discover the rest of the monsters' tunnels as well. Unfortunately, I think there are many more.

"Ogres will always try to crush you with a club. They just prefer it.

"Monster Crushers must never show fear. If they do, the monsters will sense the weakness, and the battle will be lost.

"You must find strategies to get to the leader as fast as possible."

The other warriors just watched me with a mixture of bemusement and disdain as I tripped on logs, toppled over wooden barriers, shot arrows wide, and awkwardly stabbed fake monsters with knives and spears and swords, all the while trying to pay attention to Eldon. A couple of times I missed the monsters altogether with my attacks . . . and the targets were stationary. That was not a good thing.

"Take a break," Eldon muttered after another run through the course, obviously seeing that I was taking one either way. "We'll start again in a few minutes."

"Yeah," I managed. "Awesome."

I crawled over to the nearest wall and propped myself against it, feeling my cheeks burn as some of the other Monster Crushers whispered about me in the corners. I knew that Swords were guarding my house even now, while others were scouting the tunnels all around Riverfield, trying to find out how the monsters were accessing the surface. But as Eldon constantly reminded me, the tunnels were a maze that could take years to unravel. The entrances were all hidden in the stone.

The woman with the crimson hair was back, sharpening her recently bloodied sword in the corner and sneering at me. As I sat there, I started thinking about what I would be doing right now if I hadn't found the secret door in my closet. I'd be sleeping right now, probably dreaming of Liam R. Kelp and me running along a beach together. Well, maybe not a beach. I didn't like even fantasy me in a bathing suit.

Instead I was running around a walled stone courtyard jumping over logs and getting laughed at by grim-faced warrior boys, and all so I would be ready to fight trolls and giant spiders in pitch-black tunnels. Maybe Newcastle hadn't been so bad after all.

"Hey," someone said.

I looked up in surprise as a boy dropped down beside me. He might have been only fifteen or so, but his arms were lined with hard muscle. His raven hair was full and a little curly, and there were a few small scars on his cheeks, white against his deeply tanned skin. His eyes were a soft brown, and he didn't seem as grim as the others, flashing me a smile of the whitest teeth I've ever seen.

"Having fun yet?" he asked, tying his running shoes.

I tried not to stare at his arms. He must really like bicep curls.

"Oh yeah," I said, flushing. "I think the falling is my favourite part."

He smirked. "It's not fair to expect you to do all this this quickly . . . you've only been here for two days. Not to mention you're . . . different. How old are you, anyway?"

"Thirteen."

He looked surprised. "You're quite big for a thirteen-year-old . . ." He paused, as if he had just realized what he'd said. "You know . . . tall."

I waved a hand in dismissal. "I think we're past that. I'm an ox."

"Hardly," he said. "You're stout. Good for fighting monsters."

"Except I don't want to fight monsters," I replied glumly. "I can't even hit the fake ones."

"It takes time to find our strengths. Lee, by the way. I'm one of the Monster Crushers from Canada. I figured you were an American . . . can't talk to a lot of the people here, obviously. They speak English in Derwin and a few other realms, but a lot of the Monster Crushers are from other countries. Most can speak a little English, of course, but they aren't all overly chatty anyway. Figured you might like to talk to someone."

He smiled again, revealing those sparkling white teeth. He smelled like sweat, but not in a bad way, which I thought was impossible. I guess not when you look like that.

"Definitely," I said, flustered. "Nice to meet you. Can I ask you something?"

"Sure."

I looked around the courtyard. "How come so many of the Monster Crushers and their Swords are young? I would think the elite warriors would all be adults."

Lee's smile disappeared. "You don't always live long in this job . . . especially the Swords. Not unless you're Eldon."

I followed his gaze and saw that Eldon was doing the Warrior's Way. He flew over the logs like a bounding gazelle, somersaulted under barriers, and landed his arrows right between the eyes of every target. When he stabbed a creature, he buried the sword right to the hilt, and then wrenched it out in a continuous motion. I watched in amazement as he flicked a knife at the last target, sticking it right into a fake goblin's chest.

"Who is he?" I whispered, while trying to discreetly wipe my brow. I glanced at Lee. Did he even have pores?

Lee lowered his voice. "He's the exception to the rule."

"What rule?"

"Every Sword from the Under Earth was chosen as a child. They don't even have a choice. They are selected as the best warriors and brought to Arnwell to train."

"That doesn't seem fair."

"It's not," Lee said. "But in their world, it's a great honour to be a Sword. So they were all chosen—except for Eldon Rein."

I watched as Eldon ran the course again. He was even faster this time. His hair billowed out behind him with his cloak, and his blue eyes flashed in the dim sunlight.

"He was a farmer from Eran," Lee said quietly. "He was only nineteen, but he'd just gotten married to a beautiful girl named Lily. He was happy. One day Eldon had to go to the next village over; he used to trade his crops for beef. It took longer than usual—apparently they were arguing over the trade, so he stayed the night. And when he came back, he found out that the monsters had come out of the tunnels and raided his village."

Eldon stabbed his sword through a fake ogre, driving it deep into the chest.

"The village had been burned to the ground. His parents were dead. His brother. Lily. His whole world was gone. But he told me that that wasn't what truly broke him. When he found Lily, he went after the goblins. Headed straight into the tunnels alone. He was wandering there, screaming for them to face him, when a lone goblin scout spotted him. They fought, and Eldon lost. Took a rusty spear through the leg, and the goblin left him there to die. Eldon said watching the goblin walk away was enough to keep him alive, just so he could have his vengeance on the monsters."

Eldon shot another arrow directly between a fake troll's eyes.

"After that, Eldon just showed up at Arnwell and demanded that he be trained. When the last trainer saw the anger in his eyes, he made the first and only exception to the rule. Eldon is the first Sword from the Under Earth who wasn't chosen, and he's also the greatest Sword alive."

Eldon finished the course again, sweeping his cloak around and tucking the sword into its sheath in one perfect motion.

"Can't he just be a Monster Crusher?" I whispered.

Lee laughed. "The Monster Crushers have to be from the surface world. Those are the rules. But I would keep him close." He glanced at me, casually brushing that thick black hair out of his eyes. I felt like I was cheating on Liam just looking at him, which was ridiculous for at least ten reasons. It was lucky Shal wasn't here . . . she might have literally melted.

"I know you didn't ask for this, Laura. None of us Monster Crushers do—but we all answer the call anyway, including you, by the way. It's not fair that the others blame you for finding the elevator. But you're here, and I'll do whatever I can to help you."

"Thanks," I said. "It might be nice to have at least one friend."

He smiled. "Better than none."

"Laura!" Eldon called, stalking back to the front of the course. "Start again."

I groaned and stood up. "Is he always this fun?"

Lee snorted. "This is him in a good mood."

I just shook my head and started for the first batch of logs, feeling my legs burn as I leaped over them. I was just running over the last one when I caught my foot hard and stumbled forward, crashing into the ground. My cheek smashed against the stone.

I lay there for a moment, dazed, and Eldon appeared beside me.

"Do you know what's happening right now?" he asked.

I sighed deeply. "I'm being killed by goblins."

"Exactly. Now get up and stay on your feet."

"Do I have to?"

"Yes."

I pushed myself up—ignoring the usual muted laughs around the courtyard—and started jogging toward the barriers.

"You know, you think you'd be nicer to the Monster Crusher," I grumbled.

"I'm being very nice," Eldon said. "I'm trying to keep you alive."

I finally collapsed into my bed hours later, my entire body aching and throbbing. I hadn't exercised that much in ever.

As I lay in bed, I thought about Lee's words: you don't live long in this job. Why would I possibly want to take it when those deadly warriors were being killed? I didn't have a chance against trolls and giants and sea creatures. I couldn't even run the Way.

But what choice did I have? Even now there were Swords watching my house from the woods to make sure goblins didn't swarm into my backyard. If they wanted to, the Swords could just abduct me and bring me to Arnwell to train anyway. And there was no way to move from Riverfield without telling my parents everything, which apparently was a very, very bad idea. It was official: I was stuck with the world's worst job.

As I started to doze off, something equally perturbing came to mind: Allison Black. I'd completely forgotten about our confrontation at school today. I had a feeling she hadn't, which meant I was in for a rough day tomorrow. But really, what could she do? Sure, she'd have fat jokes and ugly jokes and clothes jokes lined up for me, but I wasn't too worried. Those were a breeze.

I rolled over, sneaking a quick glance at my alarm clock. It was already four in the morning. I sighed and closed my eyes. Apparently Monster Crushers didn't get a lot of sleep. I was out almost instantly, but my dreams were nothing but yellow eyes and teeth.

Chapter Fifteen

As I had kind of guessed, my days of avoiding Allison Black's attention were over. I'd called her out in front of her friends, and I was now officially a target.

I'd also broken my own rule number one for bullied people: never draw attention to yourself. Let's just say I looked a little dishevelled. I'd slept in so late that I'd had no time for a shower, which of course meant my chestnut hair was matted and greasy. Add to that no makeup—not even my usual dab of blush—and an old yellow long-sleeve shirt I'd thrown on that had probably fit better four years ago, and I might as well have been wearing a Kick Me sign on my back.

In fairness, I had spent much of my night running— okay, mostly walking—through an obstacle course and generally being mocked for my lack of physical fitness, but I couldn't really explain that to Allison. As it was, she had plenty of material.

"I didn't know the filthy-hobo look was in," she'd said to her friends that morning when she walked by—just loud enough for me to hear it.

The seagulls enjoyed that one. Later in the hall outside of class she'd shielded her eyes and complained that the sun was so bright today. Portia used to like that one too.

This was definitely an unfortunate change, but I was taking it pretty well. When you have seven years of practice, those jokes just bounce off of you. Portia had spent entire days commenting on my wardrobe and size. And here I had Shal and Mia to talk to, so I was actually starting to think that I was going to get off easy. I was wrong. Geography was last period, and I spent most of it admiring Liam as he answered every single question while the other students snickered. Maybe he didn't have Lee's muscles or tanned skin or gentle brown eyes, but he still had . . . well, I don't know what it was. His hair was parted today, just off the middle, and held down with what smelled like hair spray. I just sniffed it when I walked by . . . that's all. Combined with those awkwardly perched glasses and a T-shirt that said Science Is Cool, he was pretty much a walking public service announcement for what nerds looked like. But I couldn't help it. I just smiled whenever I looked at him.

I was in love with a spectacled ocean plant.

Ms. Haddock was currently discussing European countries. She seemed fascinated with the subject and tried to sneak it in wherever possible, though I'm pretty sure it wasn't in the curriculum.

"Let's have a little competition," Ms. Haddock said, as if this would be greeted by raucous applause. The whole class just stared at her. "Everyone line up at the front," she continued eagerly, rolling up the world map. "It'll be like a spelling bee. If you get your question wrong, you sit down and cheer for everyone else."

Dead silence.

"The winner," she said meaningfully, "will get a gift certificate for two to the movies."

Well, it wasn't much, but provide a prize of any sort and people tend to get more excited. There were a few movies I wanted to see. The only problem was that I would have to stand in front of the class after being called a filthy hobo all day. Super.

So we all lined up at the front—Shal and Mia on either side of me—and the competition began. They started dropping like flies.

"What's the capital of Germany?" Ms. Haddock asked Tim.

He paused. "Europe?"

Oh boy. This was going to be a short competition.

"What language do they speak in the Netherlands?"

Ashley frowned. "Netherlandish?"

I really wanted to groan. Shal went out on the capital of Norway—she declined to try—while Mia got by on the language of Portugal.

"Name a country on Germany's eastern border," Ms. Haddock asked me.

I'm actually kind of a geography buff. I always wanted to travel, so I spent a lot of time looking at maps. A by-product of hating where you live, I guess. Same reason I like space so much. They both sounded a lot better than Newcastle. Everywhere did.

"Poland," I said confidently.

She smiled and rolled on.

Soon it was the fifth round, and there were only four of us left: Mia, a guy named Blake, Liam, and myself. Liam was currently standing only one boy away from me. I think I was sweating. I definitely felt flushed. Mia was up.

"What country contains the city of Budapest?"

Mia fidgeted. I could tell she was not comfortable standing in front of the class. Way too much attention for Mia Mouse. "Romania?" she guessed.

"Sorry," Ms. Haddock said, "Hungary."

The words were barely out of her mouth before Mia was sitting again.

"Okay, Laura," Ms. Haddock said, turning to me. "This is a tricky one. Name one of the two official languages they speak in Belgium."

Crap. That was a tricky one. I could see Allison whispering something to Ashley about me. They were both quietly giggling. Focus.

"French," I said.

"Excellent," Ms. Haddock said. "Very impressive, Laura."

I beamed. Hey, it was the first compliment I'd gotten all day.

Blake went out, and all of a sudden I was standing right next to Liam. Well, there was like a half-metre gap, but it was close. I could smell that hair spray again. It was like a spring meadow mixed with chemicals. I felt my skin tingling. What was wrong with me?

He nailed his question—big surprise—and so the finals were set.

Ms. Haddock stood up in excitement. "Okay, if Laura gets it wrong, Liam still has to answer his correctly. If she gets it right, and he's wrong, Laura wins."

I shot just the tiniest glance at Liam. His eyes were really blue up close. Focus!

"Laura, what is the northernmost country in Europe?"

By a stroke of luck, I had a thing for the Scandinavian countries. They always seemed really beautiful and empty, which was good for avoiding bullies. "Norway."

"Correct!"

Liam looked at me in surprise, and I felt my cheeks burning. Thankfully Allison was looking away, whispering with Carl. Ms. Haddock turned to Liam.

"What is the newest country in Europe?"

Hmm. Even I wasn't sure about that one. I had a guess, but I could see Liam was completely stumped. He shifted from foot to foot and frowned and rubbed his forehead.

"Liam?" Ms. Haddock asked politely.

He shook his head. "I don't know."

"Kosovo," she said. "Very tough. Great competition. But of course we can only have one winner, and that is Laura. Give her a round of applause."

There were some smattered claps, and I smiled shyly. And then Liam shook my hand and said congratulations. Why was my hand so clammy? I really blushed this time and muttered "thanks" and barely managed to take the movie certificate from Ms. Haddock without floating out of the classroom. I sat down feeling pretty great.

138

"Someone has a crush," Allison whispered behind me.

Uh-oh.

"I'm sure she'll forget about it soon," Shal said on the way home from school.

I wasn't that keen to walk home from school again after yesterday, but Eldon had assured me that the Swords were now watching the entire area, so I figured it was pretty safe. It was also very hard to explain why I didn't want to walk when Shal, Mia, and even my mom all wanted me to. So I just agreed and decided to walk really fast when I got to Raven's End.

"She doesn't forget about that stuff usually—" Mia started.

"Mia!" Shal cut in. "Not helping."

I sighed. "I guess she was going to figure it out eventually. I'll just try not to react and hopefully she'll assume she was wrong. Unless you want to tell Carl you love him?" I said, looking at Shal. "That might distract her—"

"No," Shal said firmly.

"Worth a shot," I muttered.

We were walking down Main Street again, and I noticed that a lot of the older people who hung out in the coffee shops and restaurants were huddled together around newspapers. In fact it seemed people were talking in hushed voices everywhere I looked.

"What's going on?" I wondered.

Mia glanced at me. "I heard the teachers talking about it on the way out. They found the hiker."

"Was he alive . . ."

Mia shook her head. "Apparently he'd been attacked by something."

I felt my stomach twist. I had a pretty good idea what had done it. Which meant the monsters were not only hunting me—they were attacking anyone else who got in their way. And that meant all of Riverfield was now in danger. There was no going back.

"Could be a bear or something," Shal said. "Or wolves."

"Yeah," I murmured, "maybe."

Shal grimaced. "Let's talk about something else. That freaks me out."

"Not Liam," I said.

"Or Carl," Mia added.

Shal paused and looked at us. "Well, that's all I got."

I just laughed and shook my head. "You're impossible. What are you guys doing this weekend?"

Shal shrugged. "Same thing as usual. Hanging out at my house eating ice cream and listening to my mom talk about parties and how much cooler she was when she was our age."

"It's the best," Mia muttered. "But my dad won't let me have people over."

"I can," I said. "I've got lots of room. Do you want to come over on Saturday?"

As soon as I said it, I sort of remembered that there was a rattling magic door in my closet and a bunch of heavily armed warriors guarding the house. But I was too late.

"Sweet," Shal said happily. "I can tell my mom I'm going out!"

"And we won't have to listen to her stories," Mia agreed, looking very relieved.

"Exactly," I said hesitantly.

As long as I got them out before ten-thirty when the rattling usually started, it should be fine. I would just have to keep a close eye on the clock. I could even pop into Derwin and tell Eldon I'd be a little late because I was having my friends over.

I pictured his face. He'd love that.

"Awesome," Shal said as we stopped in front of her house. "See ya, girls."

She scampered inside and Mia and I continued on to her house.

"That hiker," Mia said, glancing at me, "I think they said it was up by Raven's End."

"That doesn't surprise me," I muttered.

"Make sure you stay out of those woods," she said worriedly.

I snorted. "Trust me—I will."

I didn't have any homework, so I spent the evening helping Stache finish the painting in the main floor hallway. We were painting it white to cover up the old faded yellow colour and the many splintering cracks in the plaster that he'd had to fill. I actually liked painting with my dad. He'd pretend to splash me or push me into the wall, and then I'd paint the back of his shirt when he wasn't looking.

We had briefly discussed the hiker incident, but he had just said the same thing as Mia: stay out of the woods until they found the animal and got rid of it. We left it at that.

I'd always been much closer to my dad. Along with his big hands and big bones, I'd also gotten more of his interests: working around the house, sports, old historical fiction novels. When I was a kid we used to pretend to box and sword fight while my mom fussed about me wearing jeans and T-shirts instead of dresses. Don't get me wrong. I love my mom, but I think she was kind of hoping for a daughter she could dress up and shop with and do her hair. Instead she got me: a jeans-wearing Monster Crusher.

When my dad finished the last corner, he put his arm around me.

"This place is gonna be something," he said proudly.

"It's something, all right," I replied.

He glanced at me. "You liking it here, Laurabell? You know, besides the bats?"

(P.S. My dad calls me Laurabell when no one else is around.)

"It's not bad. It still looks like a haunted house, and I don't want to know how many spiders are in the basement I refuse to go into, but other than that, it's coming around."

"Good," he said, patting my shoulder. "I think I'm going to go start on the—"

"Get some sleep, Stache," I cut in.

He seemed to think about that. "All right. See you tomorrow, Laurabell."

"Good night."

I headed up to my room as well, figuring I'd take a shower and clean some of the paint off my cheeks before I went through the panel. I was just grabbing a towel from the linen closet when I heard my cellphone beep. There was a text message from Shal:

If you need to talk give me a call. I'm up.

I frowned. That could not be good. I tried to think what could be wrong. I glanced at my computer, and on a hunch, I sat down and checked my profile. No.

There I was, tagged on a Photoshopped picture. Instead of his mother, Liam had his arm around me. Well, my face on his mother's body. The words *Lovers=Gross* were written over our legs in big red font. Liam was tagged in it too.

He was going to see this. He was going to be embarrassed, and he was never going to even look at me again. I felt sick. I actually thought I might puke.

In the corner, for all the world to see, it said: posted by Allison Black.

I quickly shut my laptop, lay down on my bed, and cried.

I went through the panel late. Eldon was waiting in the courtyard with his arms folded across his muscular chest. He did not look happy.

"We need to maximize your time," he said sternly. "We don't have much of it."

"Sorry," I muttered.

He just glared at me and gestured to the Way. "Get started."

It was even worse than the day before. By the fourth time through I was walking, and Eldon disgustedly told me to sit down and take a break. Lee must have been back in Canada tonight because he wasn't in the courtyard. The crimson-haired girl was there though, and when I glanced at her, she just shook her head and went inside.

"You should be getting better every night," Eldon growled, appearing over me.

"I'm not going to get any better," I said quietly.

He turned and walked away. "I hope you're wrong."

We trained for a while longer. He walked me through sword motions and how to use a bow, though he told me I would only really be using the Iron Hammer.

"So let me practise with that," I said, frustrated.

He narrowed his blue eyes. "Only when you earn it."

So mostly I just ran the course, stumbling and tripping and failing again and again. The other Monster Crushers and the Swords weren't even laughing anymore—they just looked scornful. When I hit the ground on my tenth time through, I immediately stood up and started for the gate, my entire body throbbing with pain.

"We're not done," Eldon called after me.

"Yes, we are."

He followed me through the village, and I heard him stop as we crossed into the meadow.

"What's wrong?" he asked.

I looked back at him, scowling. "I can't do this."

"You have to."

"I can't!" I said, suddenly feeling my eyes well with tears. "Do you know who I am in my world, Eldon? A target. Girls make fun of me and call me fat and I just stand there and take it. Why? Because I'm a coward. I'm not a warrior—find someone else."

Eldon stared at me for a moment. "You're not a coward."

I wiped my eyes. "And how do you know that?"

"Because you came back," he said. He paused for a minute, but then didn't say anything more, just turned and started back for Arnwell. "See you tomorrow."

I stormed into the elevator, swung the lever, and shot back to the surface, not even saying goodbye to Porton, who was just watching me with a knowing look. He seemed to always know what was going on. When I got back to my bedroom, I climbed right under my blankets and thought about what Eldon had said, my vision still blurred with hot tears. Maybe he was right.

But if I wasn't a coward, then why I was so scared to see Liam in the morning?

Chapter Sixteen

I didn't eat breakfast the next morning. My stomach was too busy tying itself into some sort of pretzel to even look at food. I'd barely slept—which seemed to be a theme in my new house—and when I did, I had terrible dreams of Allison Black turning into a goblin and trying to eat me.

"What's wrong?" Tom asked me from across the table.

"Evil girls," I said quietly.

Tom nodded. "I figured they lived here too. Fat jokes?"

"Worse."

He seemed to think about that. "Boy jokes?"

"Bingo."

"What are you gonna do?" he asked.

"Probably take it and mope around all day. What else can I do? Punch her? Make up some nasty rumours and spread them around?" I paused. "Actually, that's not bad."

Tom looked at me with a very serious expression. "An eye for an eye makes the whole world blind—"

"Oh, shut up," I said, and he just grinned and went back to his English muffin.

But he was right. I wasn't that girl. I hated rumours and gossip, and I wasn't about to join the party now. When you spend your entire life as the subject of awful stories, you develop a certain sensitivity to gossip. Of course, Allison Black deserved all of that and more—I just wasn't the one to do it. And so what did I do? I took it and moped.

They laughed in the yard when I got there. They whispered about it during first period. They drew pictures and threw them at me. Allison started calling me Mrs. Kelp, and Tim asked if I used him as a toothpick after our dates. I was used to name-calling. I was used to things getting thrown and laughter and dirty looks. But this was different today, because Liam could see it. He could hear them calling me Mrs. Kelp.

And that made it much, much worse.

But they didn't really get me until lunch recess. I was sitting with Shal and Mia in the corner like usual, as far as possible from Allison and the other girls. It was cool today, and I had my jacket pulled up to my chin as we sat against the fence, watching the breeze rustle the leaves in the old maple tree that kept us company in the corner

"So she didn't exactly forget," Shal said soothingly. "But it's Friday. By Monday she'll have moved on."

Mia opened her mouth to say something, but she was silenced by a stern look from Shal. I just absently picked some grass and let it fly off into the breeze.

"It's fine," I said quietly. "I'm just not used to the boy jokes."

Shal snorted. "Those are usually Allison's favourite. Trust me, I've had plenty."

"I'm sure I would too if she ever had a chance to talk to me," Mia agreed.

"You really need to stop running away," Shal said, glancing at her. "It's sad."

Mia shrugged. "It's survival."

Shal just sighed and shook her head. "I'm sick of school already and it's Friday of the first week. That can't be good."

"Only ten more months to go," Mia said.

"Until the joys of high school," I pointed out. "Older Allison Blacks."

"Ugh," Shal muttered. "My mom's already talking about the changes I'll have to make. New clothes. New haircut. New . . ." She paused.

"New what?" Mia asked.

"Nothing," Shal said. "Who listens to that crazy, old pageant queen anyway?"

I knew what she was about to say. Friends. I was just about to say something when Mia suddenly stood up and took off like a puff of smoke. I watched her hurry down the fence, heading for the safety of the portables. That could only mean one thing.

Allison Black was walking toward us with a group of popular kids. I glanced across the yard at Liam, and I saw him watching the impending confrontation.

"Is it too late to run?" I asked quietly.

Shal had blanched. "Definitely."

"Hey, girls," Allison said, not even bothering to sit down this time. Clearly she was going to get straight to the point. She looked at me. "The girls and I were out buying skirts and talking about makeup last night when we realized we were being terrible friends. We should be setting you and Liam up."

Some of the girls snickered. Tim and another jock named Ian were there as well.

"I'm good, thanks," I muttered.

She waved a hand in dismissal. "I doubt it. Now, we know you like him, but I'm not convinced he likes you yet. We need to make a few changes." She looked me up and down. "First things first, you're really going to have to stop dressing like that. Boys don't like homeless girls, unless they're hot, and well . . . you aren't. A diet might also be nice. I'd say about forty pounds should do. You know what, I'm just going to ask Liam what he likes—"

I stood up without thinking, my hands balling into fists. Allison took a tiny step back, but she was still smiling. I knew why. If I hit her, I would be the one who got suspended and grounded and treated like a murderer. But I really, really wanted to.

"Something wrong?" she asked sweetly.

"Leave me alone," I said, walking by her and heading for the school.

Shal stood up and hurried after me.

"It's fine," Allison called after me. "We'll talk to him for you!"

I walked straight into the school and headed for the bathroom. When Portia used to really get to me, I'd go sit in a bathroom stall for awhile. Sometimes I cried; sometimes I just needed a place to cool down. Today kind of felt like a cry day.

"She's just an idiot," Shal said, following me in. "She gets bored and decides to . . . are you going to the bathroom?"

I closed the stall door behind me and sat down—well, I put the lid down first. "I just want to be alone for a bit," I said quietly. My eyes starting welling with tears.

"Oh, cool," Shal said, clearly not going anywhere. "I'll just hang out."

The bathroom door opened again.

"Oh, the mouse returns," Shal grumbled.

"Sorry," Mia replied.

I just sat there and let the tears spill out over my shaking fingers.

The rest of the day was more of the same. People made comments, and I pretended they didn't bother me. When the final bell went, I quickly grabbed my stuff and hurried to my locker. I just needed to get home. People walked by, called me Mrs. Kelp and muttered "gross" and laughed, and tears streamed down my cheeks as I stuffed my books in my backpack. I wiped my face with the back of my hands, zipped up my bag, and turned to go, trying desperately to hold in the next wave of tears. I froze.

Liam R. Kelp was standing right behind me.

He was going to yell at me. He was going to tell me to stay away from him. He was going to tell me I was fat and he would never like me. I tried to prepare myself.

"Hey, Mrs. Kelp," he said, breaking into a toothy grin. He shook his head. "What a bunch of idiots. I hope they didn't get to you."

"Not even close," I lied.

"Good. Worst Photoshop work I've ever seen. Awesome

job on the geography quiz, by the way. I've never lost before." He smiled again. "I'll get you next time."

I flushed. "We'll see about that."

"See you Monday, Mrs. Kelp," he said, and continued down the hall.

I watched him go, and I barely heard the nasty comments as people walked by.

That night my family went out to dinner, and as we walked through the restaurant, I saw Ashley—Allison Black's second-in-command—sitting with her parents and two younger sisters.

There's this weird thing that happens to bullied people. We go out with our families and we see our bullies with their families, and there's this moment where maybe we both realize that people aren't supposed to act like this in the real world—that it's not really okay to spend your whole afternoon trying to make someone cry. The hostess led us right by Ashley's table, and the second she saw me she flushed bright red and looked away. Hey. I was supposed to do that.

I realized that she probably thought I would call her out in front of her parents. Expose her for being so terrible. And that maybe, somewhere deep down, she was embarrassed. But I also knew that nothing would change at school the next day.

As we sat down, the waitress bustled about, making sure to unfold Tom's napkin on his lap and pouring his water first. Tom always gets doted on at restaurants. People can be a little weird around him too. Like the server will say, "And what can I get you?" before realizing a blind boy wouldn't know who they're referring to. Then they always get a little flustered and look at us for help or lightly touch his arm. I think we forget how much we talk in looks and gestures. When you take that away, people get awkward. I kind of enjoy watching it. I know, I'm a jerk.

After finally getting our orders, the waitress—a pretty woman that had Stache looking a little flustered himself— hurried off, and my mom turned to the family.

"Who wants to go first?" She gets right to the point sometimes.

"I'll go," Tom said. "By the way, is our waitress hot?"

"Tom!" my mom said in a hushed voice. "Why would you say that?"

He shrugged. "Dad's voice sounded weird."

I snorted and Stache went bright red as my mom scowled at him.

She shook her head and turned back to Tom. "How was your day, Tom?"

"Okay," he said. "I think my EA's boyfriend might be cheating on her."

She sighed. "What did I tell you about eavesdropping?"

"She was talking pretty loudly. He keeps coming home late and yesterday he smelled like perfume—"

"Laura," my mom said, cutting him off. "Your turn."

"Well," I said, "my class spent most of the day calling me Mrs. Kelp."

"Why?" she asked.

"They were implying that I was married to a boy in my class."

My dad almost spit out his beer. "What boy?"

"Relax, Stache," I said calmly. "Just a joke. A mean one. But as it turns out, it didn't bother Liam and everything is cool."

"Do you like this Liam?" my mom asked with a smile.

My dad watched me closely.

"Maybe," I muttered.

My father took another drink of beer. "No boyfriends until—"

"I'm thirty-five and living on my own." I cut in. "Yeah, yeah, Stache."

Not a real rule by the way. Though at this rate it was certainly possible.

"And don't you forget it," he said.

The waitress returned with our cutlery.

"Can I get you guys anything else?" she asked.

"I'll take another beer," Stache said, about five octaves higher than normal.

Tom giggled and my mom rolled her eyes.

Yep. That's my family.

That night I sat on my bed thinking about what Eldon had said. He did have a point. I'd gone to school today, even though I'd wanted to stay home. I'd taken the abuse, I'd cried, but I hadn't left. And because of all that, I found out that Liam wasn't even upset. Just because I stuck around.

Kind of what I should have done with softball. Instead I quit, and now I just looked at the old boxes in my closet and felt like I had let myself down.

I opened up the guide and started reading more of the Guide to Monsters section. There was some general information on the monsters, including where they came from. Daniel the Dragon Killer, the first Monster Crusher from Riverfield, had written an account of his visit.

Only a few people have ever had the misfortune of visiting the monster realms, including me. There are many of them, and all are dark and awful. Some have rivers of lava running through, casting everything in a red glow, though there are streams and lakes as well, as even monsters must eat and drink. What they eat I do not know: each other, maybe, and bats and fish and the oversized rats that scour the tunnels.

I have only been to one monster realm, which we called the Dead Mountains, since it is a cavernous place with towering mountains running through it . . . it is the closest realm to Derwin. I won a battle there against Scarab the Scourge barely.

I saw a note on the side, written by someone else.

Then he decided to go back and was killed. Bad idea.

I frowned and kept reading Daniel's account.

I don't know what the monsters really want, but they hate humans. They've been fighting each other since the moment they met, and I suspect they think of us as monsters too. They seem to only have one goal: wipe out the humans in the Under Earth so they can reclaim it as their own. But I think the goal is greater: wipe out ALL humans, so that

only monsters remain. One day, I suspect that will lead
them to the surface too. In the meanwhile, we must hold
them at bay. But the Dead Mountains is just one of their
realms: we know of many others, and who knows what
else lies beneath our feet.

Another person had written a postscript below it.

Note: He really was a cheery fellow, wasn't he?

I sat back and thought about what Daniel had written.
How many monsters were there? What if they got onto the
surface? Could we even stop them?

My cellphone beeped, and I immediately scooped it up.

Did you see Carl today? That shirt was so hot.

Thank you, Shal. The second one was from Mia.

Check your wall. Awesome.

I hurried over to my laptop and opened my profile. I
literally laughed out loud.

A picture of Allison Black was the first thing I saw.
Except it had been slightly altered. Her face was covered
with warts, tinted green, and somehow her nose had been
extended and bent. A hat had been added over her long
black hair. At the bottom it said:

The Wicked Witch of Riverfield.

It was posted by Liam R. Kelp. You courageous fool.
I had a message in my inbox. It simply read:

This is how you use Photoshop.

Did I mention yet that I love him? This sealed the deal.
Allison would probably find some evil way to get back at
him, but oh well. The picture already had eight likes.

Make that nine.

After staring at the picture for a while longer, grinning
from ear to ear, I threw on some workout clothes and headed
for the panel. I still sincerely doubted that I was going to
become a great warrior, but at the very least I wasn't going
to quit.

Sometimes you just had to stick around.

I crawled into the elevator and shot downward, now
holding onto the lever with one hand and not even worrying about screaming. Nodding at Porton, I hurried through
the village, heading for Arnwell. I noticed that the streets
were a lot quieter today, though the sun sphere was shining
brightly as ever. I stepped through the towering arched gate
and saw that for the first time the courtyard was completely
empty. The Warrior's Way stood alone, and weapons were
scattered across the cobblestones, as if everyone had suddenly left and not bothered to clean them.

"Eldon?" I called. "Hello?"

There was no response. I stepped inside the courtyard.
Where was everybody? I figured they had to be in the
castle. Maybe they were eating or something.

That's when I felt it. Something was watching me.

I slowly turned around, my muscles tensed. Then I looked up. There, crawling down the wall over the gate, was a massive, furry black spider. It bared its glistening foot-long fangs, hissing loudly as it did, and prepared to jump directly on my head.

Chapter Seventeen

I screamed and took off the other way, glancing back to see the monstrous spider drop down onto the spot where I'd been standing. It was easily a metre tall at the tip of its furry black abdomen, and its hair-covered legs spread at least twice as wide. Combined with eight beady black eyes, two grasping mandibles, and those glistening fangs, I'd never seen anything more terrifying in my life.

"Eldon!" I shouted in a panic. "Lee! Someone!"

The spider scurried after me, raising its deadly looking fangs. I screamed again and sprinted for the castle, but for the first time I noticed that the heavy iron doors were closed. There was no way I'd have time to open them before the spider attacked.

What if there were more spiders? What if everyone else was already dead?

I whirled around and saw the spider racing toward me. I sprinted to the left, trying to circle back to the gate and make a break for the village. But the spider was too fast. It moved laterally with quick little steps, blocking my path and continuing toward me.

"Eldon!"

I looked around the courtyard in desperation. It was still set up for training, so there were bows and swords and spears littered everywhere. I spotted a long silver spear propped against the wall about three metres away and made a dash to grab it. The spider chased after me. I just managed to scoop up the spear when the spider flung itself through the air toward me, hissing loudly again. I dove onto the hard stones, and the spider crashed right into the wall, its hairy legs flailing as it stood itself upright again.

I might have been able to get up and stab it with the spear, but instead, I raced back toward the gate into the village.

I was halfway there when I heard a fast-moving patter closing in on me. I looked back and saw the spider right behind me. I wasn't going to make it. In a last desperate attempt, I tried to turn around and stab it with the spear.

It didn't quite work out.

My feet crashed into each other, and I went spinning back-first toward the ground, realizing in horror that the spider was going to land right on top of me. Just before I hit the ground, I pointed the spear at the creature's soft padded underbelly as it launched itself through the air. I slammed into the stones, and the spider landed right on top of me, the spear tip piercing right through its chest and out its back.

But I didn't have much time to celebrate. The spider was still alive.

It sunk closer and closer to my face, its massive fangs gnashing in front of me, the black venom already beginning to form droplets at their tips. I tried to push it off, but it was too strong. The fangs got closer. They were centimetres from my face now.

Suddenly a long feathered arrow flew into its head, followed by three more. The spider went limp and I managed to shove it off me, using the spear for leverage.

I lay there for a second, unable to move. Then I heard it. Laughter.

Warriors started appearing on the walls, some of them holding bows. I looked around in disbelief from where I was lying in the middle of the courtyard and saw Eldon appear over the gate. Even he wore a faint smile.

I scrambled to my feet and looked at him furiously. "You sent a *spider* after me?"

"I wanted to prove you weren't a coward."

I scowled. "Well that worked. I screamed, ran away, and fell over."

"You also killed it," he replied simply. "Mostly. You said you were afraid of spiders. Now you've killed it. You should be proud."

"Proud? It almost killed me!" I shouted, starting for the door. "I'm going home."

Eldon jumped off the roof, landing in a practised crouch in front of me.

"Every Monster Crusher must kill a monster before their training can be complete. It's one of the tests. We always try to find the monster they fear most to test their courage. You've done it early. That was worth a hundred trips through the Way."

I paused. "Does that mean I don't have to do it anymore?"

Eldon laughed. "Of course not."

"Great," I muttered, walking around him and heading for the elevator. I could hear the warriors snickering on the walls. "I'm taking a break tonight."

"Fair enough," Eldon said. "But I do want to speak to you for a moment."

I glanced at him. "What about?"

"Walk," he said, falling into line beside me.

We strode through the gate, and I noticed the villagers starting to emerge from their houses, many laughing and talking to each other. Apparently all of Derwin was sharing in the joke.

"The war is intensifying in Riverfield. We are killing more and more monsters surrounding your house. They obviously want to murder you soon."

"This isn't making me feel better."

"They also seem to be searching for our tunnels, just as we are searching for theirs. At the moment we are both chasing shadows. We need to figure out where their tunnels are, and soon." He shook his head. "There is something we are missing here. The monsters have never attacked the Monster Crushers on the surface before. For some reason they're paying special attention to you."

"Lucky me," I muttered.

He stopped in front of a white stone fountain and put a rough hand on my shoulder. "We'll protect your house as best as we can. But the war is coming faster now . . . you must be ready soon."

"I don't know if I can do this," I said, meeting his blue eyes.

He smiled. "That's the one good part about these situations. You have no choice."

"That's a good part?" I asked skeptically.

"Absolutely," he said. "You don't have to worry about if you *can*. You either will . . . or you won't."

"That's very comforting."

"I try."

I shook my head and started for the elevator, ignoring the whispering villagers.

"And Laura?"

I glanced back.

"That was some scream," he said.

I scowled. "Shut up."

He laughed as I stormed across the meadow. But I was smiling as I changed my clothes later that night and plopped exhaustedly into bed. Suddenly I wasn't that worried about little spiders in my bedroom.

The rest of the weekend was pretty uneventful: Shal had forgotten she had a cousin's birthday to attend on the Saturday, so the three of us made plans to hang out next weekend instead. I spent my Saturday watching an old Western with Stache and Tom—he always enjoyed the old-fashioned lingo—while my mom read a book on the recliner.

When it was done, I went upstairs at ten and left for training as usual. It was pretty much the same thing Sunday night as well: run the Warrior's Way, train with weaponry, and learn about monsters. I again asked to train with the hammer, but Eldon told me I still hadn't earned it.

"Coming back is a start," he said, "but it doesn't make you a Monster Crusher."

And so I just kept working, and I thought maybe, just maybe, I was getting a little better. I was certainly a lot sorer. When I woke up Monday morning my legs were so cramped I basically had to crawl out of bed and warm them up in the shower. Even if I wasn't becoming the best warrior, I was at least getting plenty of exercise.

But when I climbed out of my mom's van on another brisk morning and walked into the schoolyard, I instantly knew there was trouble. Allison was already there, and she was talking feverishly with the seagulls They were up to something.

As it turned out, they had a lot of things in mind.

I soon learned that people don't usually mess with Allison. Not because they don't want to, but because she decides to make destroying you her new priority. In this case that meant all the people who had liked the page as well—Mia and Shal included.

Actually Shal had folded and taken her like back before school that morning, but it was too late. She was already on the Kill List. Of course, Liam was right up there today. But I think Allison assumed I was part of creating the photo as well because she saved me for last.

It started out normal enough. Allison and her seagulls swooped around the yard calling people names and whispering gossip. Mia ran away three times. Liam was playing his game with Paul and Steve and ignored them, but some of the other targets weren't taking the new attention very well. One girl went inside early, probably to cry in the bathroom stall.

Unfortunately that was nothing new.

But things got progressively more evil as the day continued. Allison did what any self-respecting wicked witch would do. She found our weaknesses, and she targeted them. I suspect everyone got hit in one way or another. But there were three that I saw first-hand: Shal, Liam, and of course, myself. Shal was first.

Hers came at lunch. It was pretty easy, I guess. She'd already cried in front of them about the ginger thing, and she was clearly very self-conscious about her appearance. That gave Allison her target.

"What is she doing?" Shal asked worriedly, watching Allison from our usual spot in the corner.

"I don't know," I said, not even bothering to turn around. "Something evil, I'm sure."

Mia turned to look. "She's handing something out."

I frowned and looked behind me. Most of the boys played basketball or handball against the back wall of the school, where there was a big paved area. Naturally all the popular girls hung out in the near vicinity. And it was there that Allison, Ashley, and a few of the other seagulls were walking around handing out little slips of paper.

"That can't be good," I murmured.

We watched as they handed them out to every eighth grader in the school, and then they gathered together and set off across the yard toward us. Poof. Mia was gone.

"Here we go again," I muttered.

Allison and the other girls stopped in front of us. She smiled, revealing those sparkling white teeth. "We're having a vote. Here's your ballot."

Shal and I exchanged a concerned look and took the ballots. As soon as I read it, I knew this was not going be good. At the top of the paper it said: Ugliest Ginger in the School. There was just one box with a name next to it: Michelle Webster.

Shal's hands trembled as she held the paper, and then her eyes started watering. Suddenly she stood up and ran toward the school, letting the ballot fall to the ground.

"I think she'll win even without that vote," Allison said. The seagulls giggled.

"Why?" I asked, looking at her in disgust.

She smiled. "Because I'm the Wicked Witch of Riverfield."

Mia and I spent the whole recess trying to console Shal as she sobbed in the bathroom stall. Didn't help. I was really getting sick of Allison Black.

Liam was next. I didn't know what his weakness was at first, but I should have.

His mom. She was a single mother, and he was an only child.

Allison started a rumour during last recess that his mom was a stripper. It was a fairly basic rumour, but when the boys started doing catcalls, I could see him flushing.

They broke him right before last period.

I was getting my math books out of my locker when I noticed Liam walking down the hall toward class. Tim stepped in front of him, wearing a crooked grin.

"Hey, Kelp. My older brother saw your mom last night. She put on a good show."

That was too much. Liam flushed red, dropped his books, and took a swing at Tim's head. I could tell he wasn't a fighter. His punch sailed wide, and Tim tackled him to the ground like a football player. He sat up and punched Liam in the face as every kid in the hallway crowded around and started shouting. I came running just as Mr. Lell ran out of his class and forcibly pulled Tim off of Liam. Liam shakily climbed to his feet, bloody and shamefaced, and Mr. Lell escorted them both to the office.

I wanted to cry as I watched Liam walk by, tears in his bright-blue eyes.

They both got suspended. I had a feeling it would be the first day of school Liam had ever missed. I saw his mom arrive from where I was watching through the window. She looked disappointed.

Allison saved me for last. It was a simple prank.

As I sat there in last period thinking about Liam, she took a water bottle and ever so delicately squeezed some through the hole in the back of my chair. I didn't notice until I stood up to leave and Allison and her friends burst out laughing.

I was wearing light jeans that day, of course.

Soon half the class was laughing, and I hurried out without even knowing why. When Mia and Shal told me at my locker, I felt sick. It was stupid, but I knew they'd all believe it. The fat girl had peed herself. Why not? I wrapped my coat around my waist and left to a chorus of laughter. Allison just smiled evilly.

What was my weakness? The fact that I was so used to fat jokes. Mix it up and I broke like glass.

I was so upset I didn't even leave my room when I got home. It wasn't just the prank. It was Liam's face and Shal's tears and the fact that I still couldn't stand up to Allison. Because I knew it always gets worse.

I just wanted to be invisible. I wanted them to leave me alone.

I missed dinner. I ignored my parents' and Tom's questions. I just lay in bed and ignored everything until past nine when everyone had gone to sleep. I blearily checked my cellphone. Ten missed calls, all from Shal and Mia. Six messages too:

Where are you?
Are you okay?
Do you want to talk?
I can't believe she called me the ugliest ginger.
Do you think Carl voted?
Call me.

I sighed and put the phone down. I didn't want to talk. I just wanted to lie here.

But a little voice in my head reminded me that I wasn't invisible. That they would never leave me alone. Because I could keep a low profile and hide, but I would run into Allison eventually, and she would always have something to say.

And worse, I would always be waiting for her to say it.

I wasn't invisible in the Under Earth either. I was part of this war, whether or not I wanted it. And it was time to start getting better. I threw on my usual training outfit of track pants and a T-shirt and climbed through the panel into the elevator.

When I walked out into the courtyard, Eldon turned to me, raising an eyebrow.

"You came early."

"Yep," I said.

"Why?"

I walked right by him. "Because I really love this obstacle course."

I heard a quiet laugh behind me, and then he shouted at me to start.

I plunked myself against the wall a little while later, and this time, Eldon sat down beside me. We watched in silence for a moment as two of the other Monster Crushers sparred in the ring, their muscular arms bulging as they crashed against one another.

I had read in the guide about the fifty Monster Crusher houses that were scattered around the world, ranging from Riverfield to Rio de Janeiro to Cairo. I had even read with interest that the pyramids themselves were heavily linked with the intricate tunnels running beneath the earth. That, of course, meant the other Monster Crushers were just as international: Lee had pointed out an Oskar Romanowich from Siberia, a Hu Jing from Shanghai, and a Bo Kobongo from Nigeria. There were two other Americans: one from Brooklyn and another from outside of Phoenix. There were also two Canadians: Lee and another boy, from Whitehorse, who looked like he was carved out of stone himself.

I watched them all training, or at least the ones who were there—because most had far greater distances to travel through the tunnels, they often had to devise elaborate stories of going to school overseas or oining the military. There were smaller training centres in the other realms, but Arnwell Castle was the centre, and that's where Monster Crushers spent most of their time.

"How are things on the surface?" Eldon asked quietly.

I shrugged. "The same, I guess."

I watched as Lee knocked another Monster Crusher down with a vicious sideways blow, his entire body rippling at the impact. He politely helped the other boy to his feet and then stalked off toward the Warrior's Way, slinging the wooden club he'd been using onto his broad shoulder. The Monster Crushers seemed to have a deep respect for each other: I didn't see many cheap shots or anything of the sort. I glanced at Eldon.

"Who are my Swords going to be?" I paused. "You know, if I actually complete this training. It won't be that redhead, will it? She kind of hates me."

He laughed. "Caria? No. She is one of Arnwell's Protectorates and doesn't act as a Monster Crusher's Sword. Other than the Protectorate, all the Swords that you see are matched with their respective Monster Crushers: they travel with them to Derwin and train with them. And they are under the same rules: they cannot help out at another surface location. They are all responsible for their own tunnels, and they cannot go to Riverfield, even if more warriors would be nice. If they die fighting another Monster Crusher's battles, they have left their own area vulnerable to attack.

"You won't have met your Swords yet. I have asked that they suspend their training until you are ready, or at least to come at times when you are not here. You won't meet them, in fact, unless you complete your training. We do that to protect their identities. Most Swords are from the Under Earth, but some are from the surface. They find tunnels and stumble across our world, and if they do, and they are capable of the task, they have a choice."

"Which is?"

"Join our fight or return to your world and say nothing on threat of death."

I snorted. "Pleasant."

"And necessary."

"At least they have a choice. I didn't."

He nodded. "The Swords are not chosen by a spell. They are chosen based on courage and skill. In our world it is a rare and special honour. Some preference is given to those from the surface, if they find their way here, as we believe they may have found the Under Earth for a reason. In the past I have agreed to train some from the surface that otherwise would never have been chosen. And often they turn out to be the best ones of all."

He turned to me. He was a striking man, or would have been, if there wasn't so much danger in his cold eyes. His stubble had grown almost into a full beard now, creeping down his neck and meeting his long hair at his shoulders.

"We will keep running the Way. I don't want you sparring yet, for your safety."

"I appreciate that."

"But we will begin more advanced monster training starting tomorrow. You need to know how to outthink your enemies, as well as crush them. Have you read the Tips on Monster Crushing section yet?"

"No."

"Do so tomorrow. In the next few days, we must escalate your training. I fear we may be running out of time."

I sat there for a moment, thinking. "How will you know when I'm ready?"

He smiled. "I have a feeling that fate will decide that for us." He rose to his feet like a cat unfurling and extended a calloused hand. "Ready?"

"Not really," I muttered, letting him pull me up.

"The others don't like you," he said quietly. "They ask me to send you home almost every day. To tell you to move. To tell you not to return."

I raised an eyebrow. "Why are you telling me this?"

"Because a very small part of me thinks they are wrong."

With that, he swept away toward the course, his cloak flying out behind him.

"Now do it again!"

Chapter Eighteen

The next day at school was a little strange. Allison had really gone into overdrive yesterday, and people were all a bit wary, like they were getting back into the water after a shark attack. Shal kept looking around like something was going to pounce on her. Mia ran away if Allison and the seagulls even glanced in our general direction.

People were still giggling when I walked by, but I was taking it better today. Shal and Mia knew I hadn't peed myself, and they were the only ones I really talked to anyway. If everyone else wanted to laugh, so be it. But I was very careful to check my pants every time I stood up while Allison and Ashley snickered behind me.

I was also missing Liam. I know that sounds crazy since we don't really talk to each other that much, but class felt very boring without him. No one put their hand up, and Ms. Haddock just got flustered and stopped asking questions. I might have considered putting my hand up for some, but I didn't want to give Allison any more excuses to come after me. It was time to get back to rule number one for awhile.

I was not going to call any more attention to myself.

I'd lost some of last night's courage when I showed up at school that morning. It was easier being brave in some alternate world, but I was too used to being afraid in this one. At lunch, Mia, Shal, and I went and sat in the corner as usual, propped up against the chain-link fence. Shal stared at Carl and the other popular kids in the distance.

"They had thirty signatures," she said.

"What?" I asked.

"On the petition. The ugliest ginger petition."

I waved a hand in dismissal. "People will sign anything that Allison gives them. Ashley would sign a petition naming herself the biggest idiot in school if Allison made it."

"I hate my hair," Shal muttered. "Always have."

"I like it," Mia said, her slender little arms wrapped around her knees. "It's so long and colourful. Mine is boring." She glanced at me. "You keep looking over at the portables. Are you sad Liam is at home today?"

Shal snickered.

"Yeah," I admitted. "I just feel bad. I hope he didn't get in trouble."

"Maybe you should go visit him," Shal suggested.

"Oh, yeah, he'd be thrilled."

"It would be nice," Mia said. "Just say you're there to see how he's doing."

I frowned. "I couldn't do that."

"Why not?" Shal asked.

I thought about that. Hmm. "I don't know. Maybe."

"Can we hide in the bushes and watch?" Shal asked eagerly.

"Shut up."

I noticed Mia was staring through the chain-link fence, and I followed her gaze. The same forest that wrapped around my street stretched down behind the school as well, though it was about thirty metres back through a grassy field. In the distance, two police officers were walking along the edge of the forest. They were both staring into the trees as they walked.

"Looking for the animal," Mia said quietly. "They still haven't found what got that hiker."

"Does this stuff happen a lot in Riverfield?" I asked.

Shal shook her head. "No. Well, I guess a few years ago a couple went missing in the woods. Oh, and my mom did tell me about this thing that happened like twenty years ago. Apparently four houses just outside of town were burned down. The families all disappeared. Mom said they never figured out what happened."

"I didn't know that," Mia said worriedly, looking at her.

Shal waved a hand. "That was a long time ago."

I watched as the two police officers plunged into the forest. I hoped they were keeping their guns close. There were monsters in those woods.

"Can we get back to Kelp?" Shal asked. "What would you say? Can you imagine if I showed up at Carl's one day? I know what I'd wear: my white top and those jeans with the little faded specks on the thighs. I'd probably wear my hair down. Maybe dye it brown first. But what would I say? Hey, Carl, how's it going? No, that's stupid. Hey, Carl, just thought I'd drop in. Nope."

As Shal went on about all the things she might say to Carl, I scanned the woods, looking for yellow eyes.

I made it through most of the day without any incidents, which was pretty impressive. I took Allison's little whispered comments and pretended I didn't hear them and just read the guide through class. This time I turned right to Tips on Monster Crushing.

Now that Eldon had surprised me with the spider, I was afraid he might try me out with other monsters soon. Not to mention the fact that goblins had already tried to kill me in my own backyard. I needed to know how to protect myself.

The tips section was even more disorganized than the histories. Notes were scribbled in everywhere, and it seemed each Monster Crusher had his own techniques. I started with the goblin section.

1. *Always go for the leader FIRST. Save yourself some trouble.*
2. *If you are attacked by one goblin, look behind you. They never attack alone.*

I frowned. I wish I'd read that tip earlier.

3. *Most goblins keep a knife hidden somewhere in their clothing. Make sure they don't stick you when you're not looking.*
Note: Sometimes they have two. I just got a knife in the thigh. Not pleasant.
4. *Goblins are led by fear. If you face overwhelming odds, make them fear YOU. I find shouting effective.*

175

> However, if you face REALLY overwhelming odds, you might want to run. OR:
> Challenge the leader. If you call him out, he may feel compelled to fight you one-on-one. Crush him, and you win the battle.
> Note: The monsters may also do this to you. That's how they got Daniel.

I flipped to the spider section to see if I should have done anything differently.

1. Don't get bitten. If you do . . . you're in trouble.
2. Poking at the eyes is always a good idea.
3. If you crush the abdomen with your hammer, watch out for spraying venom.
Note: Should have read this sooner. Ow.
4. Spiders don't like fire.

Hmm, I thought. Better remember that one. I flipped through a few more monsters, though I noticed the tips were sparser for the leaders. For dragons, most of them were warnings not to get caught out in the open and to try to catch them sleeping. For giants, it was pretty much the same, though Gregory the Giant's Bane had killed his giant by jumping off a rocky ledge and bringing the hammer down on its head.

Trolls seemed equally troublesome.

1. Trolls love ambushes. Be aware.
2. Do I even need to tell you about bridges?

3. They often wear armour under ratty brown clothes . . . they can absorb a lot of blows.

Note: No kidding. I barely beat the last one. Are they getting bigger?

4. *Don't underestimate their intelligence.*

5. They have thick skin almost everywhere, but not on the top of their feet. If you hit them there, they'll feel it.

I read through the rest of the tips, on ogres, imps, giant snakes, sea creatures, and those scary wolf hawk things that I really hoped I didn't run into. Actually, I hoped to avoid all of them, but considering it was supposedly my job to crush these things that didn't seem very likely. I closed the book and grimaced. This was not cool.

The bell went for recess, and I tucked the guide away and met up with Shal and Mia on the outside, trying to remember what life was like before I found that elevator.

I was just heading back into class when I realized I'd forgotten my math textbook. I hurried back to my locker, thinking that I might have been even less excited for math class than I was for training that night. My whole body was aching again, and I knew it was just going to keep getting worse for awhile until I got used to running the course.

I had just pulled the textbook off the shelf when I heard someone step behind me.

"Look how heartbroken she is," Allison said with mock sympathy. "Lover boy is home today. At least you remembered to wear a diaper."

I turned around and saw Allison standing behind me with Ashley and another seagull named Tanya, a fairly stocky girl who was essentially their muscle. She was still smaller than me, obviously, but I guess they wanted to come prepared. They both cackled.

I tried to stay calm. Rule number four was very clear: NEVER react to insults.

"It's a good thing he was gone before that," Allison continued, playing with a strand of that annoyingly shiny black hair. "Boys don't usually like girls that pee themselves. Maybe Liam does. He is a little weirdo."

I closed my locker, took a second to compose myself, and started to walk by her. There were still a few other kids milling around in the halls, but most people had already filtered into class.

Allison stepped in my way. "You don't want to talk anymore? Maybe I can give you some advice. Let's see: lose fifty pounds, buy new clothes, put on some makeup, stop peeing yourself—"

"Leave me alone," I muttered, moving around her.

"Oh, she's getting angry," Allison said. "Fine, we don't need to hang out. Better you hang out with your little brother, anyway. He can't see how ugly you are."

And that did it. It wasn't even an insult to Tom. But I don't like when he is brought up by evil girls. Ever. Like I said, I'm not a slapper or a hair puller. I spent most of my childhood with Stache, and he watched a lot of boxing.

And so without thinking I turned around and punched Allison directly in the stomach. Hard. Like her brown eyes bulged and she collapsed grabbing her stomach hard. And

Ashley and Tanya looked at me like I was a murderer hard. Ashley took off, probably to get the principal, and I just stood there as Allison clutched her stomach. She suddenly glanced up at me, and to my surprise, she was wearing a knowing little smile.

I was still standing there when the principal stormed around the corner, took in the scene, and escorted me straight to his office.

"It's lucky it's just a day," my mom said on the way home, shaking her head.

She'd had to leave work early to come get me. She was not thrilled. Tom was. She'd taken him out early to avoid making the trip back to school again.

"She's lucky it was just her stomach," I muttered.

My mom glanced at me. "You should know better. After all you went through in Newcastle—"

"Yeah, well, I'm going through it here too. I'm still fat, if you haven't noticed."

"You don't look fat to me," Tom said.

"Thanks, Bat Boy."

"You're full-figured," my mom added. "Like your father."

"That's not a good thing."

"But you're used to these girls, Laura," she continued. "They've been making these comments for years. And you know punching them doesn't help—"

"I don't care about the fat jokes," I said. "She brought up Tom."

"Who would want to insult the captain of the football team?" Tom asked.

My mom frowned in the rear-view mirror. "What?" She shook her head. "What did she say?"

I paused. "Just that I should hang out with him because he can't see how fat I am."

"That's awful," my mother said.

"I like to think I make good company regardless," Tom pointed out.

"The point is I shouldn't have done it," I said. "It was stupid. It's just going to be worse when I go back."

My mom seemed to consider that. "Well, then I hope you really socked her."

I looked at her in surprise, and she tried to hold back a little smile. My cellphone buzzed. The bell must have gone, which meant Shal and Mia finally had a chance to text.

Shal: I heard you punched Allison!!!!!!!!!!!!!!!!!!!

Mia: Are you okay?

Shal: Where did you hit her??????????

Mia: You're not in trouble are you?

Shal: I love you!!!!!!!!! Carl laughed at her. Best day ever. Want to chill tonight?

"Who's that?" my mom asked.

"Just Shal and Mia," I said. "Asking if I'm all right. And if I want to hang out." I snorted. "I guess they don't get the whole grounding concept."

"Who said you were grounded?"

I looked at her. "I'm not?"

She smiled. "I don't condone punching people. Ever. But I know they can be hard on you. And you haven't . . . you know . . . had a lot of friends come over. Why not have them over for a girls' night? I mean it's a school night, so you have until nine."

"Are you feeling okay?" Tom asked from the back.

"Yes," she said. "I'm just sick of those annoying hussies bothering your sister."

I laughed. "Did you just call them hussies?"

She sat up a little straighter. "Never you mind. Now invite your friends over."

I looked at her for a moment and then shook my head and started texting them back. It's always nice when your parents surprise you.

"This house is cool," Mia said, sitting cross-legged on my bed. "You have a big room."

"Love the closet," Shal added, peeking inside.

"Yeah, nothing special," I said quickly. "What do you guys want to do?"

"We can creep on Carl and Liam," Shal replied, walking over to the computer. She clapped her hands together. "I know. We can send Liam a message. You didn't have a chance to get over there, so we'll just write him one."

I sat down on my bed. "I don't know. What would we say?"

Shal paused. "Dear Liam, I am now also a felon. Will you marry me?"

Mia laughed and shook her head. "Just say hi or something." It sounded like the idea of writing a message to a boy was enough to get her nervous.

She wasn't the only one.

"Let's write Carl instead," I suggested.

Shal looked at me like I'd gone mad. "No."

"But—"

"No."

"Fine," I muttered. "We can write Liam."

"Excellent!" Shal opened my profile and cracked her fingers. "Dear Liam—"

"Hey, Liam," I interjected.

"Fine," she said. "Hey, Liam. Not sure if you heard, but I got suspended too."

She looked at me for approval, and I nodded.

"You'll be happy to know it was for punching Allison in the stomach—"

"That hussy Allison," I added. "Don't ask."

Shal frowned and added it. "Hope you didn't get in too much trouble. I'd love to come over and talk about it—"

"No," I cut in.

"Go to a movie—"

"No."

Shal sighed. "See you on Thursday. Love, Laura Ledwick."

I stared at her, and she deleted the sign-off. "Not bad," she said. "It says I care without making it clear that you stare at a picture of him all night."

"I do not."

She smiled. "It's okay. I stare at Carl a lot."

"A lot," Mia agreed. She turned to me. "Want a make-over?"

"A make-over?" Shal asked. "Since when do you do make-overs?"

Mia flushed. "I looked up online what to do at a girls' night."

Shal and I glanced at each other and broke out laughing.

"A make-over sounds fun," I said.

Two hours later, I was staring into a small portable mirror we'd borrowed from my mom. My chestnut hair was curled and crimped, I had black eyeliner and eye shadow on, and a whole lot of blush and concealer. I was even wearing lipstick. I hadn't quite wanted so much, but we were having so much fun that I kind of just went along for the ride.

It was my first girls' night ever, after all.

"I love it," Shal said, nodding at me thoughtfully. "Next time we're doing Mia."

Mia looked terrified at the idea.

"I could never wear this anywhere," I said.

It looked all right, I guess. I'd never even worn eyeliner or eye shadow before, and it did kind of make my green eyes stand out. And my hair looked kind of nice. But I wasn't a makeup and lipstick kind of girl. And that was before I was recruited to be a Monster Crusher. Uh-oh. I still had to go train tonight.

Eldon was going to love my eyeliner.

"I think my mom's going to be here soon," Mia said, checking her cellphone. It was almost nine. "This was fun! Let's do it again soon."

"Definitely," I agreed. "I'll walk you down. I just have to make sure Stache doesn't see me. He might pass out."

"You have to show your mom," Shal said. "She'll love it—"

And then I heard it. The rattling.

Shal stopped. "What's that?"

"Nothing," I said.

Mia frowned. "I hear it too. Is your window loose?"

"It sounds like it's coming from the closet . . ." Shal said, starting for the closet.

"No, it's the door in my brother's room," I said quickly. "The draft comes in and knocks it back and forth. Super annoying." I stood up and ushered them out of the room.

"Can I get my purse?" Shal asked.

I hurried back into the room and got it for her. "Shall we?"

She gave me a little frown but didn't ask any more questions. When they were safely driving away in Mia's mom's car, I shut the front door and rubbed my forehead. That was close. I marched back up the stairs, walked into my room, and stopped.

Tom was standing in front of my closet door.

He turned to me. "I think there's something in your closet."

Chapter Nineteen

"Why do you say that?" I asked cautiously, walking into the room. I instinctively looked at the window, wondering if the Swords were outside. The panel was still rattling.

He looked at me. "Because I can hear it."

"Right." I paused. "It's just a draft. I told Mom and Dad about it."

"I don't feel a draft," he said, frowning. "And your closet door is closed."

"Yeah, but it rattles. And since when do you just walk into my room?"

He shrugged. "Whenever I think there's a monster in your closet."

He really was a perceptive kid.

I walked over and took Tom's arm, pulling him toward the bedroom door. "Well, I'm gonna get some sleep—"

"I see the light again."

I stopped and looked at him. "What?"

"The light. It's in your closet. I was just seeing it through the bathroom wall."

I glanced at my closet. I suddenly thought back to the

"door of light" he'd seen in the woods. Were they related somehow? Could Tom *see* the openings to the Under Earth? It sounded ridiculous, but here he was, staring at my closet. I felt goosebumps snaking their way down my arms. I considered asking Eldon about it, but I decided to keep it to myself. If it was true, he might want to get Tom involved with the war, and that was not going to happen. I wasn't bringing my little brother anywhere near those monsters.

"There's nothing in the closet. Just T-shirts and boxes."

"You're hiding something," he said.

"No, I'm not."

"Your voice just changed."

"No, it didn't."

He looked at me suspiciously. "You sure, Giant Girl?"

"Absolutely, Bat Boy. Now go get some sleep. One of us has school tomorrow."

He sighed. "I wish I was a delinquent."

"Don't we all?" I agreed, leading him into the hallway. "Good night."

"Night," he said, still sounding unconvinced. "Enjoy your sleep-in."

I smiled. "Will do."

I closed the door and listened to him slowly walk back to his room. I didn't like lying to my brother, but there was no way I was telling him about the door either. He would definitely want to go through, and it was going to be hard enough keeping myself alive in there.

I decided I probably didn't have time to go clean all the makeup off. Obviously Eldon wanted to get started earlier today, but I was definitely going to tell him to find some other way to get my attention. That was way too close.

I threw on my usual track pants and hoodie and was just heading for the panel when I decided to quickly check my profile. I doubted that Liam would have messaged me back so quickly, but it was worth a shot. I opened up my inbox and almost fell off my chair in delight when I saw a new message. I clicked on it immediately.

Dear Laura,

(HE SAID "DEAR"!)

Welcome to the suspended club. It's my first time. Of course, I don't go out or do anything fun, so it was hard to ground me. I think my mom was going to take my computer away, but she took pity. At least you got suspended for punching Allison. I got suspended for missing a punch at Tim. That's way worse. Anyway, enjoy your day off tomorrow. Hopefully you didn't get grounded either. See you Thursday. Maybe you can teach me how to punch for future reference.

Liam

I read that message, like, ten times. I know, I'm a weirdo. But I just smiled from ear to ear, read it, sat back and smiled, and then read it again.

When I was finally satisfied, I signed off and headed for the closet, wondering if I would ever have the courage to ask Liam out. Or at least ask Shal to ask Liam if he would ever ask me out. Why couldn't I just be hot? Life seemed much easier for hot girls.

Instead I get to go crush monsters with a hammer.

I pulled the panel open, sparing one last satisfied look at my computer—I couldn't wait to see Liam on Thursday. Pulling the lever, I descended into the depths of the earth once again, and I barely noticed the fact that I was floating off the floor.

The next morning, I dragged myself out of bed at the usual time. It had been a particularly difficult night at training, as Eldon wanted me to work a little more on my agility— not my strong suit. Needless to say I was really tired. When I walked into the kitchen, Tom was sitting there eating his English muffin with jam. He looked at me as I put some bread in the toaster.

"What are you doing?"

"Uh . . . making breakfast?" I said, glancing at him.

He smiled. "You forgot."

"Forgot what . . . oh."

I had totally forgotten I was suspended. I guess it should have been a good thing, since I wasn't grounded and could probably go back to bed. But I had kind of wanted to go to school today. Liam was back. I slumped and grabbed the peanut butter anyway. Might as well stay up now.

"No monster in your closet?" Tom asked, taking a bite of his English muffin.

"No," I said. "Or it didn't try and eat me, at least."

"That's good."

I scanned over him. His hair was done differently today; he usually just messed it up with his hand, but he'd actually kind of spiked it. Obviously it was still a little messy, but there was no mistaking the gel glistening in his sandy-blond hair.

"So . . . how's Shannon?"

He stiffened a little. "What do you mean? Who?"

"The girl at school," I said casually.

He shrugged. "Don't know. Fine. Why do you ask?"

"New hairdo."

"Is it really obvious?" he murmured.

I walked over and adjusted his spikes. "Just got to work the gel in a little. You have a crush or something?"

"No," Tom said quickly. "Well, not completely sure. Never had one."

I finished with his hair and took a step back to examine it. "Do you think about her a lot?"

"Kind of."

"Before bed?"

"Maybe."

"When you wake up?"

"That's why I did my hair."

I smiled and patted his shoulder. "Then you have a crush."

He sighed. "I was afraid of that."

"It's no big deal," I said as my toast popped. "It just guides your entire day, enters your dreams, and generally makes you do stupid things."

"Oh," he said, "well, that's fine then. Is that how you are with Liam?"

"Pretty much. Except I also want to marry him. Hopefully you're not there yet."

He wrinkled his nose. "I just want to talk to her more."

"Good." I thought about something and glanced at him. "You think she's pretty?"

"She is in the only way I care about. She's nice and funny and smart."

"And me?" I asked, smearing the bread with peanut butter.

"A radiant beauty," he said.

I smiled and took a bite of toast. "Thanks, Bat Boy."

I spent the day helping Stache with the basement renovations, which actually wasn't that bad. Well, freezing cement floors and spiderwebs weren't great, but I did like spending time with my dad, even if that meant holding a flashlight while he screwed in a toilet.

I don't think Stache really knew what being suspended meant, since he seemed thrilled to have me at home and even got us takeout for lunch. Actually he never even really asked about the fight, except if it was a left or right punch.

But the best part of the day was a text I got from Shal at recess:

Liam asked about you!!! Mostly if you were going to be back tomorrow, but still!!!! He loves you!!!!!!!!!!!!!!!!!!

I thought about that for the entire day, and Shal and Mia called me the second school was finished. We spent a solid hour speculating about what this meant, and then another twenty minutes talking about Allison's evil doings, Ashley's risqué outfit, Carl's new haircut, and other things that Shal wanted to cover. Mia also filled me in on the homework, which was slightly more productive. Math. Ugh.

So really it was a pretty good suspension day in general, and when I got back to school on Thursday, things were right back to normal. Liam kind of nodded at me, Allison and her seagulls gave me evil smirks, and Mia. Shal, and I went right back to our spot in the corner. That became the routine again, and for awhile it started to feel like I was having a normal kid's life. Well, I was still heading into the elevator every night to train to crush monsters, but besides that.

Things in Derwin were getting a little better, though my progress was slow. The Warrior's Way was still taking me about nine minutes, and that was probably leaving half of the monsters alive to eat me—if they weren't stuffed with straw. Lee was giving me pointers, but I spent most of that time stealing glances at his warm brown eyes and wondering again why his sweat smelled like cologne. Needless to say it wasn't helping that much, and when I almost hit him with an arrow, he kind of gave up and went back to talking about normal things. The fact that he talked to me at all was kind of surprising, but I wasn't going to complain. It made training much more enjoyable.

But I was definitely getting stronger, and though I wasn't losing much weight with all the muscle I was gaining, I was starting to very slowly look a little trimmer. I think I could still have eaten two Liam R. Kelps and had room for Mia, but it was a start.

Allison was just as evil as ever, of course, and she seemed to be making it her life's mission to make me suffer. I probably cried three times through the rest of September, which really wasn't bad. I didn't punch her again at least, even though I wanted to. Liam and I talked pretty infrequently, with our longest conversation being about a math problem I was pretend having, and that was only about two minutes. So we weren't exactly madly in love like I'd hoped, but he always smiled at me in the morning and said hi, and I still looked at his profile picture more than was probably advisable.

Mia, Shal, and I spent almost every weekend together now, hanging out at my house mostly. I made sure to keep them out of the closet, and everything was fine. Thankfully there was no more rattling while they were around.

There were a couple of incidents, of course: I passed out on my desk one day at school, much to the amusement of the class. I woke up, horrified, to find Ms. Haddock asking me politely if I was feeling all right. Even Liam was laughing. Thankfully Shal said I hadn't been snoring, though she did shoot Mia a stern look right after.

I had to pretend work out in my bedroom to explain why I was constantly washing so many pairs of shorts and hoodies. Whenever my mom walked in, I started doing sit-ups and stretches, and she would just smile and tell me to keep it up. Yeah . . . on it.

And probably the hardest one to explain was when Stache asked me for help carrying some bags of concrete down to the basement, which apparently we were supposed to do together to make sure no one got hurt. He almost dropped his hammer when he saw me walk downstairs with a bag under each arm. I told him I was doing a lot of curls. He just went back to work, shaking his head.

Eldon kept me updated on the activity of the monsters around Riverfield, but as of yet, the Swords—both mine, who I still hadn't met, and those from the Protectorate—hadn't found the tunnels the monsters were using to access the surface. At least I didn't see any yellow eyes for a few weeks, which was good. Uncle Laine even started coming over a lot to help Stache, and he and I would sit in the backyard and chat. I had a feeling that even a goblin would hesitate to attack with him sitting next to me

We were sitting outside one afternoon when I asked him about the factory.

"Yeah, nothing yet," he said, sighing deeply. "Got a couple more months and that's it. Sandra's been looking, but she's been out of work for years. Between the two of us, we're a couple of dinosaurs. I've been doing the same job for so long I don't have any other skills. I might have to head out to a logging camp or something, if they'll take me."

"It'll work out," I said encouragingly, but he just smiled from behind that thick black beard and changed the subject. "Liking the house a bit more yet?"

I shrugged. "It's okay. Still looks like the setting of a B horror movie, but I haven't been eaten by spiders yet, so I can't complain."

Uncle Laine laughed, glancing up at my bedroom window. "You get that rattling fixed yet?"

"Yeah," I said, shifting a little. "It's gone now."

He looked at me for a moment and then turned back to the yard. "Nice to have the forest behind you. Even with the whole hiker thing. Terrible. You never know what's creeping around in the dark, do you?"

"No. That's why you turn a light on."

Uncle Laine laughed again. "Right you are."

As the brisk October air swept in and the forest turned a fiery red and orange, I started to think that being a Monster Crusher wasn't so bad after all. I didn't get as much sleep as I might have liked, but I was getting in shape and had friends, and even Eldon was being a little nicer to me, though he still seemed dubious about actually having me fight monsters, which was fine with me. I was still hoping to skip that part anyway.

Halfway through October I stepped out of the elevator on a quiet Thursday night, the guide tucked under my arm as usual. I brought it everywhere for reference, since Eldon was always firing monster-related questions at me while I was training. I nodded at Porton, who flashed his crooked, yellow teeth.

"Evening," he said brightly.

"Do you ever sleep, Porton?" I asked curiously.

Porton laughed. "Most of the time. That's why I have a rocking chair."

I laughed and hurried through the meadow, watching the butterflies flit across the pathway. Derwin was starting to feel like a second home. Some of the villagers had actually started nodding at me, and once a little girl even ran up and gave me a beautiful blue flower that I'd never seen before.

Most of the adults still looked at me a bit condescendingly, but at least some of them had accepted that, like it or not, I was training to be a Monster Crusher. Maybe they were even secretly cheering me on. I reached the gate to Arnwell and stopped immediately. Something was wrong.

The Monster Crushers and Swords were all standing in a closed ring against the walls, leaving the courtyard empty. Eldon stood at the far side, and he was flanked by three old men in dark, violet robes. I could see their eyes flashing at me even from here.

Eldon walked toward me, his face disconcertingly grim. When he reached me, he didn't say hello or smile or even give me his customary nod. He just met my eyes.

"Two days ago one of our scouts spotted an army of goblins moving through the tunnels. We have reason to believe they are approaching Derwin and, in turn, Riverfield."

I looked behind him at the three mysterious robed men. "So what's going on?"

"Your training is being sped up," Eldon said, sounding perturbed. "Those three men are the last of the Brotherhood, and they will determine if you are worthy of the Iron Hammer. They test different Monster Crushers in different ways, depending on their weaknesses. For you, they have chosen one particular test."

I already knew what it was, but I had to ask. "What test?"

He sighed deeply. "They want to watch you run the Warrior's Way."

"Perfect," I muttered. "When?"

He turned and strode toward the start of the course.

"Right now."

Chapter Twenty

"Are you ready?" Eldon asked, eyeing me from beside the three members of the Brotherhood. None of them had betrayed the slightest expression since I'd been there.

I looked out over the Way, feeling my stomach knot up. "Not really."

"Begin!" he shouted.

I was really nervous, and it showed. I stubbed my toe on the first log and then half-ran, half-limped over the rest of them, just trying to keep my balance. Usually the warriors would be snickering by now, but when I snuck a glance, they just looked disgusted, as if I was reflecting on all of them. The old men were still expressionless.

Next up were the series of wooden barriers that you ducked under then climbed over and so forth. I slowed right down and crawled under the high ones, and then threw myself over the other ones and flopped onto the other side. Very graceful.

I was definitely failing. The Brotherhood would send me home and forbid me from ever coming back. Maybe that was for the best. But I was at least going to finish.

Next was the archery stop, and I got my arrow within a metre, which was major progress. I stopped to admire my shot then a shout from Eldon got me moving again. The ropes were next, and I actually tried today, though that just meant swinging from the first rope right into a puddle. Great, white sneakers ruined.

I snuck a quick glance at the old men. Yep, not impressed.

After the ropes was the dagger throw, and I managed to hit the fake ogre, even though it was the hilt and it just bounced off into the courtyard. Hey, I was definitely making progress. A few days ago I missed by two metres. From there was a bunch of vertical spears that you weaved in and out of—I knocked over four instead of the seven of last time—and another set of logs that I managed to get over without falling. I would have been proud of myself if I couldn't feel all those condescending glares on me.

Eldon was just folding his arms and scowling.

The last stop was to attack a fake goblin—the one that looked like a scarecrow. There was always a sword or a spear on the little table, and you would scoop it up, charge, and stab the goblin or swing at it or whatever. The goblin was covered with holes and tears and was fraying a little on its head where the warriors had been hitting it.

I usually just lightly stabbed it in the stomach or something. Once I got the sword stuck in the leather and had to leave it there, which was very embarrassing. I decided to try a big overhead swing today. But this time there wasn't a sword sitting on the table. Or a spear. It was a hammer, and it was even more impressive than the picture.

The weapon was huge—at least a metre long with a massive double-sided iron top as big as a portable barbecue. The top was inlaid with three crimson rubies on each side, and there was a large black handle at the bottom big enough for two hands. I doubted I could even lift the thing. Was this a last joke to finish the test?

I stopped to look at the hammer for a moment, and this time I heard some of the Swords and other Monster Crushers laughing. I thought I could even pick out Caria's cruel laugh from the gate. My cheeks started burning again, and I felt that anger filling my whole body. I was really sick of being laughed at.

I reached down and scooped up the hammer. It must have been made of some special type of metal, because it was a lot lighter than it looked. Actually, it felt really good as I lifted it up over my shoulder. Kind of like a baseball bat.

My eyes fell on the goblin. I knew exactly what to do with a baseball bat.

I charged the monster, and when I got close, I swung the hammer right toward its head. The hammer connected with a massive *thump*, and the fake goblin's head exploded in a billowing shower of straw and brown wool. The courtyard fell into absolute silence as the straw slowly floated to the ground all around me.

I turned back to Eldon, catching Caria's stunned look on the way.

"Anything else?"

Eldon was the first to react. He walked over to me, giving me a quick smile on the way. When he reached me, he turned me toward the three old men.

"Well done," he whispered.

I was still in shock. I'd seen a lot of Monster Crushers hit the fake goblin. A few had even used hammers, though they never trained with the actual Iron Hammers. But for all that, no one had ever knocked its head off, never mind exploded it.

I wasn't even sure what had happened. I mean, I was a great hitter. But I'd never felt a swing like that—it was like the hammer was an extension of my arm.

The rest of the warriors still weren't speaking. Neither were the old men. Lee looked pleased at least. He gave me a sparkling smile and a nod.

"We all have to find our strengths," Eldon said loudly. "Brothers, I believe Laura has proven herself. She is not a runner or a jumper or an archer. But she is most certainly a Monster Crusher."

The Brothers stared at me for a long time, and I felt their shrewd eyes looking right through me. I shifted, unsure if they were convinced.

But finally, the Brother in the middle nodded.

"I agree," he said. "I name you a Monster Crusher, defender of two worlds."

Instantly the Swords straightened and bowed their heads. Many didn't look happy about it. Most were still stunned. But they all bowed. Even Caria.

I grinned. I didn't exactly want to be a Monster Crusher, but it was kind of nice to prove Caria and everyone else wrong.

The three robed men suddenly turned and strode into the castle without another word, and Eldon looked at me, grinning.

"I wasn't expecting that," he said.

"Me either."

"So it's official?" a deep voice asked from behind us. "She's it?"

Eldon smiled. "Yes."

"Does that mean we can show her?" he asked.

I turned around, frowning. The warriors had all gathered in a group behind us. I noticed that five new people were there today, all wearing hoods pulled down to their noses. One of them was a huge man with a thick black beard, and he was smiling.

"Yes," Eldon said quietly. "You can show her."

The bearded man grinned and pulled off his hood. I felt my knees buckle.

"Uncle Laine?" I whispered.

"Hello, sweetie," he said. "Welcome to the Monster Crushers."

Beside him the other four hooded Swords pulled off their hoods one by one. I felt like I was going to topple over. One was the waitress from the café who had given me the dirty look, introduced as Liz Boden; another was the quiet, bespectacled manager of the grocery store we went to, Steven Hale. He nodded in greeting. One other I didn't recognize, a tall man with cropped, strawberry-blond hair and a wispy goatee, Laren Elvitan, who turned out to be from the Under Earth, and the last one hesitated with her hood.

"As I mentioned, whenever someone in Riverfield finds a tunnel, they have a choice," Eldon explained, looking over the gathered Swords. "To maintain the secret, or to join the Swords and help protect both worlds. Four have joined from Riverfield, including some of our best—a rare incident, to have so many surface humans from one area. Your uncle has been a Sword for twelve years."

I just stared at my uncle in disbelief. "Why did no one tell me?"

"We always conceal our identity when someone from Riverfield is being trained," he said. "Just in case they flake out and tell someone. We only tell them when they become a member."

I noticed the last Sword still had her hood on. She was just giving me a familiar, mean little smile. I stared at her for a second, my eyes widening. It couldn't be.

The girl pulled her hood off.

It was Allison Black.

Chapter Twenty-One

I sat at the large, rectangular wooden table in Arnwell's mess hall, still completely stunned. Eldon had invited me to stay for a meal to celebrate my official naming as a Monster Crusher. It didn't really seem like something to celebrate, but I did want to know more about the Swords and why people from my town were a part of it.

Specifically the dour, raven-haired girl who terrorized me at school.

"I stumbled across a tunnel twelve years ago while I was hunting," Uncle Laine was telling me, while also drinking from a big flagon of mead. "Tripped over the edge completely by accident. Did some digging around to find out what it was and then pulled the hidden door right open. Probably should have gone home, but I was curious, so I set off down the tunnels. I was about a half kilometre down when Eldon popped out of the shadows right behind me and snatched the crossbow."

Eldon was sitting at the head of the table, listening with a wan smile. He had finally removed his cloak and now wore a simple beige tunic that was open enough at the top to reveal the lines of his muscular chest. Allison was sitting a few seats down from Uncle Laine, shooting me occasional condescending looks as she picked at a plate of roasted lamb. I still didn't understand how such an awful girl could be a Sword.

Especially one of my Swords.

"So Eldon explains everything," Laine continued, "and of course I didn't believe a word of it until he took me farther down and showed me Derwin. He told me what was happening in the Under Earth and that my home was in danger too. So I decided to join, and I've been here almost every day since, whenever I can manage. Of course I've been doing late nights since you moved here . . . I train after you go back up, usually. But yeah, been a Sword for a long time now, that's for sure. Had some close calls too. Worked with the last Riverfield Monster Crusher—the chap who lived in your house. He . . . died six years ago. Paul the Imp Chaser they called him. Nice kid. He was actually eighteen . . . bought the house himself with his inheritance. Parents had died, you see. He had something to prove maybe and went charging after those imps. Couldn't stop him."

"Was he the last one?" I asked.

"Yeah," Laine said gruffly. "Started to think we weren't getting another one. Eldon let me do some other work in the meanwhile. Scouting and guard work and so forth. That's what led to the last close call."

"Your uncle was captured four months ago," Eldon said, glancing at me. "On a mission to scout the monsters' movements. He was held for a few days, and he just barely managed to escape."

I looked at my uncle in amazement. "Did they hurt you?"

"No," he said softly. "Well, a bit, but mostly they were waiting."

"For what?"

He shrugged. "The troll, I'm guessing. They kept saying the king was coming." He took another big swig of mead. "But one of them got a bit too close one night, and I managed to kick out its legs and kill it. Used its sword to cut myself free and then took off for Arnwell. They hunted me right through the night. Not my best night ever."

I shook my head in disbelief. "I don't understand. If you knew about all this, why did you tell Dad to move to that house? You knew it was the Monster Crusher's house."

He shrugged again. "I had a hunch that you might find the elevator."

"You wanted me to find it?" I asked incredulously.

I saw some of the other Swords scowling.

"We needed a Monster Crusher," he said. "And I knew you had it in you."

I rubbed my forehead. "But why didn't you just move there?"

"Tried," he said. "Didn't work. The spells prevent the wrong people from living there. First the bank wouldn't approve the mortgage. Then the private companies turned me down. I tried to just go in and open the panel, but it wouldn't even budge. Not for me. Not for any of us." He looked around the room. "All four of us from Riverfield tried. Allison actually talked her parents into buying it, but they couldn't get approved either."

Allison pushed her plate away, looking sour.

"Of course, he didn't tell us who he had found to move in," the waitress from the café, Liz, added coolly. She had big hazel eyes and long blond hair that swept down her shoulders. "We weren't thrilled when we found out . . . you didn't exactly look like a Monster Crusher."

Uncle Laine waved a meaty hand. "They were skeptical. But you just proved them wrong."

"She hit a fake goblin," Allison snarled. "Big deal."

I turned to her. "And how did you join?"

She met my eyes. "I found the same portal as your uncle when I was ten. I demanded they train me, and Eldon agreed. He wasn't too keen at first, but I proved him wrong. I've been here since. Mostly protecting the Under Earth, but now apparently guarding you."

I stared at Allison for a moment longer and then turned back to my uncle.

"Does Aunt Sandy know?"

"No," he said quietly. "We're forbidden to tell anyone or to move here permanently. There are a few of us who would like to, but it's against the rules."

I saw Liz glance at Eldon. Even Allison scowled.

"You want to live here?" I asked. "Why?" I paused, looking at Eldon. "No offence."

"None taken," he said bemusedly.

Uncle Laine gestured around the room. "We're respected warriors here. We could have a big piece of land and a nice house. We're something here. On the surface we're just greasy line workers and waitresses, fighting to pay the mortgage. Understand?"

"Yeah," I murmured. "I guess I do."

Eldon just listened quietly. "There is great honour in what you do here."

"Just not great pay," Laine said, smirking. "It's fine. We made our choice, and I'm happy to help. I've seen what these monsters can do. We need to stop them now."

"If only we had a real Monster Crusher," Allison snarled.

"Enough," Eldon said sharply, standing up. "Laura, you better be getting back. You need to get some rest tonight. I suspect we all have some long nights ahead of us."

I followed Eldon out of the mess hall, and my uncle stood up to hug me goodbye.

"You'll be fine, Laura," he said, resting his hands on my shoulders and shooting me a comforting grin. "You're going to be great."

I smiled as he messed up my hair and went to sit down again. Allison just stared at me as I left. It was going to be fun seeing her at school tomorrow. It still didn't make sense that she was a Sword. How could someone protecting the world be that terrible? And why wasn't she nicer to me? She was supposed to be helping me.

"This is weird," I said, shaking my head as we walked out into the courtyard.

Many of the warriors were training again, and I noticed that some of the Monster Crushers were looking at me with just a tiny bit more respect.

Eldon smiled. "I told you it would get weirder."

"So what's next?"

"We continue your training. I have scouts watching the monsters' movements under Riverfield, and we will know if anything happens. They still can't find our tunnels, so

Derwin is safe. Trust me, they would love to destroy Arnwell if they could."

I frowned as we passed through the gate and out onto the road, the white stones catching the artificial light of the sun sphere. I watched as a group of children chased a ball down the street. "Why can't they find the tunnels?"

"All the entrances and exits are expertly hidden. Finding them in the darkness without knowing exactly where they are is almost impossible, unless you have the Sight."

"The what?"

"The Sight. It's exceedingly rare. There is only one man in the entire Under Earth who has it . . . one of the Brothers who you met earlier today. There hasn't been another in a hundred years. We call them Shadow Sights. With the Sight, he can find tunnels that we would never see, but he is too old and frail to venture off and search for them. So we must continue to do the best we can without one."

"Aren't there any on the surface?"

"No," he replied. "The Sight only comes to those who know the darkness."

I thought about Tom. I knew Eldon would love to know about the strange doors of lights that Tom had seen, but I couldn't tell him. There was no way I was getting Tom involved in all of this. It was too dangerous. So I just stayed quiet.

We walked slowly through the village, and I watched as a group of villagers sat together in the tall grass in a yard, laughing and talking. It was all so normal, and yet here we were, miles under the surface. The lake sparkled in the background, ships sailing lazily across the crystal-clear glass of its waters. It really was a beautiful place.

"Do you think I actually have what it takes to be a Monster Crusher?"

He looked out toward the distant cavern walls. "I don't know. All we can do is prepare and see what happens. Tomorrow you will start training with your personal Swords. You will have to become a cohesive unit if you are all going to survive."

He glanced at me.

"What are spiders afraid of?"

"Fire," I said, rolling my eyes.

"What's the best way to attack an ogre?"

"Get behind him."

"And what's the most important thing to remember when you see a goblin?"

I snorted. "They never attack alone."

Eldon smiled and stopped at the edge of the village. "Good. At least you've been reading."

"That I can do." I paused. "It's going to get worse, isn't it?"

"Yes," he said calmly. "And we will have to be ready."

I thought about that as I walked to the elevator, watching the butterflies. This was all fine and good . . . training at night and fighting fake monsters and pretending I was a warrior. But could I actually fight real monsters? Could I go into those tunnels, into the darkness, and wield that Iron Hammer?

Suddenly the cavern looked dark, and I shivered in the warm air.

I had a feeling I was going to find out soon enough.

Chapter Twenty-Two

As expected, seeing Allison at school the next day was a little odd. I kind of expected her to just ignore me, since of course she couldn't just start acting nice to me, but surely she wouldn't be as mean. On the contrary, I think she was worse. She stormed right past me in the morning, flipping me a dark look and asking if I'd ever heard of a comb.

I patted my hair self-consciously; I had kind of woken up late again and had to run out the door after my shower. It was feeling a little tangled.

"That was right to the point," Shal said thoughtfully, sitting beside me on the portable steps and immediately adjusting her long auburn hair as well, even though it was meticulously combed and curled. She snuck a little mirror out of her pocket and took a look. "What was in her cereal this morning?"

"Who cares," I murmured, leaving my hair alone.

Mia was watching Shal carefully fix her hair, shaking her head in exasperation. "She was talking to Laura."

"I know that," Shal snapped, tucking her mirror away. "But it doesn't hurt to check."

Mia and I exchanged a bemused glare. We did our best to humour Shal, but neither of us shared her love of clothes and fashion. For all Shal's complaining about her pageant-queen mother, she was certainly concerned with her looks. Meanwhile I was sitting there with worn jeans and a T-shirt that said Space Is Cool on it. Mia was wearing khakis again, a plain white long-sleeved shirt, and a jean jacket that I think Shal made her wear. But as usual her shoulder-length hair was just hanging down, looking a bit frayed, and I saw Shal staring at it longingly. She was always trying to do Mia's hair, but Mia didn't seem that interested.

"Hear anything else about that missing hiker?" I asked her.

Mia shook her head. "They never found the animal. Hopefully it's moved on."

"Or it's still out there," I said darkly.

Shal clearly wasn't listening. "Liam has a new shirt."

I instantly turned to look as Liam walked into the yard, heading for Paul and Steve. He was indeed wearing a new plaid shirt, blue and white. I sighed inwardly.

I wish I had the courage to talk to him more, but other than our random discussions about homework or the weather, we weren't getting very far.

"I just wish he had cuter friends," Shal said, eyeing Paul and Steve. "I mean Paul's all right I guess, even if he is a bit of a loser."

"As a fellow loser, I take offence to that," I replied.

She shrugged. "Fair enough. Though I'm hardly the captain of the cheerleaders, so who am I to talk?" She turned to stare longingly at Carl. "If only."

"We were thinking about a girls' night on Saturday," Mia said.

"Sure," I replied. "We can do my house again."

"We can write another love letter to Liam," Shal said, smirking.

"No."

"Come on," Shal insisted. "You still owe him punching lessons. Maybe he'd trade them for kissing lessons."

"Who would be the teacher?" Mia asked curiously.

"Thanks," I muttered. "Just drop it. I'm sure he doesn't like me."

"Why not?" Mia asked. "You're funny, pretty—"

"Twice his size," I pointed out.

"More of you to love," Shal said dismissively. "And you're not twice his size. Maybe a little bigger—"

"A little?" I asked, raising my eyebrows.

"Maybe a Liam-and-a-half," Shal admitted. "But he's also a twig."

"I guess," I said. "I don't know. Either way, I'm in for the girls' night. At least I can draw a clown face on Mia if Liam doesn't speak to me until then."

"Great," Mia said sarcastically.

"Deal," Shal agreed. "Ugh, did either of do that math homework? Mia, can I see yours so I can check my answers?"

"Do you mean copy my answers?" Mia asked.

Shal paused. "Yes."

I sat in class that day thinking about Liam. I know I had much bigger things to worry about, including a possible monster army marching around under my feet, but I couldn't help it. Shal and Mia had got me thinking. How could I be sure he didn't like me? We had a lot in common, and we always seemed to have nice talks, even if they were only ten seconds a piece. And he did smile at me a lot. In the mornings. When he first saw me.

I sighed, doodling on my notebook. There was no chance.

I wished I had brought the guide to school today, but I had already read through most of it, so I'd stopped bringing it. I tried to pay attention to the math lesson, but I was distracted by the textbook at my back, which I had put over the opening in my chair so Allison couldn't pull her little pee trick on me anymore.

"Ready for training tonight?" a quiet voice whispered.

I almost fell off my chair. Allison was leaning toward me, her pretty dark eyes narrowed ominously. Carl was busy chatting with Tim, leaving her alone.

"I don't think we should talk about this," I murmured.

"I know the rules," she snarled. "And I'm going to teach you a thing or two about combat tonight, as well. I think I can convince Eldon to let us spar."

I pictured myself hitting Allison over the head with a hammer and smiled.

"Excellent."

"Anything you want to share with the rest of us?" Ms. Haddock said politely, staring at Allison and me.

Allison sat upright immediately, flashing a brilliant smile.

"Sorry, Ms. Haddock," she said. "Laura just asked to borrow a pencil."

"Oh," Ms. Haddock replied, looking slightly embarrassed. "That's fine."

Shal and Mia shot me questioning looks from across the classroom, and I just shook my head to let them know I was fine. I could feel my cheeks burning as Liam glanced back as well.

"See you tonight, tubby," Allison whispered, kicking the back of my chair.

I sighed. What a great bodyguard. Thanks, Eldon.

Later that night, after finally finishing my math homework, I went downstairs to where Stache was now working on painting the main floor bathroom. My mom usually went to bed around nine, and Tom was reading a Braille book in his room, so it was already quiet in the house. I poked my head into the bathroom.

"Hey, Stache."

My dad looked back in surprise, and I almost laughed. His face was splattered with blue paint, especially his moustache. He raised a bushy brown eyebrow.

"Shouldn't you be getting ready for bed?" he asked, looking at his watch.

Ha. The earliest I'd gone to bed in this new house was, like, three in the morning.

"Just wanted to say good night," I said, looking around the bathroom. "Looks good. Maybe you were right about this place."

He beamed. "It's definitely coming around."

I hesitated, feeling a bit awkward. "Also, I just wanted to say thanks. Mom told me a few weeks ago that one of the reasons you moved was to give me a fresh start, and I forgot to say thanks. Been a little busy, I guess."

My dad laid his paintbrush down on the can and turned to me. "And do you still like it here, Laurabell? You seem a little . . . distant sometimes."

"No, I like it here," I said, feeling a sudden surge of emotion I wasn't at all expecting. My eyes threatened to tear up, and I tried to get myself together. Obviously I'd been holding more in than I thought, and my dad's tone was breaking down all my walls.

He gently took my hand. "If you don't, we can move again."

I looked at him in surprise. "You've been working non-stop since we got here."

"Doesn't matter," he said, squeezing my fingers with his strong hands. "I'll move ten times until we find somewhere you like."

That did it. I felt my eyes well with tears, and I quickly blinked them back. I knew how much he loved this place, and how much work he had already put into it, and he was still willing to give it up. This was my out. I could ask him to move, he would, and I could leave all this monster crushing stuff behind me. I could let someone else worry about it. And even if things went wrong, and the monsters got to the surface, we would be far away from Riverfield. My family would be safe.

But even as I thought it, I knew it didn't feel right. I didn't want my dad to give up on his dream home. Or Tom to give up his new crush. Or my mom to have to start a new job somewhere else. And more importantly, I didn't want to give up my job either.

That surprised me. I was afraid of fighting monsters. I was afraid of those things watching me from my yard. But for the first time in my life, I had something really, really special to do. Something I was chosen for. And I wasn't going to quit again. I did that once already. Whatever happened, I was going to stick around.

I stepped forward and wrapped my surprised dad in a hug. "Thanks, Stache. That means a lot. But I don't want to go anywhere. This is just starting to feel like home."

"That's good to hear, Laurabell. And now you have paint on you."

"Crap," I said, pulling away again and looking down at my T-shirt. It was speckled with blue paint. "Well, I guess I'll go change before bed."

He smiled. "Probably a good idea."

I walked back upstairs feeling much different than I had on the way down. It was one thing to feel forced into a job; it was another thing to accept it. I got to my room and closed my computer. I had laid out some of my old collectibles on the table, and I picked up my grandpa's pen and smiled. Somehow I knew he'd be proud of me. He was always telling me I was capable of doing great things. He probably meant like be a doctor or something, but crushing monsters was pretty cool too. I wondered what my grandma would say: her only advice had been to give myself a chance. I was certainly doing that.

Training that night was a little different. Some of my Swords were there for the first time: Allison, Steven the grocery manager, and Liz. Laine was watching my house with Laren, and some of the roaming Protectorate of Arnwell that helped out where necessary. Eldon didn't let Allison and me spar—I wasn't sure who was more disappointed—but he did ask her to teach me how to shoot a bow and arrow. She was like a freaking master archer, and when she was done putting another arrow between a fake monster's eyes, I decided I was happy we weren't sparring.

I ran the Way a few times as usual, and when I was suitably sweating and flushed, Eldon asked Lee to show me a few moves with a large fake hammer carved from wood.

I stood across from him in the ring, trying to copy his slow, deliberate movements. But my brain wasn't exactly processing things correctly. Like when he showed me how to do an overhead swing, I just saw that his arms really bulged and his chest got tight beneath his shirt. And when he did a forward jab, I noticed that he had a cute little frown line between his eyes. And then he tried to tell me some things about strategy, I saw that he had a dimple on his right cheek that deepened when he smiled.

"You listening?" he asked, smirking.

"What?" I snapped back into it. "Yeah. Hit stuff with the hammer."

He laughed. "More or less. Come on, take a swing."

I immediately took a few light swings, and he easily beat them away.

"I saw you blow up that goblin head," he said. "Take some real swings."

Flushing, I picked it up a little, swinging at both sides of him and even a few overhead blows. He blocked them all, but his muscles were straining and glistening with sweat as I pushed him back, and I saw h_m smiling admiringly.

"Not bad."

I grinned. "Well I am kind of a Monster Crusher you know—"

I'm not entirely sure what happened. I think I stepped on a shoelace or something, because one minute I was talking and the next I was lying face first on the cobble-stone, my whole body aching and the hammer lying on the other side of the ring.

I rolled over.

"Never mind."

Lee laughed and helped me up, and I sort of bumped into him as I stood up, my stomach pressed against his. I was about to pull away, but he held me there for a moment, his eyes serious.

"You have to be aware of everything," he said seriously. "I don't want to find out you were killed in your first battle. Understood?"

"Yeah," I said, shyly meeting his eyes. Did he actually care? "I will be."

He released me and went to scoop up his hammer again. "Let's do it again."

I felt eyes on me, and glanced over to see Allison watching me from the corner. She looked even more sour than usual, sharpening her blade on a whetstone. I gave her a mock smile and returned to training, wondering what was wrong with her this time.

Eldon let me finish a bit early and surprised me with a couple of beautiful brown horses waiting outside the gate of Arnwell. He led me over to the horses.

"What's this?" I asked, looking at him.

"I want you to see what you're protecting."

After a bit of a struggle to actually get up on the horse, I followed Eldon on his horse for a tour of Derwin, sometimes trotting along the cobblestone streets, smelling the rich scents of roasting beef and fresh bread and the perfume wafting in from the meadows. We circled the lake, our reflections staring back at us, and I saw silver fish darting along beneath the surface, their scales like diamonds. In fact, I saw a lot of diamonds. They were glinting out from exposed rocks and flashing beneath the water in the winding streams, bigger and more beautiful than any I had ever seen on earth. Eldon saw me staring.

"You value different things when you have them in abundance," he said. "We have mountains of diamonds and oceans of crude oil. For us, we value the sweet taste of a peach, which we've never been able to grow here, or coconuts, my personal favourite."

Everything rolled by in a beautiful blur, like I was riding through an oil painting. Eldon showed me some of the tunnels, including the huge one where the train came and went, currently empty except for the wooden tracks that ran off into the darkness. He showed me one of the boring machines they used—a massive steam-powered contraption with a diamond cutting wheel that sliced through the rock like butter. He said there were hundreds of those machines in the Under Earth—different sizes for different tunnels.

"Do you live in Arnwell Castle?" I asked him as we continued on.

He nodded. "I live there, along with the ten Swords of the Protectorate. We also have rooms for all the Monster Crushers and their Swords from around the world, the ones who stay here for days at a time. There are housekeepers and staff as well, of course, but it can be a cold and lonely place. It wasn't always for Monster Crushers: once it was a home for a king and his armies, a long time ago."

"Who rules Derwin now?"

"There's a mayor elected by the people; democracy is an idea we liked from the surface." He laughed. "But he's a portly old fellow who spends much of his time in the tavern. Most of the people here are farmers and blacksmiths and tailors: they like simple things, though they all have weapons, because our enemies are all around us. Monsters have only gotten into Derwin once before, and thankfully they were completely destroyed before they could share the location with others. The monsters want to destroy Derwin very badly, and end the training of their most feared enemies."

He glanced at me as we rode.

"But magic still rules in Derwin, as it always has. The Brotherhood, the three that are left, are the main authority in the five realms. The leader in Eran is a powerful man, but the Brotherhood still have the power to overrule him. But there are only three left, and they are getting very old. The Under Earth will have to make some choices when those three pass away."

As we continued our ride across Derwin, I even got to see some more of the animals of the Under Earth: many were brought from the surface—wild horses, dogs, cows—while others they had found down here in the shadows. There were rats as big as house cats, long dark lizards with flashing white eyes, and birds that soared around in the cavern, eating the rats and lizards. The birds were huge, as big as albatrosses, and richly coloured with red and blue plumage. I watched them soar overhead, weaving in and out of the hanging stalactites.

"I see why you like it here," I murmured.

"Eran is even more beautiful," he said softly. "And Oren, which is beneath your China, is the strangest and most fascinating place you will ever see. Lakes pockmark it like puddles after rain, some bubbling hot, others brutally cold. Waterfalls spill from every wall, sending a mist across the realm like a jungle. Houses are built on stilts or nestled on jutting spires, and some are even perched right on the walls. I'll take you there one day. Of course they also have the most giant spiders and that's where wolf hawks come from, so we'll wait until you're a bit better with your weapons."

"Thanks," I said, rolling my eyes.

Finally Eldon led us back to Arnwell, and I climbed off the horse, sore from the two-hour ride, but nearly speechless from everything I had seen. If his plan was to make me love Derwin enough to fight for it, then his plan had worked. I was almost reluctant to leave. There was a vibrancy here—you could feel the energy of the life that somehow managed to survive down here.

Eldon had said the people of the Under Earth had sensed the magic beneath them—and I felt like I could sense it too. The trees seemed alive, grasping always toward the sun sphere, and the waters of the many streams and the vast lake felt so crisp and pure that it almost melted my anxieties away.

"There is one more thing before you go," he said, leading me into the castle. "It's time to make you look like a Monster Crusher."

We walked through the great hall and into an adjoining armoury, where the Iron Hammer sat perched atop a stone dais, surrounded by walls of weaponry and armour.

He scooped up a large brown leather sheath with a strap attached to both ends.

"Here," Eldon said. "See if it fits."

I slid into the leather strap, which ran from my right shoulder down to my left hip. It was made of a thick, durable leather like a hauberk and fit pretty snugly across my stomach. I looked at Eldon hopefully. "Well? Do I look like a Monster Crusher yet?"

He snorted and gestured to the hammer. "Now try that."

I scooped up the hammer, thinking once again how light it was—whatever metal they used, we didn't have it on the surface. The handle itself was black and grooved, while the silver hammer top was scuffed and worn from use, the three red rubies on either side subdued in the pale light. Gripping the hammer in two hands, I stopped, looking over my shoulder at the sheath and wondering how I was going to get it in there.

"This seems a little inconvenient."

The hammer itself was about a metre long—far too long to just tuck over my shoulder. I awkwardly tried to position it with two hands, knowing I looked ridiculous. Eldon was smirking as he watched me struggle to set it in the sheath.

"Stop," he said. "The sheath is designed for someone with the strength to use *one* hand. It should be dropped in with one and pulled out with one. Grab it close to the bottom of the handle with your hand facing down."

I did as I was told, feeling the hammer wavering in mid-air. It was lighter than it looked, but it was still very heavy to try and hold with just one hand.

Eldon nodded. "Now lift it over your shoulder, put the bottom in the sheath, and let it slide in. Try not to knock yourself in the head with the hammer."

I gingerly lifted the hammer over my shoulder, my whole arm trembling. The iron top was wobbling all over the place. I tucked the bottom of the handle into the sheath, my arm straining, and then let it drop, catching it every few inches to make sure the top didn't crash into head. When the hammer was in, I was surprised to feel the weight spread across my body, almost as if I wasn't carrying anything at all. Even the massive iron top sat back enough that it didn't block my view to the left.

"It was well designed," Eldon said softly, guessing at my thoughts. "Now pull it out. You won't have time to inch it out. It has to be one strong pull, like throwing a spear. Then catch it in mid-air and face your enemy."

"Oh, that should be easy," I grumbled, adjusting my stance. I reached behind me, grabbing the iron pole just below the top, and with a tremendous effort I threw it straight up into the air. Well, that was the intention anyway.

Apparently I didn't throw it straight enough, because

the hammer was almost out when the bottom caught the sheath and the entire weapon started drifting backward. I wasn't ready for the change of weight and I toppled over, slamming into the floor and hearing a crack as the hammer split the tiles. I lay there for a moment, stunned.

Eldon just looked down at me and sighed. "We're in trouble."

I practised for a while, until I finally managed to get the hammer out in one smooth motion. Satisfied, Eldon put the hammer and sheath away and walked with me back to Porton and the elevator. He quizzed me along the way, as per usual. When I answered every question correctly, he shook his head and laughed.

"I must say, Laura, I wish my other students would read as much as you do."

"I guess they're too busy crushing things."

He turned to me. "There is more to being a Monster Crusher than brute strength. You must wield the hammer, yes. But you must be a leader. A true leader. And that requires courage, character, and the intelligence to know what risks are worth taking."

He laid a hand on my shoulder.

"You may not be the best warrior I have ever seen. But you may just turn into a leader yet." He smiled. "See you tomorrow," he said, and then turned back for Arnwell.

I climbed into the elevator and headed for the surface. I was so deep in thought that I just climbed out, shut the panel, and walked out of my closet but then stopped immediately. Tom was sitting on my bed.

"Hello, Giant Girl," he said.

Chapter Twenty-Three

"Tom?" I said, almost jumping backward through the door. "What are you doing?"

"Waiting for you," he replied calmly. "Why were you in the closet?

"Uhh . . ." Think fast. "Organizing my stuff."

He immediately folded his arms, which he always does when he knows I'm lying.

"I knocked on your door and called your name," he said. "You didn't answer."

"I dozed off," I said, sitting down beside him. "No big deal."

A frown creased his pale forehead. His short blond hair was tousled and standing on end, so he'd obviously been asleep. "You dozed off in your closet?"

I shrugged. "I've been sleepy."

He seemed to think about that for a moment.

"You've been acting strangely for the last month. Happy, I guess, but kind of like you're hiding something. You always take off for bed at 9:30 and sleep late and you never pop into my room to read for me anymore."

Tom had Braille books of course, but it was true: I used to read to him at least every other night at the old house. I suddenly felt guilty. I really hadn't been paying much attention to my little brother lately. I'd been busy, but that was no excuse. I was going to make sure I spent more time with him from now on.

"Sorry," I said sheepishly. "I guess I've just been trying to adjust."

"Me too," he agreed. "Shannon doesn't like me."

"How do you know that?"

He sighed. "She's going out with some guy named Dave. He sounds handsome."

I stifled a laugh. "What does handsome sound like?"

"Deep and confident." He paused. "Well, as deep as a nine-year-old can sound."

"What is with this nine-year-old dating people thing anyway?" I asked incredulously. "Shouldn't you be worrying about cooties or something?"

"Probably," he murmured. "But I liked her."

I wrapped my arm around his shoulders and hugged him.

"If it's any consolation, the love of my life doesn't like me either."

"Is he dating someone?"

I hesitated. "No."

"Did he tell you he didn't like you?"

"Not exactly."

"So how do you know he doesn't like you?"

I thought about that. "I don't know. I guess I don't."

"Then ask him out, Giant Girl. If he says no, squash him."

I laughed. Tom didn't know how close he was to the truth.

"I'll think about it. Now go to bed."

"You're sure you're all right?"

"Positive."

Tom got off the bed and walked out into the hall, and I started to close the door before stopping.

"Why were you in my room anyway?" I asked, frowning.

"I had a nightmare. Wanted to see if you were all right."

"What nightmare?"

He shrugged. "You were fighting a big green monster."

I looked at him, feeling nervous little tingles creep down my neck. Did Tom know anything about where I was going at night? And why could he see the openings to the Under Earth? It was all very worrisome. It was bad enough that I was involved. There was no way I was letting my little brother anywhere near Derwin or monsters or any of it. I had to keep him out of this at any cost.

I just shook my head. "Sometimes you freak me out, Bat Boy."

It took a little while to finally fall asleep, and when I did, I dreamt of big green monsters too. It wasn't a pleasant sleep. Needless to say I was a little tired in the morning, enough that I actually fell asleep during the car ride to school. It's like a five-minute drive. My mom looked over and snapped, "Laura!" and I jerked awake and blinked sleepily. Tom giggled in the back.

"Are you feeling all right?" she asked worriedly.

A sick day! Why didn't I think of taking one earlier?

"Fine," I muttered. "Just tired. Didn't sleep very well."

"Bully trouble?" she asked, glancing at me.

"Just a lot on my mind," I said. "I'm good."

As soon as my mom dropped me off, I spotted Mia and Shal sitting at their usual spot on the portable steps and hurried over, eager to get my mind off of monster training.

"You look tired," Shal said immediately.

"Thanks," I said. "Hey, Mia."

"Hey," she said brightly. "Dream of Liam all night?"

"Oh, yeah. There was a beach involved."

Shal wrinkled her nose. "I'm not sure he has much of a beach body."

I laughed. "Neither do I. Unless I've washed up on one."

Mia giggled and then instantly covered her mouth. "Sorry."

"You do your math homework?" Shal asked.

"Yeah, most of it. I think I missed a few. Did Mia do your math homework?"

Shal smiled. "You know it. And here comes Allison."

I turned and saw Allison coming around the school from the front, accompanied by a few seagulls. I expected Allison to be equally tired after a long night of training last night, but apparently she was just fine. She was wearing her raven hair in a ponytail today, which should have been less flashy, but isn't quite the same when you have perfectly curled strands hanging down around your ears and are wearing bright-red lipstick. Who wears lipstick in eighth grade? I could tell she was having an "Aren't I SO hot?" day that usually resulted in twice the bullying.

She walked by us, meeting my eyes for just a second. Mia was already long gone. For a moment I wondered if she would act differently now that I knew the truth about her. "Morning, ladies. You both look great today. Minus the ginger hair and about fifty to seventy pounds."

Sigh. I guess not.

"You look good too," I said to Allison. "Minus your sparkling personality."

Shal looked at me in shock. Allison just smirked.

"Funny," she said. "Are you a comedian now?"

"I guess that makes you the joke," I replied. Nice.

The seagulls glanced at me, frowning. Shal looked like she was about to faint.

"Look everyone, the fat girl is growing a backbone," Allison said. She leaned in close. "Just try not to grow anywhere else. We're going to have to find you a new chair."

The seagulls snickered and continued on their merry way, sending people scurrying in their wake. I saw Allison smiling and shaking her head as she walked away.

"Where did that come from?" Shal whispered.

"I don't know," I said. "I've just got it out for trolls lately."

The rest of the day was fairly uneventful. Liam was answering every question like usual, and I was fawning over him from a safe distance. We didn't even speak all day, though I did get a smile and a wave. Shal had a lot to say on the topic at lunch.

"You can't just expect him to come up to you," she reasoned, sipping from a grape juice box. "He's shy."

I made a face. "So what am I supposed to do? Ask him out?"

Shal slapped the table. "That's it. You can ask him out!"

"I thought we went over this?" I said, looking around frantically to make sure no one was listening.

She shook her head. "Not one-on-one. You still have those movie tickets you won for that geography quiz?"

"Yeah," I said, frowning.

"So me, you, and Mia will go to the movies, and we'll say my mom already bought me a pass for two, so you needed someone else to use yours on or it will go to waste. Ask him to come!"

"With three girls?"

She smiled. "Exactly. If he turns it down, his own mother will make fun of him."

I hesitated and looked across the classroom, where Liam was sitting with his two friends, Paul and Steve. The three of them were very similar: they played a lot of fantasy card games and didn't really talk to girls. They all seemed nice. I thought about something and turned back to Shal.

"Don't even say it," Shal said, putting her juice box down.

"It makes sense."

"What?" Mia asked, sounding alarmed.

"He might as well bring them," I said.

Mia looked at me. "The other two boys?" she whispered.

"But they're such losers," Shal whined.

I narrowed my eyes and she sighed.

"Fine. But I call Paul."

Mia sat back in her chair, eyes wide. "Tell me we're not going on a triple date."

It's a lot easier to talk about asking a boy out than to actually do it. I kept finding excuses. Oh, he's talking with Paul. Oh, recess is almost over. Oh, the wind is too loud, he won't hear me. Before I knew it the last bell had gone, and we were exiting the class. I grabbed my books and started for my locker, ignoring Shal and Mia as they hurried behind me.

"You didn't ask," Shal said.

"I noticed," I muttered.

"Well, you tried—" Mia started.

Shal grabbed my arm. "Do it."

I shook my head. "It's too late."

She scowled. "Do it."

I looked at her and then at Liam as he opened up his locker. My stomach was doing backflips again. I think facing the giant spider was easier.

"Okay," I said. "I'm going. Wish me luck."

I slowly walked toward him, clutching my books to my chest so hard that my knuckles were white. I could feel Shal and Mia watching. What was I going to say? Hey, will you go out with me? I mean us. I mean will you come to the movie? With Shal and Mia? And Steve and Paul? By the way, I think you're awesome and can we sit next to each other? Oh yeah, that would work great. I reached his locker. Say something!

"Hey," I said. Okay, good start. Very natural.

He turned and smiled. "Hey."

I fidgeted for a second. "Not sure what you're doing tonight, but Mia, Shal, and I are going to the movies. We're gonna see *Dinosaur Ninja* or something ridiculous like that. They already have a pass, and I have that pass from the geography quiz, so I was gonna see if you wanted to come. You can bring Steve and Paul, too, if you want."

He grinned. "It's like a triple date."

I felt myself blush immediately. "Ha, yeah, didn't even think of that. Well, no big deal if you're doing something or—"

"I'm in," he said. "Can't turn down a free movie. I'll get the popcorn. And I'll ask Steve and Paul too. We usually just play vids on Friday, so I'm sure they're free"

Did he just say yes? He said yes! Compose yourself. The job isn't done yet.

"Great," I said. "I think it's on at 7:45. Meet you guys at 7:30?"

"Sounds good. See you then."

I smiled, turned around, and slowly walked back to Mia and Shal, trying not to skip, bounce, jog, or do anything but walk naturally. They pretended to do something by my locker until I was right beside them, and then they both turned to me instantly.

"What did he say?" Shal asked, grabbing my arm.

I grinned. "We better go home and get ready The three of us have dates tonight."

Chapter Twenty-Four

We decided that a sleepover was the only possible way to deal with this new development. Actually, Shal did. I couldn't see how I could sneak into the closet to get to Derwin without the girls noticing, but I had never had a sleepover before, and Shal was making some forceful arguments, so I decided to risk it and let myself be talked into it. For one, we all had to get ready together. I'm not sure why, but Shal insisted that was a necessity for triple dates. And we had to go back to the same house afterwards so we could discuss and analyze every single thing that had happened over the course of the evening. I just had to hope my closet didn't rattle too early. And, besides, I was glad for the company.

I was also freaking out.

Mia was worse. She looked terrified. I'm not sure she'd ever even spoken to a boy before. She barely spoke to any girls. I had been hanging out with boys for the last month in Derwin, so I was at least slightly more prepared. Of course, those boys were also warriors from around the planet, so the conversation would probably be a bit different.

"Too curly?" Shal asked, turning to us from the mirror.

She'd curled her auburn hair into little ringlets that fell to her shoulders and highlighted her blue eyes. For a girl who had apparently not wanted to go on a triple date, she was putting a lot of effort in. She was wearing a new white top and faded blue jeans, and she'd been painstakingly applying makeup for the last hour and a half.

"Perfect," I said.

I had gone a little simpler. Actually I was just wearing jeans and a graphic T-shirt—same as every other day. I had allowed Shal to curl my hair just a little, and I had put on some concealer, eye shadow, and blush. It didn't look bad actually. I was just really happy Allison wasn't here.

Mia sat beside me on the bed and stared into a little oval mirror. Her hair was up in a messy bun, which she never did, and she too was wearing makeup—another first. Along with a green shirt and yoga pants that Shal had made her buy, she looked really cute.

"Are you okay?" I asked her.

"No," she said.

"You'll be fine."

"I've never even spoken to Steve," she said, looking at me with wide eyes. "Not even hi. Hello. Once he looked at me, I think. But I'm not even sure about that."

I sat down at the computer and scrolled through my profile. "You don't have to marry him, Mia. You just have to sit near him. Not even beside him, if you want." I paused. "How are we going to arrange the seating?"

Shal glanced at me in the mirror. "They're boys. They'll sit together. Your only chance will be before and after."

233

"Makes sense," I said thoughtfully.

"What if Liam wants to sit next to you?" Mia asked.

Shal snorted. "Then she'll throw us both on the ground to make room."

I stopped on Liam's old message to me and smiled. "Probably."

My mom poked her head into the room. I think she was more excited than anyone. As someone who loved to dress up and put on makeup, she was thrilled that her tomboy daughter was finally going on a date. She looked at me and hesitated.

"I still think a nicer shirt—"

"This one is fine," I said.

She smiled. "It's definitely fine. The hair is so cute. You girls all look adorable." She glanced at her watch. "We should probably get going. Don't want to be late."

"All right, meet you down there," I said.

She gave me one last happy grin and hurried down the stairs. I sighed deeply.

"She's going to talk about this for weeks."

"My mom looked like she was going to faint when I told her," Mia said.

Shal pouted into the mirror one last time before turning around. "And my dad warned me that boys are all scoundrels and to be avoided," she said. "That's what parents are for. Shall we?"

We hurried down the stairs, where my still-beaming mother was waiting by the door with her keys. Tom and Stache were in the living room watching TV. Stache glanced back as we put our shoes on.

"Leaving?" he asked.

"Yep," I said.

"Call me when the movie's done," he said. "Not a second later. Don't let those boys get any ideas. You stick around and they'll think it's kiss-in-the-moonlight time."

I made a face. "Can we never talk about this again?"

He turned back to the TV. "Agreed."

Tom looked over from the recliner. "Love the outfits, ladies."

Shal and Mia looked at me in confusion. I just rubbed my forehead.

"Thank you, Bat Boy. Can we leave, Mom?"

"Absolutely," she said happily, pulling the door open. "Come on, girls. Don't want to leave the boys waiting." Just saying that made her smile even wider.

She ushered us to the car and turned to me as we pulled out of the driveway.

"Now remember what I said—"

"Even boys like please and thank you?"

She smiled. "You'll be great."

I looked out the window, feeling my stomach turn. I really hoped she was right.

The boys were waiting awkwardly by the front doors when we arrived. I had been a little afraid that Paul and Steve might not show, since they hadn't technically agreed to come. But everyone was here, Shal and Mia were smiling nervously in the back of the van, and my mom was squeezing my hand and saying, "Have fun, sweetie."

Oh crap. I was actually going on a date.

"Thanks," I murmured.

We climbed out, said our goodbyes, and went to meet the boys. As soon as I saw Liam, some of my nervousness disappeared. He gave me a quick smile as we approached.

"Hey," I said. "Hey, Paul. Steve."

"Hey," they said.

There was a quick moment of silence. Uh-oh. What happens now?

"Should we get our seats?" Liam asked.

"Yep," Shal said quickly, walking by. "Hi, Paul."

"Hey," he said, glancing at Steve.

This was going well.

Everyone went inside, with Mia sticking very close to me and Liam heading inside with his friends. Liam shot me another smile as we reached the counter. He'd gelled his hair a little so that it was parted at the front. It should have been super nerdy. I thought it was super cute.

"Still treating me to that date?" he asked.

"As long as you're getting the popcorn," I replied.

He laughed. "Deal."

And from there it was all a happy blur. We definitely sat with the three girls and three boys beside each other, but I was at the far end next to Liam, so I didn't care. Shal looked a little miffed that Paul didn't sit next to her, and Mia just looked thrilled.

Dinosaur Ninja was an even stupider movie than it sounds. But everyone was so nervous and awkward that we laughed at everything—even the part where the ninja raptor practises a breakdance. Don't ask. Better yet, Liam and I shared a large popcorn, which meant we had seven different two-hands-in-the-popcorn-bag moments where we laughed at each other and fumbled to let the other one go first. Those were the best.

Every time I looked at him, I could see *Dinosaur Ninja* reflected in his glasses. Needless to say I now love that movie.

When the lights came back on, Steve made a joke about dinosaur feces, we all laughed, and then we awkwardly made our way back to the lobby. I called my dad, Paul called his mom, and then we gathered in a loose circle outside to wait.

It actually wasn't bad. Paul and Shal kind of talked about how bad the movie was, Mia said something like "I know," that Steve laughed at for some reason, and Liam and I just talked about the irony that a raptor was using a sword. It was very stimulating.

Paul must have lived really close, because his mom was there in like five minutes. We all looked at each other for a second.

"That was fun," Liam said. "Thanks for the invite."

Should we shake hands? Hug? Kiss in the moonlight?

They made it easy. They all just did like a little half wave and started for the car, leaving us to smile and act normal until they had safely driven away, at which point we obviously started to giggle and laugh and break down everything that had happened.

Stache showed up soon after—clearly having sped all the way—and we climbed in and started home.

"How was it?" he asked gruffly.

"Fun," I said.

He glanced at me. "How fun?"

"We didn't kiss in the moonlight," I said.

He nodded and turned back to the road. "That's my girl."

When we got home, we grabbed a bag of chips, some chocolate chip cookie dough ice cream, and proceeded straight to my room. I did get fifty questions on the way up from my mother, who had clearly stayed up way past her bedtime to find out how it went, and I gave her just enough that she went off to bed with a smile on her face. As soon as we closed the bedroom door, the gossip really got going.

"Did you hold hands?"

"Paul is a lot funnier than I thought."

"Did Steve look at me again?"

"I can't believe those babies didn't sit next to us."

"Liam looked so cute."

Yeah, the last one was me. These types of comments continued for at least two or three hours. We kind of broke it up by checking our profiles and eating ice cream and pumping the two air mattresses Stache had fished out of the garage, but it was definitely mostly talking. I just kept thinking about Liam smiling at me as a raptor did backflips in his glasses. I think it might just have been the best night of my life.

When we'd finally exhausted the conversation, we all settled into our beds and turned the lights off. I just lay there looking up at the ceiling and smiling.

"Laura?" Mia said.

"Yeah?"

"I'm glad we went."

"Me too," I said.

Shal sighed. "Now if we could just get Carl to come next time."

With that we started to doze off, and I rolled onto my side against the wall and closed my eyes. I was still way too excited to sleep. The other two were sleeping soundly, and I was still lying there, thinking about one of those great two-hands-in-the-popcorn moments. I pictured his little crooked grin as he quickly pulled his out again.

I was still picturing this when something hard bounced off of my window.

My eyes shot open.

I quickly turned to Shal and Mia, but they were still asleep. I rolled over again, shaking my head. Maybe it was just a bat flying into the window.

I was just closing my eyes again when there was another crack on the window.

Someone was out there. Slinking out of bed, I carefully stepped around Mia and opened the curtains. There, standing in the middle of my yard, was Eldon. He gestured for me to come outside and then slipped back into the shadows.

Frowning, I snuck out of the room, still wearing my red-and-white cotton pyjamas. I grabbed a coat downstairs, threw it on, and gently eased the front door open. Hurrying out into the cold night air, I rounded the house, heading for the woods.

"What is it?" I asked urgently, spotting Eldon and the others in the shadows.

I saw immediately that there were three others. Uncle Laine was there, looking ominous in the background, as was Allison, watching me from beneath her hood.

"Laren just spotted a group of goblins," Eldon said quietly, pulling me into the darkness of the trees. "It looks like they are preparing an attack."

"On me?"

"No. One of your neighbours."

I shook my head. "Why would they do that?"

"To start the war."

I blanched. "What are you saying?"

He put a comforting hand on my shoulder. "I'm saying it's time to do your job. We have to stop them before they harm anyone."

He nodded at Laine, who was holding a bundled wrap of clothing. Steven stood beside him, holding another bundled wrap with a black handle sticking out the bottom.

Eldon smiled grimly.

"Come. If we're going into battle, you had better at least look like a Monster Crusher."

Chapter Twenty-Five

Uncle Laine unfurled his bundle of clothes first, looking worried, and Eldon scooped up the items one by one. He looked at my pyjamas and scowled, obviously thinking they made for poor battle clothing. He handed me a thick brown leather vest, which I slipped over my head and fastened at either side. It smelled like dried sweat and stung my nose.

"That will at least ward off claws and arrows."

"Claws?" I murmured.

Eldon ignored me and held up a long, hooded cloak. "Monster Crushers often prefer battle armour, but for this it would be better if you just looked like a Sword. That means a cloak, your hammer, and a knife. We stick to the shadows only."

I nodded and pulled the cloak on. It was made of some sort of coarse brown wool, and the loose-fitting hood was long enough that it sat right down to the tip of my nose. It was fastened at the nape by a loop of brown string and a large black button. Though the cloak felt snug and warm, it was still light enough that I could move freely. It even sat comfortably on my shoulders and thighs, and I wondered if they'd had it custom-made.

Next Eldon picked up a short knife with a silver blade and solid black handle.

"Tuck this into your boot—" He saw my sneakers and scowled again. "I have to find you a tailor."

"These are very comfortable, you know."

Eldon shook his head and handed me a small leather sheath. "Strap it to your leg."

I did as I was told, tying the leather strap around my ankle and making sure the knife was firmly tucked into the sheath. I didn't want that thing poking me if I had to run away from a troll. It felt a bit awkward as I stood up, but I guess I would be glad to have it if my hammer wasn't close by.

"Am I going to have to actually fight something?" I asked quietly.

Eldon looked at me, his dark-brown locks draped over his forehead. "I hope not."

After putting on the large sheath and carefully placing the hammer in, I was ready to go. I was very grateful I had practised with the sheath, as the others were watching me closely. Especially Allison. I gave her a knowing little smile, and she rolled her eyes.

"Laine is going to guard your house, but they should all be safe as long as they stay inside," Eldon said. He turned to Laine. "Are you sure you don't want me to leave someone else?"

Laine drew a massive broadsword from a sheath and gripped it with one massive hand. He shook his head, his usually friendly eyes narrowed dangerously. "I'll be fine."

"Good," Eldon said. "Let's move."

Uncle Laine gave me a comforting nod, and then I followed Eldon, Allison, and Steven into the woods, grimacing as the cold wind whipped through the trees.

"Where are we going?" I asked.

"The end of your street," Eldon said. "They were gathering there. Laren and Liz are keeping watch."

"Why gather there?"

Eldon glanced back at me. "I have no idea. None of this makes any sense, but we have no choice. We need to destroy them."

Frowning, I tried to keep up as we raced through the trees. Branches swiped past my face, scratching my cheeks. I passed through a spiderweb and quickly wiped it off. Why would the monsters start attacking Riverfield? To draw me out? Was it an ambush?

Eldon finally slowed down, and I saw two cloaked shadows emerge from the darkness. Liz hurried over to Eldon and gave me a brief nod.

"They're still gathering. It looks like they might attack the first house."

Eldon looked behind her. "How many?"

"About thirty," she said. "They outnumber us five to one."

"We have no choice," Eldon replied. "I sent word back to Derwin, but Caria and the others won't be here for hours. It takes a whole lot longer without the elevator, and only the Monster Crusher can use it."

"Six of us," Allison whispered. "Versus thirty."

"And only one we need to kill," Eldon said. "Did you see the leader, Laren?"

Laren shook his head. "No, just goblins. We're going to have to find him the hard way."

"Perfect," Eldon muttered. "Show me."

We started after Laren, and Allison glanced at me.

"Ready for a real fight?" she asked quietly.

"Not really."

We fell into step beside each other.

"I've never seen this before," she murmured. "This is the first time they've ever shown themselves in Riverfield in such force. Like they want us to attack."

"Do you think it's a trap?"

"It's always a trap."

I looked at her. "So why not go home?"

"Because you need me." She paused. "Besides, if we lose, I won't have a home for much longer anyway."

"Can I ask you something?"

"What?" she asked, already sounding bored. She really was evil.

"Why do you act like that at school? I mean, you'd think someone fighting monsters wouldn't even really care about elementary school drama."

"Do you?" she asked, raising one perfectly trimmed eyebrow.

I paused. "Point taken. But I'm not evil."

Allison shook her head. "I'm popular. That's how popular girls act."

"I don't buy that."

She scowled and looked away.

"It's just how I've always been. It's how people expect me to be. Maybe I like it. I don't know. I do feel . . . guilty sometimes. I shouldn't have posted the picture."

"That was kind of mean."

"I know." She briefly met my eyes. "I . . . well, I guess I was a bit jealous that you got to be the Monster Crusher. Maybe a lot jealous. And I knew I was supposed to be helping you and that's why I was going to just ignore you, but then you called me out and the other girls were asking if I was going to do something . . . I don't know. It was dumb. I'm sorry."

I frowned. "Thanks. Can't you just start being nice?"

"Maybe. I hate school . . . I guess I'm just miserable there, you know."

"Why do you hate it at school? You're the most popular girl there."

She stiffened and quickly started after the others, leaving me behind.

"Everything I want is in Derwin. I just can't have it."

I watched her hurry ahead, and then suddenly thought back to something. A very dark look she had given me in the courtyard yesterday when I was talking to Lee.

"You like Lee."

"No, I don't," she said sharply shooting me an angry look.

"You're in love," I said.

"Shut up."

We joined the others where they were crouched down, watching something in silence. I peered through the trees. I couldn't see too much in the faint moonlight, but

245

I could hear the raspy voices. Squinting harder, I started to see the shapes forming in the trees. I could make out the mossy-green skin and the moonlight glinting off of spears and swords and metal caps. I took a small step to get a better look and stepped right on a branch. It cracked loudly, and I hunched right down to the ground, horrified. The raspy voices changed, and Eldon looked back, glaring at me. I heard shuffling in the distance.

"Good work," Allison muttered. "So glad to have you along."

"Weapons ready," Eldon whispered.

"Where are they going?" Liz asked softly.

I eased around Eldon to get a better look. The goblins were marching now, their swords and spears at the ready. I looked ahead of them and just made out the faint street lights through the trees.

"They're attacking," I said. "We have to stop them."

Eldon looked around, seeming hesitant. "This doesn't make any sense."

"We have no choice," Allison said. "They'll kill anybody who gets in their way."

Eldon paused for a moment and then nodded. "On my signal."

He slowly stood up and everyone followed suit. I felt my palms sweating on the handle, despite the cold air. But it was different than my first mission. Now the monsters were attacking my home. They were in my world. It was time to defend it.

"Now," Eldon said quietly, moving forward in almost complete silence.

The Swords crept after him, Allison pulling the bow from her back and fitting an arrow. I took the rear, and the group slowly started picking up speed, heading for the back of the goblin troop. We broke out into a jog, still moving quietly through the trees.

We closed in, and I unsheathed the hammer and lifted it over my shoulder.

Just then a hideous shriek split through the canopy. Eldon and the others stopped immediately, and I saw the goblins turn around, smiling evilly. I slowly looked up.

There, perched in the trees over our heads, were hordes of small, wiry creatures with yellow eyes and crooked, bat-like wings. Long, clawed arms clutched the branches.

"Uh-oh," Allison whispered.

Chapter Twenty-Six

We had been pulled into a trap. And with another awful, screeching howl, the imps descended from the trees like a wave of horrendous bats.

"Stay together!" Eldon shouted.

The first imp flew toward me, its clawed hands grasping for my face. I swung the hammer upward with two hands, smashing it right into the imp's disfigured grey head. The imp went sailing backward, crashing into two other imps and sending all three cartwheeling out of the air into the grass.

Another imp landed on my back, and I used the handle to smash the creature in the head. It collapsed onto the ground. I wasn't even thinking. I just had to fight.

Beside me, Allison was firing arrow after arrow into the night sky, shooting down one imp after another. For a second I thought we might win the battle easily.

And then the goblins crashed into us.

I saw Liz topple to the ground as the first wave of goblins rammed into her, her sword flying from her hand. Eldon just managed to kill a goblin as it tried to skewer Liz with a spear. I turned to help with the goblins when an imp landed on top of me, clawing deep into my arm. Blood rushed out of the wounds.

Grimacing, I elbowed the imp, knocking it off my arm. Beside me, Allison threw her bow aside and drew her sword. She cut through a goblin with a graceful swing before dispatching an imp with a hidden knife. I was glad I never got into a real fight with her.

"Laura!" Eldon cried, fighting wildly at the front. "You have to find the leader."

"That should be easy!" I shouted back, looking over the swarm of creatures attacking us in the darkness. Between the imps blotting out the sky and the goblins pouring out of the dense trees, there were monsters everywhere.

How was I going to find the leader?

The Swords broke apart, hacking and swinging and stabbing on all sides. I charged to the front of the group beside Eldon, taking a massive swing with the hammer as I did. It connected with two goblins, sending them both flying. The crimson rubies on the hammer flared to life, pushing back the darkness, and I saw the fear in the goblins' disfigured faces as it grew brighter and brighter.

I scanned the monsters, looking for the biggest one.

Finally, I saw one near the back, standing just a few inches taller than the rest. He wore the same black chest plate and dented metal cap as the rest of them, but his long green arms were corded with wiry muscle, and his crooked sword was particularly large and jagged. I saw his yellow eyes flashing as he shouted orders at the other monsters.

"There!" I shouted.

Using the hammer like a battering ram, I charged, knocking the goblins back. I saw Eldon pull an injured Liz to her feet, and Laren and Steven formed a protective circle around her. I knew we didn't have much time.

I felt every muscle in my body straining as I drove the hammer forward, trying to break through to the leader. Allison was trying to stay with me, but it was complete chaos. Monsters hacked at us on all sides, and I just kept moving forward. The goblins fell back, stumbling to keep away from the hammer, which was now blazing red. The horde finally parted, revealing the leader. His yellow eyes flashed as he lifted his sword with two hands. Gripping my hammer, I prepared to charge.

But before either of us could move, another goblin burst out of the woods and shouted something. The leader looked at it, and then turned to me and smiled evilly.

"Fall back!" it shouted.

The goblins instantly fled into the trees, while the imps flew off into the night sky, disappearing through the canopy. Eldon and the others killed a few as they fled, but in seconds the forest was empty again. I could tell Eldon wanted to chase them, but then Liz immediately dropped to the ground, clutching her side again.

"Are you all right?" someone asked me.

I turned and saw Allison looking at my cut. Blood was pooling onto my shirt and cloak, where the claws had ripped right through the material.

"Yeah," I said, cringing. "Fine."

She cut a piece of fabric off her cloak and started wrapping my arm.

I looked at her in surprise. "Thanks."

"No problem," she muttered.

"What was that all about?" I asked.

"No idea," she said softly. "But I'm sure it's bad."

"We need to get Liz back to Arnwell," Eldon said, helping her up. "Whatever just happened, at least they fell back for now."

We started back for the house, slowly picking our way through the trees. Eldon and another Sword were supporting Liz by the shoulders, but she was very weak.

Something felt very wrong about the whole attack. Obviously the monsters had been waiting for us. But if it was an ambush, why did they retreat before the fight was over? We were still outnumbered. It didn't make any sense.

"I know," Allison muttered beside me, clearly guessing at my thoughts. "I don't like it either."

We were almost to my house when I saw lights through the trees. Lots of lights. Frowning, I hurried to my backyard. Every light in my house was on. Feeling my stomach twist, my eyes fell on the back door. It had been ripped clean off the hinges.

"No," I whispered.

I sprinted across the lawn, lifting the hammer. I didn't care who saw me. They were in my house.

"Laura!" Eldon shouted.

But there was no way I was stopping. My brother was inside. I was halfway there when a hulking figure suddenly grabbed me from behind. I struggled to free myself, but a familiar voice stopped me. "It's too late," Uncle Laine said, carrying me back to the trees.

"But they're in the house—"

"They're gone," he said brusquely. "I watched them leave."

As soon as we were in the woods again, he dropped me. I whirled to face him.

"What happened?" I demanded.

"A group came at me from behind," he explained, looking sombre. His cloak was ripped and torn, as was his tunic. "I chased them back, but as I did, I heard shouting."

Eldon and the others had gathered around him. He looked away.

"They were already leaving. I went after them, but they got away."

"But they can't go in the house—" Eldon said, frowning.

"Obviously they can," Laine said. "We were wrong."

"Were they looking for Laura?" Allison asked. "Is everyone else all right—"

"They weren't looking for Laura," Laine said quietly. "They never were."

"What do you mean?" I asked, narrowing my eyes.

Laine put his hand on my arm. "They took Tom."

Chapter Twenty-Seven

I sat in my kitchen, unable to speak or move or do anything at all. The police were there, asking my parents questions and inspecting the back door. My parents had been looking for me in a panic, of course. I told them I'd heard Tom shouting and chased the kidnappers outside. Then I'd just broken down and sobbed so hard that my body was shaking and my legs were weak and they had to sit me in this chair. Eldon, Laine, and the others had fallen back into the trees, obviously unable to follow me inside wearing their cloaks and swords. I was alone, back in the real world, just staring at nothing.

And now I couldn't even cry anymore. All I could do was think about Tom.

I'd let my brother down.

Shal and Mia had already been picked up by their parents, and they'd given me quick hugs before they left. They hadn't heard me leave, so they believed the story.

I'd pulled off the fabric Allison had wrapped around my arm before I went inside, and told my parents I must have cut it on a branch or something. It was way too deep for that, but my mom was putting antibacterial cream and bandages on it so fast I don't think she even noticed. Her hands were shaking the whole time, tears pouring down her face.

She was still crying, leaning against the counter with her face in her hands and sobbing. Stache was just pacing around, unable to sit still. They didn't understand.

Of course they didn't. They couldn't. I wanted to tell them what had happened, but Eldon had quietly told me the same rules applied before I went in. If I told my parents, there would be repercussions. He said the Swords were already tracking the goblins. They'd find Tom. But that was no consolation to me. Nothing was. My brother was gone, and it was my fault. I felt tears streaming down my cheeks again.

Another officer knelt down in front of me. "You're sure you didn't see anything?"

I shook my head. "Just their backs. Two of them. One was holding Tom."

He nodded and put his hand on my knee. "We'll find them."

No, you won't, I thought to myself. I will.

It was another few hours before they left. Stache managed to install some new hinges and lock the door, and we all just sat in the living room for a while. No one slept. We just sat there in silence, and Stache rubbed my back as I sat there and wondered if the Swords had found anything. Uncle Laine had come inside soon after me, telling my father that he had seen the flashing lights, and told me when no one was listening that Eldon and the other Swords were searching for the tunnel the monsters were using.

Uncle Laine left soon after to join the search—he seemed almost crazed, clenching his fists and telling me he would come get me the second he found something. He said he had tracked the goblins a fair way and had a vague idea of where the tunnel might be. He also told me he wouldn't sleep until he found it, which made me feel a little better.

I wanted to search too, but there was no way I could leave my parents now.

When the sun was up and streaming through the windows, I told my parents I was going to try and lie down for awhile. My mom gave me a hug, tears streaming down her face.

"We'll be right here," she whispered.

When I was alone in my room, I finally let it out. I grabbed my eyes and sobbed, the tears rolling down my face like twin rivers spilling into falls. I started shaking and trembling and curled into a little ball on my bed, pulling my knees to my chest. All I could see was Tom with the monsters, and when my mind wandered to the worst, the sobbing would start again. I was completely broken.

I lay there, crying for hours, before I finally drifted off into an uneasy sleep.

I woke to someone caressing my face. I snapped awake and found my mom sitting over me, running her fingers along my cheek. Her eyes were puffy and red.

"Hey, Laura," she said softly.

"Hey," I whispered.

"Your uncle Laine is here," she said. "He invited you to spend the night at their place. Said it might be good to get you away from the house for a bit—and away from these woods." She ran her fingers through my hair. "I said I would ask you."

I didn't want to leave the house, but I knew what Laine was doing: giving me a chance to talk to someone about what had actually happened. He was giving me an out.

"I think it might be a good idea," I said, pushing myself up. "If you and Dad are going to be all right."

She smiled sadly. "We have each other for company. I've just been crying on his shoulder most of the day anyway."

I leaned over and gave my mom a hug. She buried her face in my shoulder.

"I want him back," she said, her voice cracking. "I want my baby back."

"We'll get him back," I said quietly. "Don't worry."

She pulled away and looked at me, tears streaming down her cheeks.

"Sometimes I forget how strong you are. Much stronger than your mother."

I smiled faintly. "That's because I'm twice your size."

She managed a little laugh and hugged me again.

"All right, he's waiting downstairs," she said, climbing off the bed. "Promise me you'll stay inside."

"We'll be safe," I said, not wanting to break a promise when I wasn't sure I was going to see her again. The thought brought fresh tears to my eyes, but I held them in check. She was right. I needed to be strong. "I'm going to pack my bag."

When I had stuffed a change of clothes into a duffle bag, I went downstairs and saw Uncle Laine waiting with Stache by the front door. I noticed that Laine was standing a little bit away from my dad and not really looking at him. He obviously felt guilty and probably wanted to explain to my parents what had happened to their son. I knew the feeling.

Stache gave me a hug. "You're sure you don't want to stay here?" he asked.

I shook my head. "Uncle Laine is right. I could use a change of scenery. Everything here just makes me think of Tom."

He nodded. "All right, Laurabell. We'll see you tomorrow."

I hugged them both again and followed my uncle outside to his beaten-down truck. Climbing up into the passenger seat, I waved goodbye as we pulled out of the driveway and then roughly wiped my eyes with the back of my hand. I'd done enough crying. It was time to be the Monster Crusher.

"Are you ready?" Laine asked softly, looking out the window at the setting sun.

"Yeah," I said. "Did you find the monster's tunnel?"

He nodded. "It wasn't too hard, really. Saw goblins waiting before I got within fifteen metres of it. They didn't spot me, so they won't expect us.'

"Where are we meeting the others?"

"They're going to meet us at the side of the road, directly north of where we're going. We'll just walk in a straight line south." He looked over at me, and his big brown eyes softened. "I'm sorry."

"For what?"

"Telling you guys to move here. I put you in this situation. I never thought any of this would happen. It wasn't supposed to be like this."

"It's not your fault," I said. "I made the choice to open the panel. I made the choice to keep coming back. I wanted to be something special."

"And you are," he replied. "I'm very proud of you."

"What about Sandy and the kids?" I asked. "Do they know what's going on?"

Laine shook his head. "I sent them to your grandma's on Friday. Didn't want them around, no matter what happens in Riverfield tonight. Sandy was a bit confused, but I told her I was just worried about these kidnappers and wanted them to stay out of town. It's for the best."

"I wish I'd sent Tom out of town too," I murmured.

We drove in silence the rest of the way. A few minutes later Laine pulled onto a small side street at the south edge of town, right by the woods. The sun was already falling below the trees, and the first shadows stretched out over the truck, welcoming us to the forest. Laine grabbed two hooded cloaks from the back of his truck, along with a huge broadsword and a knife. He also handed me the worn leather hauberk.

"Put this on," he said. "There will be plenty more claws and teeth where we're going."

I stepped out of the truck and slid it on. I had just wrapped the cloak over my shoulders when Eldon and the others appeared in the shadows. Laren stepped forward and handled me the bundled Iron Hammer, as well as the small silver knife and leather sheath to tie to my ankle again.

"I had to leave a few Swords to guard Raven's End," Eldon said. "Just in case. But that means there are only six of us. We will have to move quickly and quietly."

I strapped the sheath to my left ankle, pulling it tight and then tucking it under my jeans. Then I unwrapped the hammer and propped it up on my shoulder. I didn't need the sheath. This time I was keeping the hammer ready.

"Stay close," Eldon said. "We don't want to be seen before we get there."

We set off into the woods, Laine and I joining Eldon at the front, while Allison, Steven, and Laren took up the rear guard. We walked for about ten minutes, trying to move as silently as possible through the ever-darkening woods.

Finally Laine slowed down. "It's close."

We slowly moved forward, watching for shapes in the darkness.

I followed Uncle Laine, sticking close behind him. As we walked, I noticed that he was wearing the same cloak he'd had on last night when Tom was taken. The rips and tears were still visible. He was lucky they didn't go any deeper—there was no blood surrounding the tears. The goblins' swords must have just missed piercing his skin.

"There," Uncle Laine said, pointing ahead.

We all froze, and through the darkness, I saw two wiry shapes standing in the shadows. Despite the gloom, I could see just a bit of light reflecting off their swords.

Goblins.

Eldon nodded at Allison, and she stepped up beside him, drawing her bow. He did the same, moving with a deadly silence that almost made me shudder. The two of them were killers through and through. Maybe we had a chance after all.

"Now," Eldon whispered.

Two arrows sailed through the night like bats, and both found their mark. The goblins toppled to the ground, arrows in their hearts. Eldon nodded. "The monsters don't know we've found their main tunnel, so they'll be assuming we're coming through our own. But we should prepare for a trap regardless. Laura, you go in last. Laine, stay with her until she's through, just in case there are goblins nearby on the surface. Give us a few minutes to scout the tunnel before you enter. If we don't come back, don't follow us."

"Right," Laine said, stepping close to me and brandishing his sword.

Eldon looked at the others. "We move quickly. If it's a trap, fall back."

He darted forward, staying close to the ground. I watched as he reached the two bodies, his hand sweeping across the ground, looking for the hidden tunnel. He paused, finding a crack, and then heaved a massive circular opening upward, using both hands. Judging by the size of that opening, even the most massive of ogres could have entered Riverfield.

He nodded at the others, and then quickly descended the stairs. The other Swords followed, leaving Laine and me alone. Laine looked out over the woods, his eyes narrowed dangerously, his hands firmly gripped on the hilt of his sword. As we waited in uncomfortable silence, my eyes fell on his cloak again. Suddenly something else came to mind. I hadn't really thought anything of it earlier, but now that I thought about the dates, it didn't make any sense.

I frowned. "Uncle Laine, when did you say you sent the kids to Grandma's?"

"Friday," he said distractedly, looking around the woods. "Why?"

"Why did you send them away on Friday? Nothing had happened yet."

Uncle Laine glanced at me, looking confused.

"I was worried," he said. "I had a hunch."

There was something odd about the way he was reacting. Like he was nervous. I couldn't even believe I was thinking it. But there was something else that didn't add up.

"Why would the monsters take Tom?"

Laine snorted. "Who knows?"

"I do," I said quietly. "They took him because he's a Shadow Sight."

Laine stiffened for a moment. I would have missed it if I wasn't watching so closely. I felt my stomach turning in disbelief. It couldn't be.

"How did the goblins get in the house?" I asked quietly.

"I don't know," Laine said, growing agitated. "They just did. What is this about?"

"You scouted this tunnel," I whispered. "You insisted you alone watch the house. You brought us to Riverfield in the first place."

Uncle Laine looked really agitated now. "So?"

"What happened on that mission? The one where you were taken prisoner?"

Laine looked away, shaking his head incredulously. Then, without warning, he started to run. He would have gotten away, but I was ready. I stuck the hammer out and

261

tripped him, and he toppled into the grass. I still couldn't believe what I was seeing.

He turned and looked up at me, his eyes wide. "I was never going to hurt you," he said, almost pleading. "Or Tom. You have to believe me."

"Why?" I whispered.

"They tortured me. I broke. I wanted to get back to my family. So I made a deal."

"What deal?"

"I told them about the other tunnels," he said, his eyes welling with tears. "I told them they could use them to invade Derwin and the other realms. The war would be over in a day."

"Why would you do that?"

"The humans were losing the war anyway. It was only a matter of time. Months. Maybe a year." His voice cracked. "I'm losing my job, Laura. My house. I pleaded with Eldon to let my family move to Derwin, but he refused. It was the stupid rule about surface humans not being allowed to live in the Under Earth. Dungan made me a deal."

"Dungan?"

He paused, and for the first time in my life, my uncle looked afraid. "The leader of the monsters. A troll. Trust me, you don't want to meet him."

He slowly climbed to his feet, leaving his sword on the ground.

"They promised me Arnwell for my own. A whole castle, Laura. I had to take it. All I had to do was bring them Tom. I know most of the tunnels to Derwin, but I don't know the secret pathways to the other realms. They needed a Shadow Sight."

262

"You were with him," I said. "When he saw the tunnel in the woods last year."

"I knew right away that he was a Shadow Sight, but I didn't tell Eldon. I don't know why. It was the first time it had ever happened, a surface human having the Sight, and I thought the secret could be valuable. And when I was captured . . . I used the information. When I told the monsters about Tom, well, I knew I had to get him to Riverfield. I was just going to try and have him over for a weekend, but when your Dad said you wanted to move, I figured it was worth a try to see if you would get the house. Then he would just be here, and I could take him when the invasion was ready."

"And me?" I asked, feeling sick. "What was my part?"

"Just an unfortunate add-on," he said quietly. "I had hoped Tom would get your room. I didn't want you involved."

"So you lied to me . . . when you said you thought I had what it takes."

"Laura . . . you're just a little girl. I didn't want you in this war. When the invasion—"

"What invasion?" I asked darkly, gripping the hammer.

Laine hesitated and looked away. "They're invading Riverfield tonight. There's an army gathering at the entrance to another tunnel, up by the hydro towers on the north side of town. Dungan is with them. They're going to use Tom to show them the secret tunnels across Riverfield, and then they're going to invade Derwin."

"They'll burn Riverfield to the ground," I whispered.

Laine shifted uneasily. "They said they wouldn't—"

"You're the one who took Tom from my house," I said, stepping toward him.

"I wanted to do it," he said. "I knew I could make sure he was safe—"

"What about my parents?" I asked softly.

"They're safe in the house," Laine said. "I would never hurt them—"

"How could you?" I whispered.

"I had to do it for my family," he said weakly. "I didn't have a choice."

He looked toward the tunnel.

"Eldon will kill me when he finds out," he said softly.

I looked at him for a long moment, the hammer in my hands. A part of me wanted to make him pay. To have him arrested and brought to Derwin and stuck in prison. But he was still my uncle. He still had a family. And I had a feeling he was right about Eldon.

"Go to Grandma's and join your family. I don't ever want to see you again."

He met my eyes, and then he turned and ran into the woods. I watched him go. I was still stunned. It was bad enough that the monsters had Tom. But my uncle was responsible. It was almost too much to deal with.

A minute later, Eldon climbed out of the tunnel. "We're clear . . . where's Laine?"

"Get the others," I murmured. "We're at the wrong place."

Eldon narrowed his eyes. "Laine?"

I nodded. He immediately disappeared, and a few minutes later the other Swords had all filed back through the portal, looking very confused.

"What happened?" Allison asked.

"We've been betrayed," I said. "My uncle made a deal with the monsters."

The Swords looked at each other darkly. Eldon stared out into the woods. I could already tell he wanted to go after Laine.

"The leader is a troll named Dungan, and if my uncle was telling the truth, he is currently marching on Riverfield with an army," I said.

Eldon turned back to me. "Why?"

"My little brother . . . he's a Shadow Sight."

Eldon and the others looked stunned. "What?" he whispered. "How can that be?"

"I didn't want to tell you. I didn't want anyone to know. I'm sorry. But Dungan knows, and he's using Tom to show him the tunnels. He's going to use them to invade Derwin. And I'm guessing he's going to burn Riverfield to the ground on the way."

"How are we going to stop an army?" Laren murmured.

I turned to him. "We're going to crush the leader."

Chapter Twenty-Eight

We raced through the woods, heading directly for the massive line of hydro towers at the north end of town. As we hurried across Main Street in the darkness, I listened for screams, but I heard nothing but cars in the distance.

Obviously the attack hadn't happened yet. We still had a little time.

"I should have suspected something earlier," Eldon said grimly as we picked our way into the forest on the other side of the road. "He's been acting strangely for months now. I just thought he was worried about his family."

"He was," I said quietly. "Part of it, anyway."

Eldon glanced at me and then darted forward, slipping through the night like a mountain lion. I thought about Tom as I followed closely behind, knocking branches out of my way as we weaved in and out of the trees. I missed, and one sliced across my face, just missing my eye. The only thing giving me hope was the fact that if they were using Tom to find the portals, that at least meant he was all right. For now.

But if Uncle Laine was right, and there was an army

gathering outside of Riverfield, then I still had to fight through hordes of monsters to get to him. Considering we had five Swords and myself, that was not going to be easy.

"What happens if the monsters take over Riverfield?" I asked.

Eldon paused. "They will flood through the tunnels, killing everyone in their way. They'll emerge in Derwin, behind our defence lines. The battle will be over in minutes, and the monsters will claim Derwin and use our trains to attack the rest of the Under Earth. Even with the other Monster Crushers, the Under Earth will probably fall. And from there, the monsters only have one more place to attack. The surface."

He looked at me.

"If we lose tonight, both our worlds may be destroyed. Mine tonight."

We continued on, and I caught sight of the hydro towers through openings in the canopy, a few blinking red lights marking their place in the darkness. We were getting close now. My sweating fingers tightened on the hammer, itching to fight.

Allison suddenly fell in step beside me, her eyes darting to mine.

"I'm sorry about your uncle," she said.

"So am I," I replied. "But right now I just care about my brother."

Allison nodded. "Then let's go get him back."

I saw the last comforting orange lights of Riverfield passing to our right, just visible through the trees. We were very close now. The night was cool and still; even the animals seemed to be hiding, as if they could feel the building tension in the air. And then I heard them: voices, rasping and cruel, shouting orders in the distance. Ahead, the trees suddenly opened onto a sprawling, grassy field, cleared away for the line of hydro towers that swept from Riverfield to a power station miles away. Secluded and enormous.

The perfect spot to gather an army.

We stopped at the edge of the trees, hunching in the brush. I pushed a low-hanging branch aside, trying to get a better look at the monsters. My eyes widened.

The field was littered with monsters. Hundreds of them. Maybe thousands. To the left, I saw them pouring out of the ground in a seemingly endless line before scurrying to join the others. They were forming ranks, gnashing their teeth and waving their shields and clutching their crooked swords. Yellow eyes sprinkled the field like fireflies. I looked toward the back of the army, searching for Dungan. It didn't take long. The massive troll was standing in the midst of the horde, five times as big as any goblin. Even from there, I could hear him shouting orders. His horrible, booming voice shook the ground.

"Now what?" Allison whispered behind us.

Eldon scanned the area. "If we cut around the forest farther down, we can sneak behind the army and go straight for Dungan—"

He was interrupted by a piercing horn blow. The monsters suddenly straightened, tightened their ranks, and began to march toward Riverfield. In the background, the massive creature lifted someone up with his right hand, clutching him by his shirt.

It was Tom.

I knew there was no time. If we tried to go around, the monsters would reach Riverfield. Even if we managed to stop them before they made it through the tunnel, Riverfield would burn. Thousands of people would die. And that thing had my brother.

I wanted him back.

"Tom!"

Hoisting the Iron Hammer with both hands, I stepped out of the woods. The hammer must have known I needed courage more than ever before, because the rubies flared a blinding crimson red, while the pale iron caught the moonlight. I heard the Swords step out behind me, Allison muttering something, and the marching line of monsters stopped, looking uncertain. I saw them buckle as the others marched into their backs and confused shouts flooded through the army. I just stood there, trying to be brave as my knees wobbled and shook and threatened to buckle. My hands trembled. My stomach felt like it was going to jump out of me and make a break for it. But my knees didn't buckle, and my grip remained strong, and the hammer grew brighter.

"Laura!" Tom shouted. "Get help!"

"It's here!" I called back.

I heard a commotion in the monster's army, and I saw Dungan pushing his way forward. When he was about half-way through, he saw me and abruptly stopped. I saw the moonlight hit his jagged teeth as he smiled and lifted my brother high into the air, as if reminding me that he had him. Tom shouted and tried to wriggle free, but it was useless.

"Destroy them!" Dungan boomed, so loudly that the monsters around him flinched.

Lowering their rusted black spears, the army of monsters turned toward us, their feet thundering on the grass. Then they started to march.

"Do we have a plan?" Eldon asked tightly.

"Only one," I said, knowing that if I failed, everyone here would die.

I stepped forward, lifting the hammer up like a torch.

"Dungan!" I shouted. "Are you too afraid to fight a little girl yourself?"

"What are you doing?" Eldon asked quietly.

"Challenging Dungan to a one-on-one fight," I murmured.

He grimaced. "That's what I was afraid of."

But the challenge didn't work.

The monsters closed in. I saw mammoth ogres approaching from the back, and imps taking flight and darting across the night sky. We would be swept away in moments. Dungan just smiled cruelly at me from the middle of it all. I tried again.

"Some king you are!" I shouted. "Letting your minions do the work. But I guess that makes sense. I've heard that all trolls are cowards."

Yep, that did it.

I saw Dungan's eyes flash, and then he suddenly lowered Tom to the ground.

"Stop!" he ordered, his booming voice cutting over the noise.

The marching army of monsters instantly stopped and then split in either direction, forming a clear path to

Dungan. Uncle Laine had said I didn't want to meet Dungan. I think he was right.

Dungan was bigger than any monster I had ever seen—double the size of the tallest man and as broad as a pickup truck. His arms were long and lined with iron-hard muscle, protruding from a rusted black chest plate that matched his gauntlets and leg protectors. Only his massive feet were bare—disgusting boogie board–sized feet that were covered with moss and marred further by twisted yellow nails. A shock of straw-like black hair contrasted sharply with his distorted green features, while his nose was mashed in like an overripe peach, his right cheek was bulging and lumpy, and he had disturbingly large fangs that protruded from his mouth and gnashed together as he stared at me.

"Are you challenging me, girl?" he asked quietly.

I met his eyes. "Yep. Unless you're too afraid, of course. I would understand."

"I think he gets it," Eldon muttered.

Dungan laughed, shaking the earth. "Bring me my hammer."

A goblin hurried forward and grabbed Tom, pulling him backward with a crooked knife to his throat. Behind Dungan, the army parted as well, and four goblins emerged, holding something enormous between them. They could barely lift it. Dungan reached down with one massive hand and picked it up. I felt my stomach sink.

The black hammer was bigger than my entire body. The handle itself was nearly as tall as I was, while the top was the size of my desk. It must have weighed half a ton.

Dungan slowly walked forward, letting the top of his hammer drag along the ground behind him, digging into the soil. He smiled cruelly.

"I had my own hammer made," he said. "Just to crush that puny one you are holding."

I shifted, looking back at Eldon. For the first time since I'd met him, he looked afraid. I watched as Dungan's disgusting green feet crunched into the grass, and I saw the muscles in his right arm shifting as he raised the hammer up onto his shoulder.

"I'm going to crush you too, girl," he said quietly. "You've caused me a lot of trouble. More than that fool Laine predicted. Your brother is still of some use to me, of course. He's going to win me the Under Earth. And when he does, I'll crush him too."

I narrowed my eyes, staring up at the massive troll.

"You better focus on killing me first."

He laughed again. "That will be the easy part."

Without warning, he swung the hammer up over his shoulder and brought it hurtling toward me like a meteor. I jumped out of the way, and the hammer hit the grass and imbedded itself into the soil with a tremendous *thump*. The ground shook with the impact. I backed away, thinking frantically about how I was going to beat such a monster. It seemed impossible. Dungan hoisted the hammer up again, still smiling.

"You can't dodge them all," he said.

I saw Tom standing with the crooked knife pressed against his throat.

"It's all right, Tom," I shouted, "I'll get you home soon."

Dungan attacked again, sweeping the hammer horizontally with two hands toward my waist this time. Between the hammer and his enormous arms, his reach was well over two metres. I dropped flat to the ground, letting the black hammer sweep over my head.

When I jumped back up, preparing to charge, I realized that Dungan wasn't finished. He swept the hammer all the way around his back and then brought it down again over his head. I didn't have time to dodge. I just lifted my hammer with both hands and tried to block his weapon with the handle. The impact was like a thunderclap.

My arms buckled but held, and the force of the blow almost knocked both of us backward. Dungan looked down at me in complete disbelief as I stood there and held my ground, sweat pouring down my face. He pushed down on his hammer with both hands, and I felt my knees shaking. But I pushed back, fighting to keep his hammer at bay.

The crimson rubies grew even brighter, casting everything in a red glare.

I couldn't keep this up though. I had to go on the offensive if I was going to win.

I suddenly shifted my weight, pushing his hammer to the side and launching an attack of my own. I swung the Iron Hammer at his waist, and Dungan just barely blocked it, the metal ringing. I swung again and again, trying to take out his tree trunk–sized legs. The massive troll stepped back, his smile faltering just a little as I attacked wildly, fighting to get to Tom. But again and again Dungan blocked me, and I felt my arms starting to tire.

Dungan obviously sensed it, and he began to launch his own attacks again. He started pushing me backward now, his hammer crashing toward me. I blocked it, but my arms ached and strained with every blow. He was too big. Too strong. Finally, just after I blocked another powerful attack, he lashed out with his left hand, striking me across the stomach. It was like being hit by a car.

I went flying backward, the hammer slipping from my hands, then slammed into the grass, rolling over a few times before coming to a stop. I heard the monsters cheer and Tom cry out from the far side of the ring. I looked up and saw Eldon's face, a spear point jammed up against his back. His eyes were sombre.

He knew what was coming.

I tried to crawl to my hammer, but Dungan was faster. He kicked me in the ribs, and I flew backward again, my entire body flooding with pain. Tears poured out of my eyes—it felt like I was being stabbed on all sides. He must have broken my ribs. A lot of them. I clutched my side in agony as Dungan appeared over me, grabbing the front of my T-shirt with his huge, clawed green hand. He hoisted me up like I was a toddler, turning me to look directly into his pale-yellow eyes, those snake-like pupils scanning my face.

"You fought well, little girl," he said, his foul breath washing over my face with the smell of rotted meat. "But you aren't facing goblins now. You are facing Dungan, King of the Dead Mountains. Soon to be King of the Under Earth, and one day, the destroyer of the surface world."

He smiled, revealing those yellow fangs.

"Did you really think I would be beaten by a fat little girl?"

He tossed me away, and once again I was crashing hard into the ground. My broken ribs flared with pain. I just managed to roll over, and I saw Dungan walking toward me, smiling again. This time he was slowly lifting the hammer over his head with two hands. He was done playing with me. He was about to end this fight.

My body hurt so much that it was hard to think. But there was something nagging at me as Dungan stopped beside me, smiling and preparing to crush me into the dirt.

"Any last words?"

It was something I'd read in the guide. Something about trolls.

It hit me just as he lifted the hammer. Grimacing through the pain, I slipped the silver knife out of its sheath on my ankle and gripped it with two trembling hands.

"I prefer *husky*," I said, and then I plunged the blade into Dungan's disgusting green foot.

It pierced right through to the handle, and Dungan let out a horrendous roar, dropping the hammer. I knew I didn't have much time. I had to move.

I scampered around his legs as he reached down and tried to pull out the knife with his massive, clumsy fingers. The crowd of monsters was in an uproar. They were all shouting and cursing and waving their swords and spears at me.

Ignoring everything, I scooped the Iron Hammer up off the dirt and turned back to Dungan. He was still hunched over, roaring in pain and trying to pull the small knife out of his foot. Hunched over like that, he was just short enough that I could reach his head.

I charged, pulling the hammer behind me with both hands. I had one shot.

Dungan looked up just as I swung it with every ounce of strength left in my body. The hammer connected squarely with his broad forehead, and a massive wave of invisible energy leapt outward from the impact, knocking the watching goblins to the ground and sending the Swords tumbling after them. It passed around me, but Dungan went flying, the incredible force sending him soaring through the air. He slammed into the ground, motionless. There was no doubt the second I saw him land. Dungan was dead.

All around me, monsters slowly got back up, wide-eyed and disbelieving. I slowly turned in a circle, gripping the hammer with two hands. It had worked once before—I figured I might as well try it again.

"Who's next?" I shouted.

The monsters all looked at each other, and then without another word, they all turned and started running for the tunnel. The shouts and cries and warnings fled through the army, and like a retreating tide they pushed over each other in a desperate rush to flood back into the Under Earth. I let them go. My body was throbbing with pain, and all I wanted to do was collapse. Instead I limped over to my brother, making sure he wasn't trampled in the retreat, and pulled him close.

"Are you all right?" I said, my voice cracking with emotion.

"I'm fine," he said, burying his face into my shoulder. "I'm sorry. Dungan said he was going to kill you if I didn't help." He pulled away. "You killed him, didn't you?"

"I did."

"And Uncle Laine?"

"I let him go. But if he ever goes near you again, I'll crush him too."

Tom smiled. "Can we go home now?"

"Yeah," I said, turning to the Swords. "I think it's about that time."

I walked over with Tom, ready to speak to Eldon, when Allison suddenly wrapped me in a hug.

"I'm sorry I doubted you," she said in a rush. "You are definitely the Monster Crusher. It's going to be different at school from now on. I promise."

I tried not to gasp as my ribs throbbed in pain in Allison's strong grip, and turned it into a laugh instead. "Don't worry about it. Suddenly fat jokes don't seem that important."

She just smiled as Eldon limped over and laid his bloodied hand on my arm.

"I thought you might have what it takes to be a Monster Crusher," he said quietly. "Now I know you have what it takes to be a great one." He smiled. "Take Tom and go home. Come to Derwin when you're ready."

"What are you going to do?" I asked.

He looked at Dungan's massive body and sighed.

"We've got some cleaning up to do."

Tom and I stepped through the front door, and my mom looked over the couch and screamed. She bolted out of the living room and snatched Tom up in her arms, already crying. Stache came running out of the kitchen and wrapped them both in a hug, and I even saw tears in his big green eyes for the first time in my life.

He turned to me. "What happened?"

Eldon had wrapped my ribs with some bandages and cleaned the blood off my face, so I was at least semi-presentable. But I was still covered in dirt and leaves.

I hesitated. "Uncle Laine and I went looking for Tom, and we found him walking through the woods. He said he got away from his abductors. We brought him straight home."

Stache looked outside. "Where's your uncle?"

"He wanted to give us some time," I said. "He went back home."

Stache hugged me, running his hands through my hair.

"I'll have to thank him," he said gruffly.

"Yeah," I muttered. "You do that."

We all stood there for a few minutes, hugging and crying. I was in a whole lot of pain, but I tried to keep it from showing. Thankfully they were both pretty distracted. Eldon said there was nothing to do for my broken ribs except give them time to heal. Stache finally went to call the police and tell them Tom was home, and my mom went to get him some food, though she was reluctant to let go of his hand. When we were alone, Tom looked at me.

"I thought I was going to die," he said softly. "When they came and took me."

I nodded and laid a hand on his shoulder. "I'm sorry, Bat Boy. I should have been honest with you. But I wanted to protect you. I guessed a few weeks ago that you were a

Shadow Sight. I thought I was the only one who knew. I was obviously wrong."

"It's not your fault," he replied. "How are we going to explain Uncle Laine?"

"I don't know. I have a feeling he won't be coming around here anymore anyway. Eldon is going to pay him a visit and make sure he doesn't bother us ever again."

Tom shook his head. "How are we going to just go back to school and pretend everything is normal?"

I laughed and messed up his hair. "I don't know. But I can't wait to try."

"So when can I come to Derwin?" he asked casually.

I scowled. "Never."

"I'm a Shadow Sight," he replied. "They need me down there."

I lowered my voice. "You were almost killed by a troll, remember?"

He smiled. "I know. But that's why I have a Monster Crusher to protect me."

"Maybe in a few years."

"I could make your job a whole lot easier," he pointed out.

"Tom . . ."

He looked right at me, as he sometimes did, with those big blue eyes. "I could be important down there, Laura. I have the Sight. Can you imagine? Being wanted for the one thing I always thought was my biggest weakness? Don't you know what that's like?"

I sighed. "Yeah. I guess I do. But you're my Bat Boy, and I want to keep you safe. That's all. I'll tell you what:

just let me make sure everything is under control down there, and then we can talk, okay?"

"Okay."

I wrapped him in a hug, being very careful not to put any pressure on my aching ribs, and he eventually had to pry himself away from me.

After we had a family meal, my mom crying all the way through it, the police came by to confirm Tom was home and ask him some questions. Of course it wasn't hard for him to say he hadn't seen the abductors, so they just left a squad car in front of the house and left us alone. When I finally said good night around three in the morning, I went up to my room and looked out the window. There were no yellow eyes, and no Swords. Things were finally going to go back to normal.

I lay down in bed, thinking that there was no way I was going to be able to sleep after everything that had happened that night. But the second my head hit the pillow, I slipped into the most restful sleep I'd had since I'd moved there.

Chapter Twenty-Nine

I went back to school on Tuesday. My family spent the Monday together, just watching movies and eating ice cream and relaxing. Even Stache just hung out and did nothing, which was pretty much the first time ever. My parents said Tom and I could have the week off, but that's the last thing I wanted. I was ready to get back to my normal life and hang out with my friends and pine after Liam and even do my math homework. It's amazing what you miss when you think you might not get to do it anymore.

Tom was a little more reluctant to go back, but he told my parents he was sticking close to me. He also told them he had decided to take up photography so he was back to normal.

Mia and Shal were waiting by the portable steps like every other day, and I joined them and gave them both a hug, wincing just a little. They'd been calling and messaging non-stop the last two days and I was very appreciative. It was nice to have friends. When the hugs and reunions were over, things quickly got back to normal. I sat and listened to Shal gossip about Paul, who was standing with Steve and Liam on the other side of the yard. Apparently us all going to the movie didn't mean we were a group now, which I'd kind of hoped for, but Liam did give me a little wave. I felt my cheeks flush.

"Laura Lovesick is at it again," Shal said, smirking.

Mia giggled. "Think you guys will go on another date?"

I picked a piece of grass and let it float off in the breeze. "I hope so."

"Really?" Shal said, looking past me and shaking her head. "On a Tuesday?"

I followed her gaze and saw Allison Black walking into the schoolyard, wearing a long, flowery summer dress and a white shawl that contrasted sharply with her raven hair. It was quite the change from her Sword's uniform. I was guessing she was trying to go back to normal too. I smiled knowingly as she walked straight toward us.

"Morning, girls," Allison said. She was flanked by Ashley and another seagull as usual. The seagull, a girl named Carly, looked at me haughtily.

"Love your graphic T-shirt," Carly said. "Very original. It's like Haute Fat Couture."

"Shut up," Allison said.

Carly and Ashley looked stunned.

Allison just smiled and walked away, followed by two very confused-looking seagulls.

Mia poked her head around the portable. "Did that just happen?"

Shal and I broke out laughing.

The rest of the school day was normal enough, except for right at the end. I was just packing up my backpack when I noticed Liam walking toward me.

I straightened immediately and tried to act natural. "Hey."

"Hey," he said.

His hair was up in kind of a cowlick today, and he was wearing a new striped blue shirt that really brought out his eyes.

"Just want to say thanks again for the movie. It was fun."

"Yeah, totally," I said. Totally? Ugh. "We should all do it again sometime."

"Yeah, I was going to say the same thing." He paused. "Maybe this weekend?"

Was Liam R. Kelp asking me out? I felt my knees wobbling.

"Yeah," I said, sounding ten times too eager. "I'll tell Mia and Shal."

He grinned. "Awesome. See you tomorrow."

"See ya," I said, trying not to run around skipping as he walked away.

Liam wanted to see another movie with me. Well, and the others. But still. Best day ever. I hurried back to my locker, thinking that eighth grade might just be a great year after all.

"So, how was your day?" my mom asked, scooping some mashed potatoes onto her plate.

I glanced at her. "Good. Liam asked if I wanted to go to the movies again this weekend."

Stache shook his head.

He hadn't managed to finish the house, but it was definitely coming along. The kitchen was all done now, and the bathrooms were painted and polished. There were still a few hallways that were cracking and yellowed, and the dining room was still just a massive pile of boxes. But it was getting there, and it was starting to feel like home.

"I don't like this kid already," Stache grumbled.

"I think it's cute," my mom said. "More potatoes, Tom?"

Tom was busy feeling around for potatoes on his plate. "Maybe a scoop."

"How was your day?" she asked, plopping some beside his fork.

"Pretty good," he said casually. "My EA broke up with her boyfriend. Found an email. Not good. She went to the bathroom to cry for awhile."

My mom sighed. "Anything else?"

"Not really. Football tryouts are next week, so we better start playing catch in the yard, Dad. I heard they have a pretty good quarterback already, but I think I can take him."

My dad just nodded. "Sounds good, Tom."

"I've been thinking," my mom said, glancing at my father. "With the kidnapping, and the disappearances, maybe we should have a family discussion about moving again—"

"No!" Tom and I said at the same time.

My mom looked taken aback, while Stache just grinned.

"I told you, honey. When I was done with this place, they'd never want to leave."

"Exactly," I said, and saw Tom smile and dig into his potatoes.

Later that night I was lying in bed, staring at the ceiling, when I decided to go check in on Derwin. Eldon had told me to take a few days and get some rest, but I wanted to know what was going on. After plummeting down in the elevator, not even holding onto the lever anymore, I emerged to find Porton sitting in the old rocking chair as usual, wearing a knowing grin through that thicket of bushy white hair.

"Welcome back, Monster Crusher. I hear you've been busy."

I snorted. "You could say that."

He looked at the elevator thoughtfully. "They've been talking about you. Saying you saved Derwin from certain destruction. And all this from the girl who almost ran away." His grey eyes twinkled as he looked at me. "What do you think of yourself now?"

I shrugged and started into the meadow.

"I can swing a mean hammer."

I heard him laughing as I strode across the meadow, taking in the scenery fully now: the scent of fresh grass; the darting, dancing butterflies; and the sounds of laughter and song in the distance. I had helped save something magical, and that was a pretty good feeling. When I walked through the village this time, people waved and called out my name. Children ran up to give me flowers, and soon I had a whole arrangement bursting between my fingers, purple and red and gold. Even the men by the tavern, the ones who had always looked at me so scornfully, raised their glasses and shouted cheers. I didn't even know what to say. I just waved and hurried on, smiling.

When I finally reached Arnwell Castle, it seemed that nothing had changed. The Monster Crushers were training with their Swords in the courtyard, stabbing fake creatures and jumping over logs and swinging on ropes. But when

I walked in, many started clapping and cheering, and Lee even gave me a hug, which had me blushing so much I tried to brush my hair over my cheeks.

"Well done," he said, flashing me a smile and shaking my shoulder.

I muttered something like thanks, meeting his eyes for a second and then quickly looking away. Oh, Lee. Not quite Liam R. Kelp, but definitely something.

I spotted Allison watching from the courtyard, and I waved and walked over. She glared at me as I approached. Was she actually jealous? That was laughable in itself.

"What were you talking about?" she asked sharply.

"Cupcakes," I said. "What do you think?"

She just scowled and folded her arms. "He always talks to you."

"So why don't you go talk to him?"

"Me?" she said, flushing just a little. "And say what?"

I couldn't believe I was having to do this. She was acting like Mia Mouse.

"I don't know . . . hello? Ask him to hang out sometime."

She shifted, and then nodded. "Okay. I can do that."

I watched as she approached, wondering how a girl that looked like that would ever be afraid of talking to a boy. Of course, Lee was probably the cutest boy I'd ever seen. Ugh. They were perfect.

They spoke for a moment, and then Allison stormed back toward me, her small dark eyes flashing dangerously. I raised my eyebrows. Why weren't they in love already?

"What happened?"

"He said girls were a distraction," she hissed. "He said

that he wouldn't be able to spend any time with me anyway, since I was your Sword. It wouldn't be proper "

I glanced at Lee, and he gave me a shrug and a smile. I couldn't help it. I laughed.

Allison just glared at me. "I hate you," she muttered.

"But you have to protect me."

"Shut up."

"Besties?"

She just scowled and scooped up a bow. "I'm going to go kill things."

I laughed as she stormed off. Even Allison Black couldn't get everything, I guess. I watched as she shot a feathered arrow into a fake goblin's forehead. She was a difficult girl sometimes, and kind of mean but I was very glad she was one of my Swords.

Eldon soon appeared, striding toward me from the castle. He looked different now: the heavy bags under his eyes were gone, and he'd shaved the thick stubble that had been creeping across his neck and face. His hair was loose, falling past a rare smile.

"Hello, Laura," he said. "I was wondering when you might pop by."

"Figured I'd get some rest."

He nodded. "Derwin is in a full celebration, as are the other realms. Many of the Monster Crushers used the battle here as a cover to push their own enemies back, so we have peace . . . for now. The Brotherhood are planning a celebration for you in Derwin a month from today. It seems they have a medal for you "

"Sweet," I said. "I haven't won anything in awhile."

"And probably nothing like this," he said proudly. "I was wrong, you know."

"About what?"

"The spell being broken. Magic is strange sometimes . . . your brother might have been the target of the monsters, but you ended up being their bane. You've done well."

He suddenly grew sombre.

"I paid Laine a visit. The Brotherhood wanted his head, but I told them you asked for him to be spared, and they reluctantly agreed. He is forbidden from re-entering Derwin, or from going near your home. I believe he's currently planning to move. I told him that would be a good idea."

I nodded sadly. "I still can't believe it."

"Neither can I. But it's a reminder that we always have to watch our backs."

"So what now?" I asked.

He shrugged. "The war isn't over, I'm afraid. The monsters have fallen back, and it will take them some time to find a new leader. Months, maybe years. But they will return eventually, I'm sure. We'll just have to be there when they do. And there are other monsters to watch out for of course, so we'll stay busy. Speaking of which, your brother . . ."

"No."

"I understand, Laura," he said. "I do. I lost my family to the monsters. It's natural to want to protect them. And he is very young, I know. But when Tom gets older, I would love to sit down with him. He could play a big part down here, Laura. He has the Sight. He can help us."

"I'll think about it," I grumble. "He's already asking about it."

Eldon laughed. "I'm not surprised. I suspect I will see him in Derwin before too long."

Eldon glanced at me, as if remembering something.

"By the way, Caria mentioned she found some spiders by a tunnel entrance. Probably just followed the army up—I'm sure it's nothing to worry about. Let us know if any wild monsters pop up in your world. That's part of your job now: getting rid of them again."

"I look forward to it," I muttered.

He smiled. "Are you going to continue your training?"

"Probably should," I replied. "I might take the week off, if that's all right."

He nodded. "You earned it. Go get some sleep, Laura Monster Crusher."

I raised an eyebrow. "Laura Monster Crusher?"

He laughed and started for Arnwell.

"That's what the people of Derwin are calling you. They're singing it in the streets. Laura Monster Crusher: the girl with the mighty swing. She may be young, she may be small, but when she swings her hammer, monsters fall."

I heard him laughing across the courtyard, and I smirked and shook my head.

"Small?" I asked incredulously. "That's a new one."

Saying goodbye to some of the other Monster Crushers, I went back to the elevator. Laura Monster Crusher. I could get used to that.

When I returned to the surface, I closed the panel behind me and was just starting to change for bed when my cellphone rang. It was Shal and Mia.

"We were just talking about you," Shal said.

"Why?"

"How you were probably dancing around your room thinking about going out with Liam on the weekend."

I paused. "I got tired."

Mia giggled. "We knew it."

"I still can't believe Allison was nice to us today," Shal said.

"I can't believe Mia witnessed it."

"Me either," Mia said.

"Speaking of which," Shal said, "did you see Carl's hair today?"

I sighed. "Here we go again."

"It was really cute."

"I'm going to bed now," Mia said.

"Me too," I agreed. "Good night, girls."

"But it was spiked differently," Shal persisted.

I laughed and hung up the phone. Lying down, I thought about everything that had happened since I'd moved here. I knew my life had changed now, and not just because I was a Monster Crusher. Somewhere in all of this, I stopped wanting to be someone else. Did I want to be skinnier? Sure. Did I want to be prettier? Absolutely. But I think I was a little braver, a little smarter, and maybe even a little more of a leader than I ever would have imagined. Not to mention Liam technically asked me out. That was awesome.

Like I said, I've had a lot of names: Laura Largebottom, Laura Lardo, Laura Lovesick . . . the list goes on. But as I closed my eyes, I realized my new name described me best now. The one that reminded me that sometimes our most obvious weaknesses are also our biggest strengths. Laura Monster Crusher.

And for now, I was just happy that things were back to normal.

I was just closing my eyes when I heard a strange noise. It was like the pitter-patter of little feet against glass. I glanced at my window, frowning. Easing out of bed, I slowly crept toward my window. I gently pulled the curtains apart and almost fell backward. There, crawling up my window, was an enormous, furry black spider.

I sighed. Sort of.

Acknowledgements

I would like to thank Lynne Missen and the team at Penguin Random House Canada for taking on this project and giving life to a character that I know readers will love. Laura Ledwick is a representation of all the strong, self-deprecating, amazing women in my life and I certainly learned a thing or two by walking in her shoes. Working with Lynne to polish the draft and create a more cohesive book has been a pleasure, and I am also grateful to the team at PRH Canada for the amazing design work.

I would also like to thank my agent, Brianne Johnson, who just plain rocks. Thank you for your support in the early days of this project and for your endless enthusiasm and encouragement.

Thank you to my wife, Juliana, for not divorcing me while I was swinging a sword around pretending to be a Monster Crusher. Though if the call ever comes, I will definitely be ready. Thanks to my family and friends for their continued support. It is always appreciated and even more now with a move and a little more distance between us.

Lastly, I just wanted to reflect on the dedication. My Opa, Rolf Mueller, passed away a few years ago to join my Oma in a better place. He was a proud man who had a soft heart for his family, and he was much like Laura's father: a big, burly guy who loved nothing more than to build with his own two hands (and to do it right the first time). We all miss him and my Oma greatly, though we know somewhere there must be a fabulous garden bordered by the sturdiest fence ever conceived, and that they might just be sitting in it now with a couple glasses of wine and some Lawrence Welk playing in the background. From Adam, Eric, Carola, Tom, Juliana, Dianne, Roland, Farida, Sharlene, your two new great grandsons, and myself, we love you guys and miss you very much.